Death
by Chocolate
Pumpkin
Muffin

Death by Chocolate Pumpkin Muffin

SARAH GRAVES

KENSINGTON PUBLISHING CORP.
kensingtonbooks.com

KENSINGTON BOOKS are published by

Kensington Publishing Corp.
900 Third Ave.
New York, NY 10022

All Kensington titles, imprints, and distributed lines are available at special quantity discounts for bulk purchases for sales promotion, premiums, fund-raising, educational, or institutional use. Special book excerpts or customized printings can also be created to fit specific needs. For details, write or phone the office of the Kensington Special Sales Manager: Attn. Special Sales Department, Kensington Publishing Corp., 900 Third Ave., New York, NY 10022. Phone: 1-800-221-2647.

Library of Congress Control Number: 2024951805

ISBN: 978-1-4967-4414-2
First Kensington Hardcover Edition: May 2025

ISBN: 978-1-4967-4416-6 (ebook)

10 9 8 7 6 5 4 3 2 1

Printed in the United States of America

The authorized representative in the EU for product safety and compliance
is eucomply OU, Parnu mnt 139b-14, Apt 123
Tallinn, Berlin 11317, hello@eucompliancepartner.com

Death
by Chocolate
Pumpkin
Muffin

One

"What d'you mean, the house is haunted?" I paused on my way out of the Chocolate Moose, the small, chocolate-themed bakery that my friend Ellie White and I owned and ran on Water Street, overlooking Passamaquoddy Bay.

"You mean haunted by *ghosts*?" I pressed nervously, pulling the door shut behind me and locking it.

It was a week past Halloween, and all over the island town of Eastport, Maine, pumpkins on porches were softening and sagging into even scarier faces than their carved ones had been.

"*Actual*," I went on to Ellie, who had backed her car out of its parking spot and now waited impatiently for me, "ghosts?"

A big orange moon hung low over the bay, shedding yellow light onto the fishing vessels in the boat basin. Wisps of mist drifted in the dark spaces under the dock pilings, and the air smelled like salt.

"Will you please hurry up?" Ellie urged. "We're late."

Outside the Coast Guard building on the dock, a couple of state police cruisers idled; there'd been an actual drug bust on the water earlier, a rarity for Eastport.

With one hand I stuffed my keys into my pocket while with the other I balanced a tray of half a dozen chocolate pumpkin muffins, all elaborately frosted and decorated.

"I mean what exactly are we talking about here, and why did you wait until we were leaving to tell me?" I asked once I was in the car.

The brightly lit windows of shops and galleries on both sides of Water Street displayed dried cornstalk bundles, red maple leaves, spilled apple baskets, and a motley assortment of left-over pumpkins, witches, and black cats.

"Our new client is Hank Rafferty," Ellie said, ignoring my question as she turned uphill onto Washington Street. "He just bought Stone House."

The name rang a bell, but I couldn't place it. Stone House, though, was a different story. Why anyone would buy a home that was said to have at least one long-dead tenant still stubbornly in residence was beyond me, but now it seemed someone had.

And they wanted muffins. "Great," I said, not meaning it. "And you didn't mention which house it was to me because . . . ?"

"I knew you'd freak out," she replied, and in this she was absolutely correct.

Ghosts never used to be high on my "things that are real" list, but then my ex-husband, Victor, who'd eventually died in the guest room of my house here in Eastport—he was awful, but by then he was alone and he was still my son's father—appeared to me as I was coming out of the bathroom late one night.

To be clear, this was weeks after he'd died, and suddenly my feeling about ghosts went from take-'em-or-leave-'em to one single certainty: nope. I'd seen him, I knew it for sure, and as soon as I did know, I understood something else, too:

He looked harmless, but he was dead. I had no clue what he could or would do and I didn't want to find out. But if the ghost supposedly infesting Stone House turned out to be real, I might find out anyway, I now realized with a sinking feeling.

On our way out of town we passed the IGA and the Bay City Mobil station, lit up like beacons in the night, then swung around the long, dark curve past Sunrise Campgrounds, its tree-sheltered campsites and lawns for RV parking shadowy and still.

"Jake, we need this job," said Ellie, her eyes scanning the dark road ahead. "And I know it's short notice, but catering a post-Halloween party is perfect for us."

Sure, a job only two days from now wasn't impossible; that is, if it didn't come with a side of fright. Still, she was right: winter was imminent, and Chocolate Moose business always dwindled to a farthing once the weather got cold.

Not only that, but our cooler's compressor needed replacing pronto, or when it rattled and wheezed for the last time we'd be flat out of refrigeration space, and thus out of business until however long it took to get some.

"Fine," I gave in, and put ghosts firmly out of my mind; later, of course, this turned out to be a colossal mistake. "But tell me again why we need it enough to go out there and audition for it?"

The tantalizing aroma of warm, fresh muffins wafted from the tray. We'd never supplied samples before, but now here we were, baking free muffins and delivering them, too.

"I mean, why is this particular job so important?"

Ellie had gone all out on the muffins, even getting her talented teenaged daughter, Lee, to decorate them with bats, tombstones, and grinning jack-o'-lanterns.

Now Ellie made a face. "Lee's friend, Arlene Cunningham, has a huge crush on Hank Rafferty," she admitted reluctantly.

"Ohhh," I breathed, catching on. I already knew that Hank Rafferty starred on a TV home-repair reality show whose internet presence had somehow caught fire, attracting armies of adoring fans. There were online clubs and contests, chat rooms, fan fiction and art . . .

"And Arlene thinks we might finagle a way for her to meet him, is that it?"

"Yup," said Ellie, squinting ahead to look for the driveway that ought to be right . . . there. "Not that there's any chance of that."

At last she spied the turnoff, a short, sharp right over a culvert and then, it seemed, straight uphill.

"In fact, I shut down the whole idea and told both girls they'd better keep quiet about Rafferty being here, or else," she went on, gunning the engine of her little old Toyota sedan.

Avoiding publicity about Rafferty's presence would've been impossible elsewhere. But this was Eastport, where people can still keep their traps shut, and they do.

We slowed for the turn. "But I still thought I might try getting an autograph or something for Arlene," Ellie said. "Poor kid's kind of a lost soul, you know?"

I opened my mouth, then shut it again as bright lights appeared suddenly from behind us, blazing straight at us; we were still in the travel lane, right in their path. Massive white headlights lit up the passenger compartment and a horn blared, its sound splitting the night.

Ellie swung the steering wheel hard and hit the gas just as forcefully. Our tires howled and I smelled burning rubber as the Toyota bump-bumped across the culvert just in time.

A diesel engine's roar, a vast, invisible shove from the big truck's backwash, a smear of running lights . . . as it went by, we hit the steep-hill portion of the driveway and started up.

Straight up, it felt like; the Toyota's front end rose abruptly. I fought to keep the muffins steady while the rest of me fell back into the position I imagine astronauts must assume right before liftoff.

"Ellie?" The car kept climbing, but very slowly; I really didn't see how it managed to do it at all.

Ellie muttered words I'd never heard out of her before, meanwhile dropping the car's transmission into low gear. Then she let the clutch out slowly, keeping one hand on the emergency brake and her other foot on the gas pedal.

The little car hesitated, chugged and nearly stalled, then crept doggedly uphill once more, and have I mentioned that Ellie has nerves of steel?

Slowly . . . I gripped the tray and gritted my teeth, silently willing the car not to roll back down into the path of another eighteen-wheeler. Finally we reached the incline's top, rolled up over it, and stopped on level ground, both of us staring.

Ahead, the orange moon still hung huge in the night sky. In sharply cut silhouette against it stood a house, very large and starkly black. No lights or sound broke the nighttime hush.

"Welcome to Stone House," Ellie murmured faintly.

I kept staring. "I'm not sure I feel welcomed."

Tall, narrow windows, turreted corner towers, and a carved wooden front door that, caught in our headlights, might've come from a medieval castle . . . The place looked so haunted, I half expected a flock of ghosts to come flapping out the windows like bats exiting a cave.

"Yeeks," I said quietly as we drove on into a paved circle with a white stone fountain at its center. "Maybe they should just get Entenmann's or something."

Ellie didn't dignify this with a reply. The fountain was dry. No one appeared to greet us, and no other cars were in the driveway.

"He said he'd be here," said Ellie into the silence.

A small wooden shed stood in the moonlight at the far end of the driveway circle, backed by massive old white pines that someone had planted here long ago. We parked the car and crossed the driveway to the shed.

"Hello?" I aimed the penlight I always carried through the shed's open door, saw no immediate dangers, and stepped in.

Old wooden shelves full of dusty tools and clutter lined the walls. A workbench boasted decades' worth of nicks, dents, and gashes; sawdust filled the chinks between floorboards.

A rough platform bed in one corner was messily heaped with blankets and a disreputable-looking pillow. The woodstove felt cold but the shed's dim interior smelled sweetly and recently of cherry tobacco. I went back outside.

"No ghosts," I reported. Ellie rolled her eyes. "But no one else, either."

We walked back to the car. The hundred-plus-year-old stone part of the dwelling had been added to later, I saw from this angle. Nicely, too; a wood-and-glass, one-story addition jutted from the rear of the flagstone terrace on the water-facing side. It looked sunny, breezy if you opened the windows, and overall like a delightful spot.

"Probably that's where all the living people hang out," I joked weakly, still battling the lingering fear that something scary was about to jump out at me.

In the fountain's dry pool lay a pipe wrench, a pry bar, and some other tools, as if someone had tried fixing the fountain's workings. I looked around: no plumber.

No people at all, in fact. The house could've been vacant, abandoned for years, for all the life it showed at the moment. But at least I wasn't getting a creepy feeling. The house was a mishmash of architectural styles—balconies, cupolas, arches, columns—but it wasn't menacing-looking, and nothing had jumped out at me.

"I'll just take the muffins in," Ellie said, retrieving the tray from the car. I stood by the fountain and watched her stalking across the flagstones of a wide veranda with umbrellaed glass tables spaced widely on it.

But she came back minutes later looking annoyed. "Jerk," she uttered once we were back in the car.

We drove around the rest of the driveway circle at a speed that expressed very clearly and thoroughly her deep irritation, then slowed for the steep downhill driveway.

"He left," she said, shoving a scrap of paper across the passenger compartment at me, "this note."

" 'Sorry,' " I read in the dashboard light's glow. " 'Door open. Kitchen straight back and to the right—Hank.' "

"Pitch dark, nobody home," she fumed, touching the brakes as we started down. "I left the muffins on the porch."

We slowed again, not as much as I would have liked. "And here we were doing him a favor, too," she gritted out.

Personally, I've found that favors can have a way of blowing up in people's faces, which of course I didn't say, and I also didn't remind her that I hadn't made the arrangements with Hank Rafferty, she had. After all, she was currently driving us down a hill so steep, it was like descending the side of a building.

Or falling off one. "Last time I help anyone out," she grumbled, glancing up into the rearview mirror and frowning in surprise at whatever she saw there.

I would've asked about it, but suddenly the burning rubber smell wafted up again, stronger, like we were driving through a smoldering dump.

Then we began rolling faster. A lot faster, and the brakes didn't help because they were already failing due to, I had to assume, being on fire.

At the foot of the hill another big truck roared by like a warning of our impending doom. Grimly Ellie threw the car into neutral and pulled the emergency brake.

Not hard. Just a touch. "Ellie? Are you sure this will—?"

"Nope." Gripping the brake lever, she kept her thumb on the release button. If we rolled too fast, she applied the brake; when we slowed, she released it. Gradually we ceased careening; the smell of burning brakes became a stink, then a stench.

Until finally we were down, idling at the highway's edge. Ellie closed her eyes, took a deep breath, and exhaled hugely.

I let my head loll back. "You're my hero."

"Ha." She managed a laugh. "Never a dull moment, huh?"

My heart was still thumping lickety-split. "Where'd you learn that brake thing?"

She pulled out onto the highway. "You know those reality shows where giant tow trucks go out in blizzards to haul other trucks out of ravines and so on?"

Oh great; she'd just saved us from pulverization by trying a trick she'd seen demonstrated a single time on TV.

On the other hand, the trick worked. "Anyway, I'm going to have a word with our client," she said as we sped back toward Eastport. "Two words, actually: we quit."

Reminding her that we didn't even have the job yet seemed pointless—wasn't that what the samples had been about?—so I kept quiet as we passed the fire station, the ambulance bay, and the youth center, then turned left onto Key Street.

Two blocks later, she stopped outside my house, a two-hundred-year-old white-clapboard Federal with three chimneys, twenty-four old double-hung windows, forty-eight old park-bench-green shutters, and an ell whose large open loft my husband, Wade Sorenson, used for repairing antique guns.

"You should've seen your face coming down that hill."

The street lamp she'd parked under glinted in her reddish-blond hair and lit her freckles with tiny gold gleams.

"Yeah, I always look that way when my life passes before my eyes," I retorted. "But listen, we're not really firing Hank Rafferty before he's even hired us, are we?"

Because not counting the driveway, the scariest thing I'd seen at Stone House was that fountain-fixing project.

"I guess not," she conceded. "I was just frustrated, is all, and that hill . . . Anyway, don't forget that we're seeing him later to finalize everything," she added.

"Right," I agreed with my hand on the car's door handle, and got out into the chilly evening.

Maple branches shook fretfully over the street; thin clouds streaked the moon. From inside my house came the usual

sounds of barely controlled chaos: a dog barking, a baby crying, a video game bloop-blooping, and someone stubbornly
trying and failing to play the Baby Shark song on, God help us,
a kazoo.

Then as I started for the porch steps, I realized that what
with all the thrilling events we'd experienced this evening, I'd
forgotten to ask Ellie one very important question.

I knew Stone House was supposed to be haunted. Everybody in Eastport did. What I didn't know was the rest of the
story.

That is, who or what was supposed to haunt it?

The kitchen in my old house was last remodeled some eighty
years ago, and that's fine with me. Scuffed hardwood floors,
beadboard cabinets and wainscoting, and a tin ceiling stamped
in the fruit-and-grape-leaves pattern all give it a 1930s look that
some people call dated or inconvenient, and I call home.

My elderly housekeeper-slash-stepmother, Bella Diamond,
was at the old soapstone sink washing dishes when I went in.
Wearing a sleeve-raveled sweater over a green cotton house-
dress, rolled-down support hose, and battered moccasins, she
sprayed a rack full of cooking utensils with enough steaming
hot rinse water to sterilize an operating room.

"Work went late?" she asked. She was skinny and raw-boned,
with long, ropy arms and grape-green eyes; her frizzy, henna-
red hair stuck straight out from her head, so she stuffed it into a
hairnet, mostly, and she was wearing one now.

A pink one. We all loved her extravagantly. "Yes," I said,
opening the refrigerator where I found a cold beer. I popped
the top just as from somewhere nearby came the crash of that
kazoo being hurled against a wall. My grandson, Ephraim, was
trying to learn to play it but not having much luck.

This most recent attempt had happened in the annex: the in-
law suite I'd had built onto the house, where Bella and my dad

now lived. And that was problematic; I hadn't meant it for a playroom but it had become one, and sooner or later I would have to do something about it.

But not right now. "Ellie and I visited Stone House today," I said after another swallow of cold beer.

Bella turned, dishcloth in hand. "You drove up there? You went *in*?" she demanded in that rusty-screen-door voice of hers.

"Why wouldn't we?" I plucked a string bean from the pot of them that she'd just set to boil and crunched into it.

"Don't tell me you think it's haunted, too," I said. She was the last one I'd thought would ever get spooked.

Bella gave the dishcloth a good wringing-out and draped it over the faucet, looking troubled.

"Sometimes it's good to know when to leave well enough alone," she replied darkly, but when I pressed her about this she was too busy fixing dinner to talk, or so she claimed.

Twenty minutes later, she called, "Come and get it!" and from all parts of the house came the sounds of a stampede. Soon all nine of us were at the heavy old oaken table in the dining room, ready and eager; Bella was a magician in the kitchen.

Candles shone on the table and from the mantelpiece and a low fire flickered in the hearth, casting a glow over the hot beef sandwiches, mashed potatoes and gravy, and steamed string beans that were being dished out.

For a while the clinking of serving utensils was the only sound. I wanted to ask Bella what she'd meant by leaving Stone House alone, but with small children present—Nadine was three and Ephraim five and depending on what Bella said there could be nightmares for weeks—it seemed unwise.

But then she brought it up herself. "Stone House," she pronounced out of the blue, "should be torn down. A person could get hurt in there, everything all collapsed and rotten."

The house hadn't appeared derelict to me, just vacant, and I said so; she shot me a dark look. "Just wait," she said.

My son, Sam, looked up from the end of the table where he and my daughter-in-law, the black-haired beauty, Mika, were trying to get their offspring to eat more than a few mouthfuls while also managing to get a bite in here and there themselves.

Mika was only picking at her food, and she looked pale, as if she didn't feel well. I was about to ask her about it when Sam spoke up.

"You talking about that big old place stuck way up on a hill, all towers and turrets and so on?" He had his father's curly dark hair, his long, lantern jaw and hazel eyes; luckily, though, he did not share many other traits with Victor.

"We just did some work out there," Sam said while spooning strained carrots into his infant son's open mouth. "That driveway's a killer," he added as the baby's pursed pink lips spewed the carrots back out again.

Sam had grown part-time snow shoveling and lawn mowing into a full-service landscaping and property maintenance company with vehicles and employees.

"Yeah, could your guys please fix it in two days?" I was only partly joking. "A little digging, a little grading . . ."

The baby grabbed a handful of strained carrots and flung it. Orange glop spattered my dad's cheek; calmly, he scraped it away with his finger and ate it while the baby laughed.

Then for a few minutes we were treated to the sight of an elderly man with a stringy gray ponytail, a face like a carved walnut, and a ruby stud glinting in his left earlobe, shakily spooning pureed beef and gravy into a baby who ate it eagerly.

Mika watched in amazement, as if my dad had just floated down from heaven and was doing miracles right here at the table. My husband, Wade, looked on surprised as well, a bemused smile on his craggy, weatherbeaten face.

It must be hard for him, I thought not for the first time as he passed a big hand over his blond-going-silver brush-cut hair. With so many of us living here, it felt even to me like all the doors and windows might blow out, sometimes, from all the commotion.

But as Wade's eyes met mine across the table, I could tell that right now, anyway, he thought it was worth it.

That is until pixie-faced little Nadine, jealous of the attention her baby brother was getting, let out a howl fit to break glass. In the silence that followed she looked around at us smugly, then deliberately upended her milk cup all over the uneaten meat and potatoes on her plate.

Well, mostly worth it.

"So tell me some more about this guy Rafferty," I said an hour later as Ellie and I drove down Key Street.

"Oh, come on." She turned left past the redbrick Peavey Library and then the Tides Institute, at last right into the fish pier's parking lot. "Don't you watch TV at all?"

"Yes, of course, but . . ."

But I'd gotten enough home repair for a lifetime since I'd moved into my old house, and teen girls' fantasy love interests weren't my thing, either, for the most part.

She parked under the statue of the fisherman in the yellow slicker and sou'wester, cradling a fish in his big hands like it was a small bomb he was thinking of hurling. The risen moon had gone dime-sized, the clouds streaking it as thin as spider-webs.

"Hank Rafferty is only the most popular reality-show star in the country," said Ellie as we got out and walked toward the Horn Run Brewery, across Water Street from the Chocolate Moose.

The breeze off the bay was damply penetrating; inside, we sighed happily as the warm air hit us.

"Zillions of fans," she said, looking around. This late on a week-night in autumn, the large, rustic-looking room with its high, beamed rafters and exposed redbrick walls held only a few customers watching football on the huge TV behind the bar.

Sitting alone at one of the empty tables was a slim, clean-shaven fellow with a lot of blond curly hair, wearing a white shirt, open collar, navy slacks, and loafers. A tan jacket that looked too light for an Eastport autumn hung on his chair.

As we approached, he got to his feet with a smile full of perfect teeth. His handshake was warm and dry, not too tight and with none of that smarmy holding-on-for-an-instant-too-long.

"Good to meet you," he said. "I'm so sorry about earlier. I got . . . called away unexpectedly."

His face was open and frankly apologetic, and he'd said the right thing, right off the bat. Ellie, mollified by his prompt mea culpa, went to the bar for a sampler of Horn Run's specialty beer, returning with a tray and four small glasses of brew.

"I hope you'll give me another chance?" Rafferty said hopefully, raising a glass.

Frowning, Ellie tipped her head uncertainly. Hank waited, his eyes twinkling and his smile winsomely appealing.

"Well, I suppose . . ." she said slowly with a grudging smile of her own; he was being very charming.

". . . we accept your apology," she said, and swallowed some beer.

I drank some, too, finding it dry and refreshing. Also, I was guessing, it packed a considerable punch.

She set her glass down. I generally let Ellie do most of the talking when it comes to business.

"Now, you mentioned muffins," she recited crisply, "but we didn't decide anything for sure. So how about if now you tell us exactly what's wanted and when, and we'll say if we can do it in that amount of time, and what it costs."

And that was Ellie, from scolding to sales in two seconds flat. Meanwhile, I could see why Rafferty attracted legions of female fans. He was tall, tanned, solid but not muscle-bound, and blessed with a mop of yellow hair that practically begged for a set of fingers running through it.

More than that, though, even on first meeting his smile seemed to hint at a private joke, his eyes daring you to share it with him. Smart, too. He listened well, stated his needs succinctly—he'd tried one of our samples and it was just what he'd hoped for—then agreed to our price.

Or anyway he agreed at first. But then a crease showed in his forehead just below where a stray lock of blond hair fell boyishly. Looking thoughtful, he laid money on the table, then got up and started for the door. Puzzled, Ellie and I followed.

"Look, just so you know," he said when we were all outside. "The party's for colleagues who all think I'm nuts for moving into Stone House."

"Too far out in the sticks?" Ellie asked as we walked back toward the fisherman statue. Eastport was three hours from Bangor and light-years, it often seemed, from anywhere else.

He nodded. "I don't think they understand how lucky I feel to have inherited the place, so far off the beaten track."

Heck, with all those adoring fans, he'd probably enjoy a nice, quiet condo on the moon. Interesting, though, that he'd inherited it; I saw Ellie thinking so, too.

"And these people who'll be coming—my agent, my show's producers, heck, even my wife—their opinion matters. To me, to my show's staff, to my work in the future . . ." He let out a sigh. "So I'm hoping that good food and drinks in an interesting atmosphere might help change their minds."

"And your wife's?" I asked, and he winced slightly.

"Well, I'm hoping she gets used to it," he allowed.

Hey, it might even work; Eastport has a way of getting under people's skin, for good or for ill.

"We understand," Ellie assured him, then confirmed the party's details a final time: when, where, how many, and how much. But at the last part he balked.

"I'm not going to tell you what to charge," he said. "You know your business. But . . . look, how about if I pay you what it would cost me back in Los Angeles?"

I eyed him doubtfully. Baking, delivery, setup, cleanup—maybe he knew a bargain basement LA caterer who'd do it all for pennies.

Then he named an amount of money that could've bought those muffins a dozen times over, plus a van to drive them around in. I blinked, not sure I'd heard correctly, but Ellie stepped right up to him with her hand out.

"Deal," she pronounced, and they shook on it.

A thought hit me. "Hank, these important guests of yours, are you going to make them drive up that steep driveway?"

He nodded alertly. "Good thought," he said, but didn't say if he meant to act on it.

"Well, congratulations on your inheritance, anyway," said Ellie. "That's a very nice piece of property."

He nodded vigorously in agreement. "You've got that right. I'm so lucky to get it, and the property's lucky to get me."

Ellie tipped her head questioningly at him. This was the cheeriest he'd been since we met him in the pub.

"I love it," he said, and I could see in his face that he really did. Downeast Maine takes some people that way, the whole land-sky-and-sea thing waking the sense of wonder that—much to their surprise, sometimes—has always been in their hearts.

"I'll tell you one thing," he declared, "it's never going to be subdivided—I'll make sure of that."

And then we were done. Clouds had gathered while we were in the pub and now a thin drizzle blurred the street lamps' glow. I wrapped my arms around myself, shivering, while Ellie finished talking to Rafferty and he crossed to his car.

A Land Rover, of course. "You do forgive me, though?" he called to us from its window. "About the house being empty?"

I couldn't tell if he was serious or joking; the latter, I thought. "No worries, we definitely forgive you," I said, mostly so I could go home and get into some warm pajamas.

Then from the passenger seat of Ellie's car I watched him drive away, still not quite able to believe the windfall we'd stumbled into. But Ellie just sat there, her fingers drumming the steering wheel until I looked a question at her.

"He's lying about something," she said. "And that means I have a confession to make."

She pulled out onto Water Street. All the little shops were closed and silent; only the pub's windows still shed light onto the sidewalk.

"Jake, the house wasn't empty," said Ellie. "Someone was there. I'm sure of it."

"That's your confession?" Water Street narrowed as she drove, winding between shingle-sided houses with sharply peaked roofs and gingerbread-trimmed front porches.

"But the lights were all out, and if no one came to the door, how do you know . . . ?"

The drizzle stopped suddenly. Ellie turned the wipers off. "I know because I saw someone." She took a deep breath. "In the rearview mirror as we were driving away. She was in the window of that tower thing with the funny top, what's it called again?"

"Turret," I said absently, trying to make sense of what she was saying. Maybe the figure she'd seen was Rafferty's wife? Who, I thought, might avoid answering the door for any number of reasons.

But then why was the whole place all dark, and why hadn't Rafferty said anything about his wife being there?

Actually, he'd said the opposite, that the place was empty. "Could you see anything about her?"

The houses thinned out at the island's southern tip where she pulled over onto the grassy shoulder. Across the black water the light-spangled International Bridge gleamed distantly.

"She was tall and dark-haired," said Ellie, "and she was

wearing a long white robe or gown with some kind of smock over it. Or an apron, maybe."

"And you didn't tell me because . . . ?" On the bridge a single car moved slowly toward Canada.

"When I first saw her in the rearview mirror I already had my hands full with the car and the hill."

Ah, yes, our swift descent. At the memory my foot pressed down hard on an imaginary brake pedal.

"And then I thought, well, no sense upsetting Jake. Maybe we won't get the job, or we won't take it if it's offered." She took a big breath, let it out. "But now we have it, and I know you hate ghosty stuff, and. . . ."

Right, ever since my dead ex-husband started romping around this earthly realm; it was just that once but the experience had stayed with me. So now Ellie was allowing me the chance to veto the whole thing, if it was too nervous-making for me.

"With her arms raised, her sleeves were like wings," said Ellie. "And her face . . ."

I stared out at the black water. The lights on the bridge glittered coldly. Something was coming, I thought very clearly; something bad.

And then it did. "Jake," said Ellie, "the thing is, I'm pretty sure that woman was screaming."

Later that night, I sat out on the porch with Bella in the wicker chairs that I kept meaning to bring in for the winter. We wore thick jackets and woolen blankets draped over our laps, and cupped mugs of hot spiced cider in our hands.

The night was silent. At Ephraim's insistence she'd lit the poor old jack-o'-lantern whose eyes had collapsed into its pointy teeth, but now it had guttered out.

I wondered if a direct question would work. "Bella," I said quietly after a little while. "What do you really know about Stone House, anyway?"

Bella had come to work for me soon after I got to Eastport, when Sam was a rebellious tween-ager and I knew for a certainty that he and the big old house I'd just bought here would be the death of me.

But soon after her arrival, as if by magic the house shone with cleanliness and order, balanced meals full of local produce appeared regularly, and Sam had a list of chores and the rewards he could earn by completing them.

Which to my amazement he did. Bella met challenges in much the same way as a locomotive meets snowbanks, and I believe Sam took one look at her and simply gave in rather than lose a long battle.

Also, I learned that she would rather jump nude off the end of the fish pier than discuss her feelings, but she understood mine, no problem.

"You don't want to go in there," she said now. Stone House, she meant. Under the porch light, her thin, lumpy fingers moved steadily, wielding a pair of knitting needles.

"But why? What exactly is supposed to be . . . ?"

I hadn't told her about the woman that Ellie saw. I didn't know what to make of her, myself. But Bella didn't need anyone, screaming or otherwise, to tell her what to think.

"Haunted," she said flatly. "And I suppose you'd better hear about it if you're going in anyway, which I know you are."

When my dad reappeared in my life after thirty years—it's a long story and I'll tell it another time—Bella accepted him, then befriended him, and at last married him in a small ceremony in our front parlor.

Afterward we were all in the dining room having cake and champagne when Bella looked out and spied a rat in the backyard compost pile. A derelict house had been torn down nearby and the vermin, I gathered, were scouting for new homes.

Bella put her plate down, strode out there still wearing her wedding suit, and got herself a good, stout shovel from the shed. Carrying it, she stomped out to the compost heap and used it on the rat: *whomp!*

Then she came back in and calmly ate the rest of her cake She was not a hysterical person, in other words, nor likely to be unnerved by anything short of nuclear war.

Looking out into the drizzle, she set the knitting aside. Out in the street, fog-wraiths marched under the street lamps.

"The woman who built Stone House wanted it kept the same, forever," she said.

Out on the sidewalk, a man smoking a cigar and his small black dog strolled through a puddle of lamplight, the cigar's smoke twirling upward like vapors from a genie's bottle.

"So no remodeling, then," I said, thinking I knew what was coming. The fountain, the circle drive, and the flagstones below the balcony had all looked new, and one whole side of the house had been torn into when that modern addition was put on.

Bella's chair let out a comfortable creak. "She put it in her will that if anyone changed the house, she'd haunt them out of it."

"You mean nobody's modernized anything on the inside?" It seemed unlikely that no plumbing or wiring had been updated in a hundred years.

"The first fellow tried. Thought he'd live there. That was, oh, fifty years or so ago? It stood empty before that."

Bella gathered her knitting things. It was raining again, fat droplets shining as they fell. We got up to go in.

"After the old lady who built it died, I mean," she said as I held the screen door for her.

Inside, everything was quiet: kids in bed, adults likewise, except for Mika whose light tread sounded in the hall upstairs.

In the kitchen, I dumped the dregs of my tea down the sink. "So did she haunt him? That first guy, who . . . ?"

"The one who replaced all the plumbing and wiring? No one can say for sure," Bella replied.

She pulled a pair of shot glasses from the cabinet and got down a bottle of her homemade blackberry cordial.

"He hung himself one night from one of those high windows," she said, pouring. "That's all anyone knows."

The hairs rose on my arms as I knocked the cordial back. By the night-light's dim glow, Bella's bony old face looked cut from driftwood: long, bumpy nose; jutting chin; high cheekbones over a mouth full of corn-kernel teeth.

"Why now, though?" I asked. "Someone's already redone the place once, wouldn't that have broken the . . . ?"

Spell. Curse. Hex. Whatever. Bella shook her head as she poured again. "But that's not what the new owner's been doing." She sipped. "What I heard is, he's not remodeling Stone House. He's putting it back the way it was when it was built."

Except, I hoped, for the plumbing and wiring, which you will understand if you've lived with a 1920s-era chain-flush toilet for very long. Anyway:

"How do you know that?" I asked, surprised. Lately the only place she and my dad ever went was the Senior Center, so how—?

But the center's dozens of elderly residents and guests got together every day, I realized, all talking a mile a minute. New bits of Eastport info were prized, and shared eagerly.

Bella's nod confirmed my guess. "I learn a lot when I play mah-jongg," she said with a sly eyebrow lift.

In the nightlight her henna-red hair was a peculiarly vivid shade of purple. "Evelyn Carney's son was the general contractor for the work." On Stone House, she meant. "They had old photographs of rooms and they put it all back to the original right down to the knobs on the cupboard doors."

I followed her out to the annex, a snug hideaway equipped

with a radiant-heat floor, airtight woodstove, all accessible fixtures, and a no-slip ramp leading out from the back door.

Green plants in pots grew exuberantly on the windowsills, prints and paintings adorned the walls, and my dad's chess set stood ready as always in case a challenger should come along.

It all looked just as cozy and comfortable as I'd hoped. Unfortunately, right now it also looked like a bomb packed with toys, books, games, pacifiers, musical instruments, and tiny socks had exploded in it.

But turning the annex back into the retreat I'd planned was a talk for later; now I returned to my earlier one.

"But Bella, for Stone House still to be haunted now doesn't make sense. I can see why an original builder might not want any renovation done. I might not, either."

Maybe she'd just loved the house the way it was and wanted it kept that way, for her vision to live on, so to speak.

"But if Evelyn Carney is right," I said, "then Rafferty hasn't renovated anything. He's *restored* what—"

Bella put her finger to her lips as we tiptoed past the annex's bedroom door. My dad had turned in for the night, or so we thought until moments later when his footsteps thumped up the ramp outside.

Bella pulled a towel from a hook in the tiny kitchenette and hurried to meet him, exclaiming over his hair beaded with raindrops and his wizened old face pink with chill.

But the watery blue eyes beneath his bushy white eyebrows still shone with pleasure. "It's fine out there," he enthused through the towel that Bella rubbed vigorously over his head. "Beautiful," he said. "Fresh air, cool and foggy."

Bella kept rubbing and tut-tutting exasperatedly. With her around, he'd live to be a hundred.

"This woman who built Stone House," I said, trying to keep her on topic, "why would she go on haunting it, do you suppose, now that it's back the way it was? It just doesn't make sense."

Bella finished drying my father's hair and wiped his face tenderly with the towel, then took his damp jacket from him and turned to me with it in her hands.

"Who," she demanded, "says ghosts have to make sense?"

Two

Early the next morning the cooler's compressor bit the dust, so our Stone House decision was made for us. Ellie and I got right to work on the muffins, even though we both felt more like going back to bed; Mika had been up most of the night with a stomach upset so I'd been up, too, listening to her suffer, while Ellie had been awakened at three to get Lee and Arlene from Arlene's house because Arlene's parents were fighting.

Leaning over our kitchen worktable, I averted my mind very firmly from what a stomach upset had meant the last time Mika suffered from it. Instead:

"Does Rafferty remind you of anyone?" I asked, pulling another wet mess of stringy innards out of the pumpkin I was preparing to bake. Canned pumpkin, Ellie had informed me, was good enough for samples but not for the real thing.

She looked up from the pile of walnut meats she was chopping. "Hmm," she said, squinting. "No, I don't think I . . ."

Suddenly the compressor let out a final, despairing wheeze that they could probably hear across the street. It startled me, whereupon the name popped into my head.

"Lillian Boyd," I said. She'd had a bakery in Eastport, too, specializing in bread, rolls, and homemade pizza crusts. But after her husband died, she'd retired and moved to a house in Quoddy Village, and we didn't see her as much after that.

"What was her maiden name, though?" I asked, pulling out a bag of flour, a canister of sugar, and more spices than you could shake a stick at from the dry goods cupboard. Chocolate pumpkin muffins can be bland, or filled with the sort of no-holds-barred pizazz that makes your taste buds happy, and we made the latter kind.

Ellie, frowning in concentration: "Okay, now, I know this." She knew everyone in Eastport and they knew her. "It was . . ."

But in the end she also drew a blank. "Hank does look a little like Lillian, though," she allowed. "Especially around the eyes, and you know, that hair."

Lil's had been white when I met her but there was lots of it, growing in ringlets like Rafferty's. "You don't suppose . . . ?"

"They're related, somehow?" Ellie shook her head. "I doubt it. I wouldn't buy a house anywhere near my relatives if I wanted a getaway spot, would you?"

"Good point," I allowed, and after that we worked in companionable silence for a while until it was time to open the shop. Today it was my turn, so I went to make sure the coffee was brewed, the cash register and credit card reader were operational, the display case was full, and that the cooler's compressor was really most sincerely dead.

"All set out there?" Ellie called from the kitchen.

My last-minute inspection took in the shop's exposed red-brick walls, wide-plank wooden floors, and front bay window. A vintage ceiling fan's wide, paddle-shaped blades slowly stirred the sweet-smelling air over my head, and Vivaldi's *Four Seasons* tootled sweetly from the sound system.

A little too sweetly, if you asked me, but customers seemed to like it. "Looking good," I called back to Ellie.

In fact, a few customers were waiting outside right now. I turned the sign on the door to OPEN and unlocked it, and the first ones came in, followed by a few more . . .

And more after that; even in October we still had a bit of a morning rush. Forty minutes later when it had dispersed, I came up for air and a gulped cup of coffee and spied a familiar face at the table near the front window.

When I got there, Eastport police chief Lizzie Snow looked up at me from a report she was reading. "Hey. Good to see you."

She patted the chair beside her. "Sit down, I'm just finishing this. Couple of geniuses tried bringing in ten crates of assorted drugs to sell all around the county, the paperwork is atrocious. Anyway, I was hoping you might have a minute."

In gray slacks, a maroon turtleneck, and a black leather jacket with her badge pinned to the breast pocket, she looked slim as a switchblade and was just as deadly when she had to be, much to some people's surprise. Her dark red lipstick and short black curls didn't soften the vibe, and she didn't want them to.

"There was a fire at Stone House last night," she said as Ellie came out of the kitchen. "The owner said you two were there earlier, so I wondered if you noticed anything unusual."

Ellie and I very carefully didn't look at each other, sure that a woman screaming from a window qualified as unusual but not wanting to talk about it. Because ghosts, you know? She'd think we were crazy, I felt sure.

"How big a fire?" Ellie asked, wiping her hands on a clean dish towel.

"It was a shed full of old house parts, wooden mantels and bannisters and so on that they didn't use in the restoration. Would've spread to the house if the fire crew hadn't arrived."

A thought hit me: that driveway. "How'd they get up there? And is there a—?"

"Hydrant?" Lizzie made a face. "No, of course not. You couldn't isolate that house better if you built it on the moon."

"Then how—?" Ellie looked puzzled.

"They've got their own fire system," Lizzie explained. "Big pump, all put in when the house was first built. The fire guys hooked their hoses to it, once they'd made it up that funhouse slide they've got for a driveway out there."

She finished her coffee and got up. "Place has its own well, too. Poor guy," she added, meaning Hank Rafferty. "He was on the phone with his insurance company when I left."

She glanced out the front window at the flags snapping on the breakwater. "But neither of you saw anything?"

I looked at Ellie again. She said nothing. It seemed we'd decided without much discussion to make the dratted muffins and deliver them and be done with it, so that's what we were doing.

No ghosts, no worrying about ghosts, no being gossiped about for having seen/not really seen ghosts. But now . . .

Ellie's eyes and mine agreed: go for it. Lizzie might need to know. "Okay," I told Ellie, "then about I take shop duty and you talk?"

Because probably the woman in the window—if she'd really been there, that is, and wasn't just the moon reflecting in the old glass, or something—and the fire weren't connected.

Probably. But still. "Just tell Lizzie everything you saw," I emphasized. "I'll bring more coffee."

Because I'd suddenly recalled that last night's moon had risen in the northeast as usual, of course, not on the driveway side of Stone House, so Ellie couldn't have seen its reflection.

Nope, she couldn't have seen it at all.

By the time Lizzie Snow left the Moose, it was after ten in the morning. Ellie stood at the butcher board worktable putting eggs, oil, vanilla, baking soda, salt, and baked fresh pumpkin pulp in the bowl of a stand mixer.

Next she assembled a small mountain of maraschino cherries and began chopping them while I started a batch of mandarin-chocolate macaroons; even with our big muffin order under way, we still had to bake for the shop as long as it was open.

"Weird, huh?" The fire at Stone House, I meant. I held the orange liqueur bottle's mouth to the tip of my finger, touched my tongue to the moisture. Essence of orange peel, citrusy-sharp, filled my head.

"Uh-huh," Ellie said darkly. "And Lizzie filled me in on a few things we didn't know, also."

My ears pricked up; the fee Rafferty had promised would not only buy a new compressor, it would cover the Moose's overhead for the coming winter, as well.

I was beginning to plan for it, in fact, and hoped I didn't have to stop. "What things?"

Ellie's fingers dripped crimson cherry juice. "You know the shed that burned? Full of building materials?"

"Mm-hm." By now I'd added the egg, flour, sugar, and salt, and was scraping the last of the orange-flavored coconut strands down the side of the bowl. Dipped in chocolate and cooled, these were so good they should've come with a warning label.

"Like Lizzie said, full of unused vintage house parts. The leftovers from the renovation. Or un-renovation."

I'd already told Ellie what Bella had said about Rafferty returning the house to its original state.

"Lizzie says those pieces were worth a fortune. That's why Rafferty was on with his insurance guy, probably," said Ellie.

I put the macaroons in the refrigerator, then turned to a bowl of brioche dough I'd set aside earlier. There's little so pleasant, I think, as a warm yeast loaf; kneading it feels as if something is coming to life under your hands.

"She said she told him she'd be asking the fire marshal to have a look, and he didn't like that," Ellie went on.

The brioche dough was plump and smooth as a baby's bottom. After kneading it again I put it into a lightly oiled bowl and set it on the shelf above the oven right next to some chocolate crescent rolls Ellie had just taken out of the freezer.

"Wouldn't you think he'd want to know whether or not the fire was set?" I asked.

Of course he would. That is, if he didn't already. Ellie started creaming brown sugar into softened butter.

"He said he thought people who were there for the party wouldn't be able to park near the house if a lot of official vehicles were there, too."

"Hmph," I said. "He should worry they don't all roll back down that hill and get creamed by an eighteen-wheeler at the bottom."

Unless he'd taken my query about it to heart and set up a chair lift. I doubted he had, though; for one thing, there wasn't time. Thinking this, I turned to the final task of the morning: chocolate-chip pumpkin cookies.

I might've used canned pumpkin for these, except that my dad had grown the big orange vegetables in our garden that summer, planting seeds he thought were spaghetti squash only to find that he'd raised a dozen ginormous jack-o'-lanterns.

Ellie got her phone out while I put cookies and a coffee into a bag for a customer. The little bell over the door tinkled and he departed just as Ellie put the device away again.

"Rafferty's not answering his phone," she said.

Outside, the sky over the bay was the hard, clear blue that precedes winter. At 10:30 a.m. the fishing boats were all coming back already, each one swinging into the boat basin and casually reversing into a space only a few feet longer than it was.

Then two more customers came in and I waited on them; three dozen chocolate pinwheel cookies for one, a chocolate cannoli for the other.

Ellie turned worriedly to me when they'd gone. "I think we'd better go out there."

To Stone House, she meant. "Why, do you think some-thing's happened to him?" It seemed unlikely.

"No, but you know, it just hit me that maybe our nice, prof-itable muffin-baking job went up in smoke last night, too."

My heart fell, but of course she was right. With the loss of all those expensive architectural pieces that his insurance might or might not pay for, even a big TV star like Rafferty might not feel like throwing a party now.

"So maybe before we do any more baking, we should make sure this shindig's happening at all," I agreed.

Then Ellie thought of something else. "By the way, you didn't happen to get a deposit from him last night, did you?"

Our usual was half up front, and it was my job to collect it. But I'd been so stunned by the amount Rafferty insisted on paying that I'd forgotten.

I said so. Ellie frowned. But: "Fine, we can talk to him about it now," she said. "And if it turns out the party's not happen-ing," she added with her typical glass-half-full optimism, "we can sell the muffins right here in the shop."

I sighed, thinking about driving up that driveway again, not to mention somehow making our way down. But we did need to know, and if Rafferty wasn't answering his phone . . .

Ellie pulled off her apron. "Let's go," she said, sounding more urgent than I thought the situation warranted, and I was about to ask her if she had something more to tell me when her and George Valentine's daughter, Lee, walked in.

At fifteen, Lee was a tall, athletically built young woman who played soccer, tennis, and basketball and was the only girl on the high school's cross-country team. She was saving for college, too, working every after-school job she could find.

Now she jumped at Ellie's unexpected offer of a few paid hours keeping the Moose open, then peered into the kitchen.

"You want me to move those pans from the rising shelf into the oven when they're ready?" she queried.

"Yes, please, I said." Besides being bright and ambitious, Lee was responsible and confident, traits she wore as unselfconsciously as her freckles or her masses of auburn hair.

So she'd be fine here. "And if Hank Rafferty calls, just forward him to my phone, okay?" Ellie asked.

Lee worked her cell phone like someone who'd had one in her crib, and from hanging around Lee so much, so did Ellie. I, by contrast, worked mine like a person who's been unconscious for a century and thinks party lines are the latest and greatest.

"Okay," Lee said as we went out into a cool, sunny morning, full of the sort of thin, bleak light that always shows up here in autumn. Ellie pulled out of her parking spot and started off in the opposite direction from Rafferty's; I thought she must want us to stop at her house on our way, and didn't comment.

But she drove with her lips pressed tight and her hands clamped on the wheel, which was unusual for her.

"You seem determined," I said finally.

"I am determined," she replied. "There's just something so strange about all this." She glanced at me. "I mean, what was that all about last night? I saw someone, Jake. A woman, she was there."

"It is weird," I admitted. "We should ask Rafferty about it. And we do need to know right away if we should bake any more muffins," I added.

Heck, maybe the party wasn't even happening, in which case I could forget about screaming women and everything else that went along with historically unfortunate Stone House.

As we neared the north end of the island, the houses thinned out; white birch clumps studded the grassy landscape. The last dwelling before Water Street dead-ended at a cliff was a large, red-roofed farmhouse with a long, flat driveway that reminded me, suddenly:

"Say, how are we going to deal with Rafferty's driveway, anyway? From the way your brakes burned the last time, I'm not sure I trust them to do it again without failing."

She pulled up to the farmhouse and parked outside the garage. "You'll see," she said, getting out of the car.

I followed her across the wide lawn toward the two other vehicles on the property—a red Dodge pickup, its tailpipe held up by a wire coat hanger and fenders patched with silver duct tape—downeast chrome, they call it around here—and a small yellow bulldozer-type thing, its plow blade detached and lying beside it.

Her husband, George, used the vehicle in construction work. I'd heard him say it could go anywhere, climb anything, and turn on a dime in tight spaces.

All of which it was welcome to do without me. "Ellie," I said, "don't you think this might be going a bit overboard?"

Because clearly she meant for us to ride this contraption; meanwhile, I'd sooner have climbed into a cannon and been shot out of it. I'd have said we should take my car but the idea of driving the vintage Fiat up and down that cliff was a no-go; a few grains of sand in the pistons and cylinders and the Fiat's next trip would be to the shop for an engine rebuild.

Then a new thought occurred to me. "Listen," I said, "you didn't by any chance tell Lee that *she* could go to this party, did you?"

I was sure she wouldn't have, but Lee's welfare was the only thing I could think of that might provoke so much anxiety in Ellie.

In reply she looked rueful. "No. But I said maybe she could help us out when we went there," she admitted. "And we'd pay her for it, I mean."

I kicked one of the little bulldozer's huge tires. Except for its color, the chunky-looking yellow contraption looked as if it ought to have anti-tank weapons mounted on it.

"But Lee took your 'maybe' as a promise, is that it?"

Ellie nodded troubledly. "Naturally she did. She's fifteen, it's what they do. But that was before I saw . . ."

Right, before she'd seen the woman in the window, and now on top of that there'd been a mysterious fire there.

"So you want to look the place over in daylight, talk to Hank once more, get a better feel for things . . ."

She looked gratefully at me. "Yes, that's it exactly, I knew you'd get it. I'm checking out that whole situation again before Lee gets anywhere near it," she declared.

So if the party was still on, she would know if Lee could be there or if she would have to forbid it, a thing I knew she hated doing, and her motherly reasoning melted my resolve not to ride any earthmoving equipment today.

Then I noticed the bulldozer's seat, a high, black, pseudo-leather one with room for only a single backside. And that meant only one rider, didn't it?

Sure it did. "Okay," I said, my mood brightening. "You go to Rafferty's. If the party's still on, get the deposit and talk to him, see how you feel. Ask him about last night, even, and I'll wait here so we can discuss it when you get back."

Ellie shook her head stubbornly. "Alone? Forget it."

Drat. "Oh, come on, we can't both ride this thing. It goes what, two miles an hour?"

Rafferty's place was two miles away, at least. But Ellie wasn't listening; she'd decided what to do, she wanted to go do it, she wanted me along, and that was that.

"Come on," she said, waving me nearer, the small earth-mover looked less like a miniature war weapon and more like a bright yellow cartoon character. I hoped I wasn't about to incur any cartoon injuries.

"Get up there," Ellie said, shooing me. "On the bench be-hind the driver's seat. Face backward."

Okay, okay . . . I tried the vehicle's metal step-up, but its height was apparently set just right for an eight-foot-tall person. I stretched my arm toward the hand grip that someone had considerately mounted on the leather seat back but it was out of reach, too.

Finally I thought I might clamber up one of the tires, but instead Ellie seized me impatiently from behind and lifted me so I could scramble on, then swung nimbly into the driver's seat.

When she turned the ignition key, the diminutive vehicle felt like a thrill ride in which a special-effect volcano erupts underneath you, complete with earthquakes and billowing smoke.

"Ellie?" I coughed, waving away the stink.

"It's all right," Ellie said a little frantically from in front of me; I got the feeling that this might be the first time she'd driven the bulldozer.

Also, it was not all right. The fumes were so thick, anyone watching would've thought we were vanishing in a puff of smoke. But then it began clearing, she shifted into first gear without too much grinding, bucking, or stalling, and we lurched forward, sounding like a cross between a riding mower and a Sherman tank.

"George isn't going to like this!" I shouted over the roar as we trundled out onto the road.

A car went by and the driver stared. I couldn't have felt more conspicuous if I'd been riding a baby elephant.

"He won't know!" Ellie shouted back.

In Eastport, George was the man you called for a collapsed foundation, a broken pipe, or a nest of skunks under the porch. The rest of the time, he worked on nearby construction sites and road crews.

"Why not?" I yelled. I mean, it's not like he wasn't going to notice it was gone if he drove by. But Ellie was focused on operating our transportation and didn't answer.

So I just sat there, bouncing on the hard seat. By then we'd traveled four blocks; only thirty-six more to go, I thought, imagining that this was how women on wagon trains must've felt as the slow miles rolled by.

Still, nothing terrible had happened, the day was warming up and becoming pleasant, and I was even starting to feel better about the whole traveling-by-bulldozer thing when Ellie eyed the rearview mirror and frowned.

In the next instant, a blue pickup truck with a dangling front headlight and a star-shaped white crack in the passenger-side windshield roared up behind us.

"Eep," I said, feeling around behind me for somewhere safe to retreat to and finding none as the pickup edged nearer, its banged-up front grille now only inches from my favorite knees.

There was nowhere for Ellie to pull over to except into the ditch. But probably this guy was in a hurry to do life-saving brain surgery on someone, I thought uncharitably, and if that bumper of his got any closer to my knees, I'd need surgery, too.

Suddenly he pulled out around us and roared past, hurling back words that I fortunately couldn't hear and brandishing a middle finger that I wanted very badly to bite off.

But then it was over, and I put it out of my mind. Even though we were actually moving at a sprightly four miles per hour instead of the two I expected, I guessed I should have figured there'd still be a few irritated tailgaters.

When we reached Route 190, Ellie switched on the emergency flashers and plugged an orange flag into the bulldozer's flag-mounting hole. Reflected in the convenience store's wide plate-glass windows on our way out of town, we looked as if we were sharing a Really Very Large mobility scooter.

Soon the road widened, curving along rocky shoreline where the maple trees' last leaves fluttered between stands of white pine. At the causeway, sunlight glittered on water the exact same color as blue jeans, the tide slopping onto the embankment with a sound like gravel sliding around in the bottom of a pan.

A quarter-mile later, the horrendously steep driveway we'd

climbed the previous night appeared, but with one big change. Ellie pulled over onto the culvert, blinking in surprise.

"Wow," she said, regarding the half dozen wooden saw-horses blocking the ascent. A sign tacked to one of them read NO ENTRY.

"Okay," she added after a moment, then shoved our little ride back into gear and gunned it across two miraculously empty traffic lanes before starting back the way we'd come.

A hundred yards or so later we spotted a recently cut track through the small scrub trees lining the highway, and then into the gently sloping fields that lay downhill from Stone House.

And here, too, something was different. Ellie pulled the little bulldozer to a skidding halt.

"It looks," I said, "like they're building a road."

Fast, too; it hadn't been there at all yesterday but now no machines were even left on the site, and the drainage pipes were already in the ditches ready to be buried.

"A driveway," Ellie corrected thoughtfully. "This must be the rush job George's crew got moved to yesterday. He said it would take all afternoon, maybe into the night, but it was key that they get it finished, 'cause there was a bonus."

She sighed. "So today he's back on the first job without any sleep," she added.

Ah, so that's why he wouldn't know we'd commandeered his machine. Ellie revved the engine and turned us onto newly built but as-yet-ungraveled dirt road. The gentle incline here made a fine change from the earlier vertical one, and soon Stone House appeared, a massive pile of dark granite looking out over the bay and the Canadian islands beyond.

Near the top, we made our way between patches of wild-growing sea lavender, sawgrass, and other native plants so hardy they could live on the moon. Working amidst them was a crew I recognized from Sam's landscaping business, with tender-looking trees and shrubberies in their truck's bed, ready for planting.

"Good luck," I said, and Ellie shook her head, too. There were reasons why only tough plants lived out here: wind, salt, and a nearly-all-sand soil composition, for instance.

"Sam wouldn't have sold Hank that stuff, he knows better. Someone must've ordered it from somewhere else," I went on.

We entered the circle drive with the empty fountain in it. The tools were gone, I noticed. Then I looked upward and gasped.

The house loomed right over me, shockingly near. Each tall, prisonlike window peered down narrowly, each curved black-iron balcony-railing's bars resembled thin, sharp teeth.

Something very much like a person tumbled out one of the windows, skirts fluttering. I gasped . . . but no, it was only a drapery panel, fluttering in the wind. Someone pulled the long green length of cloth back inside and closed the window behind it.

"All right, now," said Ellie, "let's get all this settled once and for all." She climbed down and strode away from me across the flagstone terrace. Moments later the metallic smack of a heavy metal door knocker cut through the silence around the house.

Happy to let Ellie do the talking, I climbed down from the bulldozer's bench seat to work a cramp from my knee. As I bent, the fountain spurted startlingly to life, fire-hosing skyward.

And then of course the water came down on me. Sputtering, I decided to follow Ellie in hopes of finding a towel, but instead the shed caught my eye, its blackened ruins hunkering balefully. Its dark interior seemed to beckon me, and I wondered again just whose hand had pulled that green curtain back into the house.

All at once I wanted very badly to get back onto the little bulldozer. The silence here was like the pause before the pounce and I didn't feel a bit like sticking around to learn what came after that.

But just then Ellie came back from around the side of the big house, and have I mentioned that her head could bash through a brick wall when her mind is made up?

"I can't find anyone. But if I'm going to say no to Lee, I am also going to be able to tell her the reason," she insisted. " 'I've got a bad feeling' just won't cut it. She deserves more."

I had to agree; Lee was a thoughtful, responsible kid, and old enough to know the "why" behind the "no."

Ellie looked around the deserted driveway. "And if we could find Rafferty," she went on vexedly, "it would take only a few minutes. Just to get a better sense of him, is all."

Yeah. A few minutes. All she needed.

Famous last words.

"Sorry, I didn't know you were here. Quite a mess, huh?"

Just as we were about to leave, Rafferty finally emerged from the house and crossed the driveway toward us.

"And no, I have no idea how it started," he said, shoving pale curls back from his forehead. "Or how I'll get the place cleaned up before people start arriving," he added bleakly.

He looked awful, his eyes red, his face puffy, and his expression just about as cheery and bright as you might expect. Possibly he was grappling with what he'd have to pay for all those vintage architectural pieces left over from the Stone House restoration, ornamental panels and mantels and moldings that no one carves anymore, not for any price.

Burned, blackened, ruined. But—it hit me suddenly—no water damage. "Hank, I thought you called the fire department?" I said as he came glumly up to us.

"Right. But by the time they got up here and had the hose set up, the shed was gone, and it never spread to the house."

We went around to that massive, medieval-looking front door. "Go on in," he said, standing aside.

So I did, pausing just past the threshold to let my eyes adjust to the gloom.

Then: "Grr," said a small, fluffy white dog. His delicate feet were defiantly planted just inches from mine and his neck hairs bristled as stiffly as white fluff can when it's growing out of a one-foot-tall animal.

Just as he must've hoped, though, he did look ferocious, which right there is quite a trick for something that weighs only about five pounds. In pink embroidered script, his collar tag read PUNKY.

"Grr, yourself," I told him dismissively—heck, I'd eaten hamburgers bigger than he was—and moved on past the angry little animal into a vast, echoingly bare front hall.

At one end of it yawned a gigantic stone fireplace, so tall I could've stood up in it. High above hung four moldy-looking oil portraits in elaborately carved gold frames, their subjects peering dimly through the gloom and a thick layer of grime.

The real showpiece of the otherwise echoingly unfurnished hall, though, was a grand staircase curving as gracefully as a shell up, up, and around to the second floor.

The family quarters, I supposed, and you'll forgive me for imagining myself floating ethereally down those stairs in some frothy confection, pink tulle, maybe.

Punky yapped as I went on gazing around, but I paid no heed until I took another step onto a soft, deeply luxurious-feeling Persian rug, whereupon he yapped sharply again and sank his tiny teeth into the toe of my sneaker.

Thus the name, I supposed sourly, reaching down to pry the charming creature off. Then a sound from nearby made me snatch up the dog and glance up, startled, into the hall's long, iron-railed gallery.

Electric candles mounted on brass sconces hung on the walls

up there, between narrow windows shedding thin bars of light. But nothing moved and no more sounds came until Punky whined and wriggled strenuously to be let down.

I let him scamper off, then turned back toward the exit. Going deeper into the house all alone felt . . . unwise. Ellie was there talking to Rafferty as I stepped back outside.

"Fine, then you're keeping your plans just the same," she was saying.

So it was down to brass tacks. She made a checkmark in her scheduling notebook. "Friday night, we're here by seven thirty, party at eight o'clock. Forty muffins, no serving, no cleanup."

Hank nodded firmly. He was clearly upset, as who wouldn't be, but he seemed fully—if very unhappily—in control. Even when Ellie mentioned the deposit money, he was right on top of it, producing a checkbook then and there.

"Might as well nail this to the kitchen table," he said, waving the checkbook before tucking it away again.

It was true, I thought as I goggled at the size of the check he'd just written us. Besides us, the new-driveway crew, and the landscapers who would also need paying, all the fire clean-up remained.

But that would have to wait until after the fire marshal's visit. Hank walked us back inside; no sign of Punky, I noted.

"Kitchen's back there," Hank said, pointing to the hall's right rear wall and a propped-open door leading through it. Past the door I glimpsed black-and-white floor tile, an ancient gas range, and a mop bucket with a mop standing in it.

"The lounge and the music room where the guests will be gathering is that way," Rafferty said, pointing to the opposite side of the hall. "Between those rooms and the kitchen there's a back hallway that leads outside," he went on.

Great, I was suddenly remembering every haunted house story I'd ever read. There was always a secret corridor; next we'd be hearing about the forbidden rooms, frightening attics, and maybe even a dungeon, or better yet, a crypt.

But of course we didn't. "You two can come in by the kitchen door, across the deck at the back. It's closer to where you'll park," Rafferty informed us.

Also, although of course he didn't say this, it ensured that guests never met caterers or kitchen help. Which was fine; it meant I wouldn't have to dress up.

We glanced into the kitchen, so bleak, chilly, and bare that I thought it ought to have scullery maids, and perhaps a skinny crone stirring a cauldron. But we'd only be putting together plates and cups of muffins and dipping sauce—have I mentioned that these come with chocolate dipping sauce?—not roasting a leg of lamb, so it would be fine.

The lounge and music room were better: chairs and settees upholstered in green brocade, draperies held back by thick gold cords, and another fireplace, smaller and surrounded by delft tiles. The music room was similar, including the requisite vast, antique-looking Persian rug, but held an upright piano.

And then to my relief we were done, crossing the back over the hall's elaborately mosaic-tiled floor. The whole place felt heavy, darkly oppressive; as I walked out through that big old carved wooden front door I felt as lighthearted as if I were leaving the dentist's office.

"So, Hank," I said when we were in the driveway again. The breeze had dropped off and the smell of charred wood hung in the air, along with men's voices from the landscapers.

"Those plantings they're putting in," I went on, waving downhill at the tender saplings of species that weren't meant to grow here and would croak if you tried making them.

Meanwhile, I kept wondering when Ellie would start asking her questions about women screaming from windows and mysterious fires that nobody knew how they got started. But she stayed silent, so I went on.

"The plants you've got there won't work," I said. "They're too delicate. But I know Sam would help you to exchange them for things that are more suited to—"

A woman's voice interrupted. "I chose the plantings. And who," she inquired icily, "would you be?"

Her harshly imperious tone matched the frown on her face, which was blue eyed, porcelain pretty, topped with very short, platinum-blond hair. But she was only about twenty years old, so she was having trouble carrying off the whole outraged-matron act convincingly.

Meanwhile, all I could think about was how glad I was not to have asked Hank about screaming women. This young woman fit Ellie's description nicely: tall, fair, slim as a willow switch.

"Honey," Hank said with the air of a man who is tiptoeing through a minefield, "these are the dessert caterers. Jake and Ellie, this is my wife, Melissa."

Melissa looked sourly unimpressed as we proclaimed that it was lovely to meet her.

"Yeah, charmed," she muttered insincerely, then turned on her sandaled heel and strode back into the house while a stony-faced Hank watched her go.

Ellie let a breath out. "Hank, listen to me, now, if this is just all too much for you to have on your plate—"

The house restoration might be complete but from what we'd seen, it wasn't ready for a party. Also, the new driveway was still unfinished and the fire-ravaged shed needed taking down and hauling away; otherwise the place was going to keep on smelling like a doused campfire.

And finally, Rafferty's wife, Melissa, was what Sam would've called a major buzzkill.

"—or if it's too much money," Ellie was saying, "under the circumstances."

"Really," I put in, "please just say so." I pulled the check he'd given us from my pocket, trying not to stare again at the (for us, anyway) eye-popping numbers written on it.

We'd have extended the same refund offer to anyone. But he seemed especially vulnerable; partly, I think, it was his grim intent to go on with his plans despite obstacles that made him into a sort of underdog for me.

"Are you going to try to pull the rest of the shed down yourself?" I asked. "You'd save yourself some money."

His big claim to fame was, I gathered, a home-repair show on which he did, you guessed it, a variety of home repairs, and demolishing a shed was just a lot of the same only in reverse.

But he was looking at me like I'd spoken to him in Greek. His face crumpled into laughter.

"You think I'm going to . . . that I could . . . oh no. Oh, that's funny." He wiped at the tears of hilarity in his eyes. "You know," he said when he could speak again, "you really shouldn't believe everything you see on TV."

Then I noticed how clean and cared for his hands looked. No bruised nails, no scars . . . a suspicion struck me, and in the next moment he confirmed it.

"I'm an actor, okay? I got this TV gig by auditioning."

"So you're not also a handyman? That is, in real life?"

A sad smile spread on his face. "Honest truth? I can't tell one end of a power saw from the other. In fact, when it comes to fixing anything in real life . . ."

A familiar female voice cut in. "My husband," Melissa said from behind us, "can't do anything useful with his hands."

The acid in the remark could've burned through steel. When I turned, Melissa Rafferty stood there with her tanned, slender arms crossed and her sandaled toe tapping impatiently.

"You'd better do something about that," she told him with a jerk of her blond head toward the shed's ruins. "Unless," she added, "you want your precious guests to show up to a party that stinks like a fire at the dump."

Rafferty said it was all arranged, that workers would be coming to deal with the fire aftermath, but his face said he was just this close to losing his temper.

I looked at Ellie: *Let's get out of here.* Then we hopped onto the little bulldozer, which suddenly didn't look so bad to me anymore.

Hey, I'd have hopped onto a rocket launcher if I thought it would get me out of here. But just as the bulldozer's engine roared to earsplitting life, a rattletrap of an old pickup truck clattered into the circle drive behind us and stopped.

An old *blue* pickup truck with a dangling headlight and a banged-up front grille . . .

A big whiskery guy in faded blue jeans and a red-and-black checked flannel shirt with the sleeves torn out jumped from the truck and swaggered toward us. He had big, meaty hands, a bear-trap grin . . .

This was the guy who'd nearly crushed both my knees with his truck's terminal-diseased-looking front bumper.

"Henry! My man!" he enthused as he neared us, and then I saw his eyes: ice blue, unamused, and focused on Rafferty like a set of crosshairs fixed on a target.

"You going to be okay?" I asked Rafferty, who was visibly screwing up his courage at the sight of this guy. His hands, which looked as if he'd never thrown a punch in his life, hung clenched at his sides.

"Yeah," he said resignedly, "I'm fine. But if I'd known that son of a bitch was living anywhere near Eastport, I'd never have come here."

Now the guy was upon us. "Henry," he boomed in a voice like a foghorn, "long time no see!"

Not long enough, Hank's face said. He stuck his hand out reluctantly. "Hey, Steven" he said, "good to see you again."

Melissa had disappeared and I wanted to, also. Ellie took a long last look at the courtyard with its flagstone terrace extend-

ing back into the shade, the spewing stone fountain still spatter-
ing everything nearby, and Stone House itself.

Dark and many-windowed, with turreted towers at each
front corner and iron-railed balconies on the towers, the house
seemed to scowl down at us as if it resented inspection.

Wind chimes tinkled somewhere. A crow flew over, cawing
urgently. Suddenly I'd had enough. "Come on, let's go."

The paycheck I'd tucked into my pocket might make this
whole job financially worthwhile, and I no longer thought
ghostly ladies yelled crazily out the upstairs windows—the
more I thought about it, the clearer it seemed that the woman
was Melissa—but Stone House still looked and felt about as
cheerful as an opened grave.

Behind us the guy from the blue pickup truck—Steven, his
name was—gripped Hank's shoulder and was shaking it a little
too hard while Hank laughed insincerely. With a glance at each
other, Ellie and I decided not to interrupt them, instead waving
our goodbyes and getting off the Stone House property as
swiftly as possible.

"Did you ask him about Arlene?" Lee wanted to know when
we got back to the Chocolate Moose.

The ride had been interminable and that hard metal seat on
the bulldozer hadn't gotten softer, either. Now it was two in
the afternoon, much later than we'd planned to return.

"Oh, honey," Ellie confessed distractedly, "I forgot. And
listen, there's something else I have to tell you."

As she spoke, she was already well into her usual Chocolate
Moose entry sequence: wash hands, don apron and hairnet, roll
sleeves, wash hands again.

"I'm sorry about this," Ellie said as hot water rinsed soap
from her hands, "but you're not going to be working at the
party tomorrow night."

Lee's answering look was outraged. "Mo-om," she protested, "you promised!"

Ellie rubbed a clean cotton towel over her arms and hands. Surgeons in operating rooms could learn handwashing technique from her, I thought.

"It just isn't," she said, "a good place for a young person to—"

We'd talked it over once we'd gotten off the bulldozer. Ellie wouldn't be able to keep track of Lee in that big house, and who knew who Rafferty's guests might be? Then there was the fire, its origins still unknown, and the clear tension between Rafferty and his much-younger wife, who really did seem quite unpleasant.

But it wasn't easy to explain any of that to a fifteen-year-old girl. "You don't believe all that ghost stuff, do you?" Lee demanded. Her eyes narrowed. "You do, don't you?"

Looking betrayed, she ripped off her hairnet, flung down her apron, and grabbed her jacket.

"Thanks a lot," she uttered flatly, and stomped out.

The little silver bell over the door was still jangling as we watched her stalk off past the Moose's front bay window.

"She doesn't want to disappoint her friend, probably," I said, tying on my own apron; more muffin-making awaited, but first I'd promised Bella we'd send the Senior Center's bake sale those trayful of macaroons.

"Maybe they were even plotting how Lee would get Arlene into the party to meet Rafferty," I said.

"Yes, and that's another thing," said Ellie, "Lee told me this morning that Arlene's getting strange about it. Rafferty's all she talks about now, Lee says."

"What's Arlene's mother think?" I asked. Brilliantly, Lee had spotted the macaroons in the refrigerator and started the chocolate melting; now I got the pan of chocolate and brought it and the chilled macaroons to the worktable.

"I'm not sure her mother knows." Ellie got out the brioche

that Lee had also taken care of, shaping and baking the tender loaf, and began wrapping it in a linen towel.

After that we worked a while longer, Ellie putting together more chocolate pumpkin muffin batter and me dipping macaroons into warm melted chocolate and carefully setting them on a nonstick tray.

"What's up with Melissa Rafferty, do you suppose?" I said finally. Dipping the macaroons was easy; not eating them all was hard.

Ellie's nimble fingers plopped paper cupcake cups into muffin tins. "Let's see," she replied, "she's young, thin, pretty, rich, bad-tempered, and likely not a fan of the rural isolation he's dragged her into." She looked up. "Does that about cover it, you think?"

Isolated was what people called Eastport if they didn't like living out here at the back edge of beyond; the ones who did like it said it was almost—but not quite—far out enough.

"She could stay in Los Angeles if she wanted to, though, I would imagine," I said around a mouthful of macaroon.

Ellie sniffed. "Alone, and him stay here? I know people do it, they have to for their work, or whatever. But . . . well, sure, if she hated it here enough. Time will tell, I guess."

Her own husband, George, stayed away on jobs, sometimes, if they were too far to commute. But that was an occasional matter of days, and not thousands of miles of distance.

"I'm starting to feel sorry for Rafferty," I said.

I'd run out of chocolate and started melting more. "Big old house way out in the sticks," I recited, "imminent guests for an important party, an unhappy wife, and—oh, there was also the fire that destroyed a lot of pricey antique wooden pieces . . ." It was a lot, that's all. "Who was that guy who showed up, do you know?" I asked.

"In the pickup truck when we were leaving?" Ellie shook her head, intent on leveling a cup of cake flour with the edge of a butter knife. "Don't know," she said. "Same guy as in the cemetery, right?" She dumped the flour into a mixing bowl. "Rafferty didn't like him, I could see that much. Or appreciate being manhandled that way, either."

The chocolate I was stirring began leaving melted streaks in the butter. I turned the heat off and kept the spoon moving.

"I do wonder what the guy was doing there," Ellie mused. "I thought at the time he didn't seem like the type Rafferty would be pals with."

Yeah, me too. Rude, crude, and unpleasant to be around . . .

And I already had an unhappy premonition that we hadn't seen the last of him.

Three

The Chocolate Moose ticked along smoothly for the rest of the day, with the overhead fan's big flat paddles stirring the warm, cocoa-perfumed air and the sound system making its way through *The Art of Fugue.* By late afternoon we'd done another batch of party muffins and Lee was back, decorating them.

I angled my head at the girl with her colored frosting cups ranged out in front of her on the table by the window, her dark auburn head tipped intently over her work.

"All straightened out?" I asked Ellie quietly. She nodded, rolling her eyes in a look of relief.

"I realized it was really the money she was upset about," Ellie said. "I mean, she's scraping and saving so hard. So I offered to pay her for the muffin decorating at the rate Hank Rafferty would've paid for it in Los Angeles."

"Aha," I said. "Very nice." When in doubt, offer cash; it's a rule I've been following for most of my life, and it works.

Ellie glanced out at Lee again. "The thing is," she went on in a different tone, "she wants to have a car with her at school so she can come home on weekends."

And I'm sorry, but if that's not the most heart-melting message a teenage girl could send—*I like being at home*—I don't know what is. Meanwhile, if I'd told Sam no about anything back when he was that age, he'd have bitten my head off and yelled down my neck, as his dad so charmingly would've put it.

An hour later, when the first muffin batch was decorated and Lee had gone home, I was puttering around the shop and Ellie was busy putting together the cookie press, a task I find similar to modeling the human brain using Legos.

"Wow," I said as I lingered at the front window, dazzled by the afternoon lengthening outside.

"Hmm?" she asked distantly, intent on fitting a star-shaped cutter onto the end of a stubbornly not-star-shaped nozzle.

I waved out at the fish pier, the harbor and the boats, and the long, quiet bay with Campobello on its far side, stretched in the setting sun's glow like a long bar of gold. You couldn't have made it all look more like Maine if you decorated a lighthouse with a blueberry-spitting lobster and set it all on top of a moose.

"Heaven," Ellie agreed dreamily when she'd taken a look, and the two of us enjoyed at least another three to five seconds of luxuriating in good old-fashioned downeast Maine eye candy before Lizzie Snow burst in, looking urgent.

She'd traded her gray uniform trousers and leather jacket for a little black dress with a short, frilly skirt and a plunging neckline that cleverly made the most of her top half without actually showing much of it.

"Zowie," I said. Short, curly black hair, big, beautifully made-up eyes, and a tight, compact figure with more curves than a scenic railway all came standard on Lizzie, but she rarely got what Bella would've called "all dolled up."

She had now, though, and meanwhile the clock over the kitchen doorway said it was nearly five, just about the right time for a couple of cocktails and a nice dinner out.

A date, in other words. I angled my head toward the street. "Hudson out there?"

Dylan Hudson, Lizzie's longtime significant other, was a quirky cross between a tough ex-homicide cop, which he was, and a brooding, tender-but-tortured he-man hero straight out of a fantasy/romance novel, which he also was.

"Yes," she said impatiently, "he is. We were going to the Lilac Club for supper. Until I got a call."

Diamond studs flashed dangerously in her earlobes, and I smelled Guerlain; she'd pulled out all the stops.

"Rafferty got a guy to pull down the rest of that burned shed for him," she said. "Did it this afternoon."

"But that's great," I began, "he's following my—"

Advice, I'd have finished, but she cut in. "The guy found a body in there."

Oh. Not so great, then. Ellie came back out from the kitchen. "Wait, what? Whose body? Somebody died in that fire?"

"State cops and the fire marshal are on the way now, and an ambulance to collect the remains," Lizzie confirmed. "They still need to identify the victim and find the cause."

"And you're telling us all this because?" I asked. I was starting to get a bad feeling, and not just on account of the faint whiffs of smoke drifting from the kitchen.

Ellie sniffed, too. "Oh crap," she pronounced distinctly, and hurried back out there again, leaving me with Lizzie.

"Look, I'm sorry to dump this on you." She glanced at her wristwatch. I hadn't quite realized anything was getting dumped.

"When the medical examiner's people get here, they'll need paperwork signed. Chain of custody, and so on," said Lizzie.

For the body, she meant; now I saw where this was going. Sadly, I dismissed the idea of the short ribs that Bella had been braising all day in savory wine sauce.

"Which would be your task," I told Lizzie, "but you want us to do it so you and Dylan can go out as planned."

You got me, her face replied.

"And maybe just a little bit of some canoodling afterward?" I pressed.

She rolled her eyes, huffed out a breath at me, but too bad; if I had a nickel for every time she'd told me she'd never even look at that bastard again . . . well, you know.

"Come on, will you do it or not? You just wait for somebody with a pen and clipboard, sign where they say."

I rested my chin on my thumb, tapping the side of my face with my index finger as if debating the matter.

"Don't worry, you won't have any trouble, I'll tell them to expect you," she said.

I hesitated a moment longer, but then, "Oh, of course I'll do it," I gave in, and she turned upon me the ravishing smile she'd be using later on Dylan Hudson. I feared for his soul.

Then from the kitchen came Ellie's voice spitting a swear word, followed by two more. But then she stopped, and since swearing loudly and repeatedly was, alas, a pretty common thing in our kitchen, I forgot all about it.

"Thanks," Lizzie told me sincerely as Dylan came in behind her, tall and dark-haired with the tall man's habit of crouching as he passed through a doorway.

Lean, jagged profile, dark, hooded eyes . . . "Hi, Jake."

His grin showed sharp canines that gave him a feral look; the five-o'-clock shadow on his lean, narrow jaw was, quite frankly, to die for, and the light blue oxford cloth shirt, navy jacket, and loose tie he wore all looked like a million bucks.

"Hi, Dylan. You clean up nice." He wasn't my type, but even I had to admit: something about that grin, especially, was quicker than liquor in the gosh-he's-cute department.

Lizzie turned back as they went out, pressing her hands together in a gesture of gratitude. When they'd gone, I flipped the sign in the door's window to CLOSED and shut off the lights in the front of the shop.

And then I noticed that the burnt-sugar smell was stronger; much stronger. "Ellie," I began as I hurried to the kitchen, and stopped. Standing at the stove wearing a mask and safety goggles was my partner in chocolate-themed bakery operation and oh, was she ever mad.

"Ellie? What happened?" The stove, the ventilation hood, and the sides of all the adjoining cabinets nearly all the way to the ceiling dripped brown stuff that looked about as thick and sticky as honey.

"Caramel?" I guessed, and she nodded, fuming.

"I set the jar on the pilot light to warm up a little," she said. "But I didn't loosen the lid, and the jar got warmer than I planned."

Yeah, like almost to boiling, it appeared. And now there was no other help for it but soap and hot water, plus massive amounts of elbow grease.

Scrub. Scrub-scrub. We applied lots of both of those, but still very little of the hardened sugar-syrup was dissolving. Finally I tossed my useless scrub rag at the sink.

This job needed real tools. "Hey, where's that little blowtorch that we used to flame those baked Alaskas that time?"

Ellie didn't react, still scrubbing. The baked Alaskas with chocolate meringues had been for a wedding-rehearsal dinner.

"And instead we torched the tablecloth and centerpieces?" I added.

The bride's father had been horrid about it, and of all the others present only the bride and groom laughed, raising a toast, when at last we'd smothered the flaming desserts.

"Brava," they'd cheered, thus saving the whole evening, but unfortunately not those baked Alaskas. Anyway I found the little blowtorch at the back of the highest kitchen shelf, dusted the spiderwebs from it, and began fiddling with it.

You attached the torch to a propane canister by means of a hose with a quick-connect plug, I recalled. I always expected an explosion whenever I connected it; even now I had to stop my-self from cringing away from the thing.

But it didn't explode this time, either; so far, so good. I pushed the ignite button, and that went mostly okay, too. Blue flame shot out of the gadget's business end, just as required. The trouble was, the flame was at least two feet long and aimed in the wrong direction.

"Yikes!" Ellie blurted, leaping back while somehow I got my fingers onto the control knob, then turned it the wrong way; flame *roared* from the device.

"Okay, okay," I whispered to myself, trying not to panic as I twisted the knob once more; this time, the fiery stream shrank to a candle flame.

Ellie let out a breath. "Jake, can I do it with a scrubber, please? Would that be okay?"

"Oh, of course you can," I said generously, my heart full of the happiness that just barely not causing a major fire always brings. Speaking of fires:

"But I guess first we'd better go and wait for the medical ex-aminer," I said.

At Stone House, I meant, and went on to explain the whole errand that Lizzie had requested. I'd thought Ellie would go, too, but as she listened, dismay filled her face.

"Jake, I'm sorry. But I absolutely promised to be at Lee's basketball game. George usually goes but he's got a job over in Millinocket starting tomorrow, so he's leaving tonight."

It would be the first time that Lee didn't have at least one parent at a game, said Ellie, and it wouldn't hurt in the mother-daughter fence-mending department, either.

So tonight I'd be going to a reputedly haunted house to sign away a dead guy's body, and I'd be doing it . . . alone.

All my instincts immediately said, *What are you, kidding?* but of course my mouth said, "Don't worry about it. Sounds like I'll just be sitting around waiting, then signing and leaving."

I began turning off the shop's devices one after another: the sound system, cash register, the credit card reader, the laptop that runs the furnace and air conditioner.

Ellie put away ingredients and shut down the kitchen, washing, rinsing, wiping, mopping. A sparkling kitchen is at the heart of every good day, Bella always said.

Of course, she also thought it was at the heart of eternal salvation, world peace, reversing climate change, and the solution to the famed three-body problem in mathematics. I tended to take her opinions with a grain of salt approximately the size of my head, but Ellie was a believer.

Finally, though, the big overhead fluorescents flickered off and she emerged through the beaded curtain. Shade down, door pulled tight . . . when we were out on the sidewalk with blue dusk deepening all around us, she turned to me again.

"Listen, I'm really sorry I can't—"

"No, no," I assured her, "there's nobody waiting at home tonight, anyway. It's fine for me to do this."

Bella and my dad were playing bridge at the Senior Center, my kids and their kids would be at the high school basketball game that Lee was to play in, and Wade had a Port Authority meeting to plan for cargo ships' arrivals and departures (Wade had to pilot those, too) in the upcoming weeks and months.

"It'll be a piece of cake," I assured Ellie of my planned trip to sign a dead guy's travel papers. "I'll call you when I get back," I promised as she got into her car. Feeling as if I needed some fresh air, I started walking home.

At the corner where the lights of the little business district came to an end, I turned up Key Street under the maple trees' bare branches. Uphill on both sides of the street, a few jack-o'-lanterns still glowed sullen orange, evidence of small children living in the houses, kids who would melt down epically if the pumpkins, now looking like mashed muffins, were removed.

At my house, the porch lights were on but the windows

were dark, as expected; in the yard lamps' glow sat my car, an old Fiat 124 Sport Spyder with an apricot paint job, a black rag top, five speeds forward, and a habit of blowing head gaskets, breaking timing belts, and dropping mufflers into the fast lanes of major highways.

Top speed was 140 mph if you had a death wish, 90 if you didn't. Also, the car was a natural antidepressant; I swear I could handle almost anything if first I could get behind that leather-covered steering wheel and go far enough, fast enough.

Running my hand affectionately over the rear fender, I debated putting the top up, decided against. After the day I was still in the throes of having, I figured a few minutes of cold, fresh air slapping me in the face would be a good thing.

Besides, for all I knew, the medical examiner's van had already arrived, and heaven forbid the dead guy shouldn't get sent off in proper style, complete with paperwork.

So I'd just make sure whoever it was got signed, sealed, and delivered without delay, I thought (translation: let's get this over with). Sliding into the Fiat's bucket seat, I turned the key and the engine fired up with a throaty growl that turned to a wicked snarl as I backed out into the street.

And once the dearly departed got posthumously posted, I'd be scramming out of the Stone House mysterious-fire scene so fast, it would be like I'd never been there.

I hoped.

Five minutes later I was making my way in the Fiat up the new, improved dirt driveway to Stone House. They hadn't yet put lights in along the drive and tonight a cloud bank blocked the moon, so the climb, while not as steep as before, was extremely dark and seemed to go on forever.

While I negotiated the curves without, I hoped, veering blindly off the road, I wondered what I would find at the top. Melissa Rafferty hadn't seemed very solidly strung together, if you asked me, emotional-fragility-wise, and Hank had suffered a fair amount of bad luck recently, to put it mildly.

And anyway, learning about a body in your shed was enough to ruin anybody's day. In the circle drive I parked and got out.

The terrace and driveway area were empty; no one else was here but a lonesome-looking Eastport deputy. I wondered why he couldn't have signed the paperwork himself, then spotted the large, padded bandage wrapping his right wrist.

I guess he wasn't expected to have to fire his weapon, just be able to swear nobody had tampered with the corpse. I hadn't thought to ask when the M.E.'s van could be expected. I mean, it wasn't like the poor guy they were collecting would be checking his watch or anything, was it?

So now I might be here for a while. Overhead, the clouds were breaking apart, letting shafts of silvery moonlight into the courtyard. The fountain splashed in the silence.

Finally I began walking toward the house, but halfway to that massive wooden front door I stopped, reluctant to spend who knew how long making small talk with Hank and Melissa Rafferty. Besides, being out here alone and apparently unnoticed had its advantages, didn't it?

The cop in his squad car was looking at his phone. Casually I sidled toward what still remained of the shed. The teardown had stopped with the discovery of the dead man, though a section of roof was there with the sky visible through it.

The body still lay where it was found when the fallen shed sections were lifted from it, I imagined. This didn't give me a good feeling about its likely condition. Luckily, there was no reason for me to go in and see it, I thought with relief. But just then the little white dog with the pink Punky collar dashed across the driveway at me.

I'd been standing there with my hands in my pockets but now I yanked them out, thinking I'd grab the dog; skunks, foxes, and coyotes roamed out here at night, and they were all hungry. He had other ideas, though, and swerved suddenly, scampering past me straight into what was left of the ruined shed.

Furthermore, yanking my left hand from my pocket pulled the check Rafferty had written us out, too. Then a little breeze captured it and twirled it, up and away.

I snatched at it, missed, and staggered forward, the check bobbing away up and down like a leaf. It sailed across the drive-way with me chasing behind it. Then the dog reappeared and started running in circles underneath it, yapping.

I glanced over at the cop in his squad car. He didn't look up from his phone's glow. When I looked back the check had floated down; now it was nearly in the dog's waiting mouth.

"No!" I cried. Ignoring me, he snatched it out of the air and dashed back between the shed's two charcoaled door posts with it fluttering between his teeth.

I glanced around once more. Who knew what might happen to that check, in there with a dog and a dead guy? And I wouldn't be allowed to retrieve it until after the body was gone.

I mean, assuming I asked permission. Thinking this, and before I could talk myself out of it—the rest of that roof could be hanging by a shred the size of a toothpick—I dug out my trusty penlight and ducked inside the burnt, sagging remnants of the little building.

Inside, heaps and piles of old wooden shapes lay blackened and warped; stairway bannisters, mantel pieces, bits of trim and moldings and doorframes.

It all looked expensive and beyond repair; this old, dry wooden stuff burned hot and fast. A smell hung in the air with the remains of smoke fumes; I wasn't sure what it was. Under my feet the floorboards were crunchy-powdery as they crum-bled, and on a workbench burnt down the middle and col-lapsed into itself, long blackened trails showed where runnels of flame had raced.

I spotted the flown-away check resting atop half-burnt shingles and roofing paper. The dog was back outside already. As I picked up the fallen slip of paper and turned to go, the penlight's thin beam caught the edge of another kind of shape.

Under the broken workbench, a man's body lay on its side with knees drawn up and fists raised like a prizefighter's. The man's shape was entirely blackened, his clothing mostly absent.

I wondered who he'd been and how he'd died, and why no one had been looking for him. Maybe while he was escaping, something fell—from that roof, perhaps—and hit him, knocking him out.

After that it would've been all over. Through the crisp, darkened skin and matted hair, I could make out the substantial deep-red gash in his forehead, confirming my theory.

"Sorry, guy," I said. I was, too. "Bad luck."

Then I turned and walked smack into Hank Rafferty, who was standing behind me.

"Oh!" I blurted, dropping the penlight, and suddenly there I was in pitch darkness with (a) a dead guy, and (b) what the hell was Hank doing out here sneaking up on me, anyway?

I asked him, perhaps not very politely. Being startled has never been my favorite activity; my heart slammed the inside of my rib cage like it was trying to break out.

"I could ask you the same thing," he said, snapping on his own flashlight. We made our way back out into the driveway by its glow, his quick retort having silenced me on account of its being so super-annoyingly correct.

"So what I've heard about you and Ellie is true, then," he said, stopping to gaze down the long, dark driveway. The nearly full moon made the fresh white gravel seem to glow, and showed me the look on Hank's face.

Fear, no question about it. He looked past me. "They're here."

Sure enough, at the very end of the driveway, a white box truck was turning in from Route 190 and starting up.

"I apologize," I told Hank, "for being in there without asking you. I was just chasing this."

I held the check up. He managed a faint smile, recognizing it. "And if you've heard what I think you probably have, you're right," I went on. "Ellie and I are well-known around Eastport as the town busybodies."

Not that I'd have put it that way myself, but it was what people called us. "But I still shouldn't have entered the shed."

He shrugged, watching the medical examiner's vehicle climb the driveway. "Forget it," he said, his tone suggesting that he had worse things to worry about.

"D'you know who it is?" I angled my head back at the shed while the box truck's headlights brightened. "In there?"

"Nope," he replied. We watched the white vehicle pull into the circle drive and stop.

He hadn't asked why I was here, so I yanked on his jacket sleeve hard enough to drag his attention momentarily from the two young guys dragging a gurney from the back of the truck.

Then I told him who'd sent me and why. His eyes narrowed slightly when I mentioned Lizzie; it seemed he hadn't expected police involvement in what was, after all, a simple accidental structure fire.

Simple until a body turned up. "I see," he said. Then the box-truck fellows waved him over while I waited some more.

Soon other techs showed up; they set up lights and began moving purposefully around in the ruins, wearing white paper suits, caps, gloves, and booties. A camera flashed repeatedly. Notes, samples, and measurements were taken. The lights made the driveway area resemble a stage set for a cheap slasher film, all harsh whites and sinister shadows.

Finally, after lifting the body onto a tarp, the tarp onto a gurney, and the gurney into the box truck, one of the techs came over to me with a pen and clipboard.

"Here, here, and here," he said, handing me the clipboard and a pen, so I there, there, and there'd, and handed them back.

And that was it. The techs strung yellow tape around what had been a shed, closed up the box truck, and went away down the drive with the other techs in cars behind them, leaving me and Hank Rafferty in the chilly moonlight.

He looked troubled and very young. "Okay, that's it," he sighed, sounding as if he would very much like to go inside and go to bed, ideally with a glass of warm milk.

Me too. I started walking back to the car. Hank came, too, heading for the house, with the little dog following him.

On the doorstep he turned. "Thanks. See you tomorrow."

"Right." I got into the car. Hank opened that big wooden front door. Suddenly from inside the house, someone screamed.

The voice sounded familiar. His shoulders sagged. But then he lifted his head, squared his shoulders, and stepped inside.

Something flew past his head, shattering on the flagstones outside. The door closed at last with a final-sounding thud.

I stuck the copies of the papers I'd signed in the Fiat's glove box, Then I drove down the new driveway, thinking all the way that I'd be back here at Stone House again twenty-four hours from now for the party, and then . . .

And then never again.

Ever.

The morning of the Stone House party dawned bright and cold, with frost on the grass and thin ice on the birdbath in the backyard; my coffee plumed steam as I stood on the deck getting ready to face the day.

"Happy Halloween!" yelled my adorable grandchild Ephraim, waving an empty paper bag with a jack-o'-lantern drawn on it. "Trick or treat!" he yelled, marching around the kitchen in his pajamas. "Candy! Put your candy right here!"

Well, more adorable at some times than at others. He waved

the bag some more, causing his baby brother, Lawrence, to wail
and pound his spoon angrily on the high-chair tray. Then little
Nadine ran in while blowing in and out through a harmonica,
and if there's a musical instrument more annoying in this world
I don't know what it is, except maybe the zither.

"Here, now." Bella caught the hem of little boy's pajama top
in her hand and reeled him in with it. "Bare feet, you'll catch
your death," she scolded, but he wiggled away and ran out to
the annex, and Nadine followed with the cursed instrument.

A moment later I heard my dad, who hadn't dressed or had
his coffee yet, greeting Ephraim with a lot more patience than
I'd have been able to.

Which reminded me. But I'd have to say it carefully. "You
know, if you ever want the kids to stick around more here in
the main house, maybe not just running in and out whenever
they—"

"Oh no." Pouring coffee with one hand while she got down
a box of All-Bran from the cabinet with the other, Bella
brushed off the suggestion as if she'd never heard of such a
thing.

In the annex, Nadine was playing her own new arrangement
of "Pop Goes the Weasel."

"We love having them," said Bella, cutting a grapefruit and
spooning the sections into a bowl.

Her good breakfasts gave her energy, she said; what they
gave me was a strong desire to go back to bed. I quietly shoved
the rest of the chocolate doughnut I was eating into my mouth
before she spied it. What I needed today was the kind of energy
only high-quality chocolate and carbohydrates could provide.

I tried again. Going at Bella head-on with the notion of
keeping the kids out of the annex was a guaranteed loser, I saw
that much. "Well, but if you ever want me or Mika to—"

My dad came in, wearing a red U MAINE hoodie and green
sweatpants and with Ephraim clinging desperately to his leg.

"Want what?" he asked, making a beeline for the coffeepot while Ephraim dragged behind him.

"Ephraim," said Mika, coming in with her glossy black hair pinned and her makeup on. "Don't pester your grandfather."

She went over and hauled the little boy off my dad while the old man smiled benignly and sipped his coffee, looking like some wizened old kitchen elf in his colorful outfit.

"You look great," I told Mika while Bella dug into her bowlful of gravel-like nuggets. Hearing her chew them reminded me of Hank Rafferty's gravel driveway.

Mika sat her son down at the table and gave him a Weetabix like the one the baby was messily gumming; giving the bigger boy one of whatever his small sibling was enjoying was a sure way to calm him, we'd all discovered.

Then she glanced at the clock. Now that the baby was old enough, Mika wanted to go back to work. For her interview today at the community college she was wearing a white silk shirt, flat black shoes, and slim black slacks plus an heirloom pearl necklace that my mother had owned.

Under her makeup, though, she looked pale and worried. It made me want to question her, but before I could she grabbed her bag and a jacket and was out the door.

Ephraim slid down from his chair and took his gnawed, mushy-edged Weetabix and Nadine's harmonica back out to the annex. A moment later came the unmistakable sound of a child with a mouthful of Weetabix tooting madly on a harmonica while also jumping up and down on a sofa.

But neither my father nor Bella turned a hair, and since I was not about to be the bad guy here, and Lee would soon arrive to help with kid-wrangling duties—the way that girl worked, you'd have thought she was saving for a heart transplant—I was now free to go down to the Chocolate Moose.

So I did, first putting the top up on the Fiat because rain was forecast. I hoped it would stop before Rafferty's party; not only would rain dampen the guests' spirits, but I really didn't want to transport four dozen muffins in a deluge.

What I thought about most, though, was the scene I'd just left. I wished I knew what Mika's worried look was about . . . or maybe I didn't, if it was what I feared. And I thought about Ephraim, the harmonica, and the jumped-on sofa, all examples of the kind of thing that'd been bothering me so much lately. I'd built the annex for the old folks, for Pete's sake, not for a playroom.

But that's what it had become, and I wasn't sure what to do about it. Mulling this, I got out of the car to the mingled sounds of gulls crying, boat engines rumbling, and small waves slopping the dock pilings in the harbor across the street, and went into the Moose.

Ellie was in the kitchen packing dream bars—coconut, butter, crushed graham crackers, vanilla pudding, chocolate, nuts—into plastic storage containers.

I parked myself on the stool by the counter where she was working. I'd called her the night before when I got home and filled her in, so she knew what had happened. I hadn't told her about seeing the body, though, figuring there was no sense in both of us having nightmares.

So now I did that, and described Melissa Rafferty's rage-fit, too.

Ellie listened impatiently; it was almost time to open the shop for customers, and there was still a lot left to accomplish before tonight. Finally:

"One last thing," I said. "The worktable in the shed, what was left of it." I described how the fire seemed to have run in thin streams down its middle.

"And there was a smell," I said. I hadn't been able to name it at the time, with my head all full of burnt stuff, a dead guy, and a very large paycheck trying to escape. But now:

"Turpentine, maybe," I said. "Or maybe linseed oil? Some

flammable stuff, anyway. Still, I guess that's what would be in a shed. Paint, tools . . ."

"Hmph," said Ellie skeptically, sliding dream bars into the cooler. It had miraculously started working again somehow, but now it sounded like it urgently needed a new lung and a couple of heart valves.

"I may not be a fire marshal," Ellie said, "but when I see a fire and smell turpentine, I know what I think must've . . ."

Happened, she'd have finished, but just then Lizzie Snow rapped sharply on the shop's still-locked door. I let her in, noting her expression which did not suggest that she's had a lovely evening the night before.

"Hi," she said as I relocked the door behind her. Today she wore a blue dress shirt, black leather jacket, navy uniform trousers, and black utility shoes. Her badge gleamed from the jacket's front pocket. "Thanks again for helping out last night."

Ellie came to the kitchen door, wiping her hands. "Have a nice time?" she asked.

"Yeah." She didn't elaborate, instead glancing out the front window. Past her I spotted Dylan Hudson's car waiting in the fish pier parking lot across the street.

"But I thought I'd just let you know," she said, "since you two are working out there tonight . . ." At Stone House, she meant. "I got a call from the medical examiner a little while ago."

"Huh. He's up early," I said. "And?"

An oven timer went off in the kitchen and Ellie went to deal with it.

"Did the guy die of smoke inhalation?" I asked, hoping he had. I didn't like thinking about the alternative.

But Lizzie shook her head. "Turns out our mystery man—no ID on him, no prints on file, they'll have to try dental records or DNA—never breathed any smoke."

An unwanted image of a blackened shape with knees bent and arms drawn tightly hit me. "So he was alive when—"

"Nope, not that either." She brushed back her black curls tiredly with a beautifully manicured hand; Lizzie didn't let cop work get in the way of her grooming routine.

Outside, Dylan Hudson got out of his car and started across the street toward us.

"Didn't burn, didn't smother," said Lizzie as I unlocked the door again for Hudson. I didn't like the unhappy note in her voice, and I liked it even less when Dylan caught the gist of my question as he came in and answered it.

"Two in the head, one in the heart," he said flatly.

Bullets, he meant. So of course, now the big question for the cops would be . . .

"Yeah," said Lizzie, seeing my face. "Who done it?"

She walked over to the cooler, cocked an ear at the sounds of distress emanating from within. "I thought cop shop business might slow down with the cooler weather," she said resignedly.

Dylan stepped up to the counter. I was dying to ask how the date last night had gone, but given that Lizzie still looked like ten days of rain, I didn't dare to.

"While we're here," Dylan asked, "can I have a couple of large coffees, two plain doughnuts, and put a couple of those chocolate-filled ones in there, also, will you please?"

We'd made them as an experiment, and they sold out so fast that we'd kept on. Now Ellie began filling a pair of white paper bakery bags as Lizzie spoke again.

"So I've got to go out there and deal with the state cops, the fire marshal, the county people, and the crime scene folks." Lizzie made a face. "Not that they're going to want to say anything interesting to the likes of me."

State cops' general attitudes toward small-town police varied widely, ranging from benign dismissiveness to flat-out contempt. I thought law-persons who worked way out here in the boonies deserved a medal just for getting up in the morning, and I'd like to see one of those state cops put a drunk, combative longshoreman behind a patrol car's perp screen single-handed, as I'd watched Lizzie do a few evenings earlier.

"Anyway, I thought I'd give you a heads-up," said Lizzie.

I was starting to wish that the Rafferty party was being held far out to sea, ideally somewhere in the Bermuda Triangle and definitely without me.

Then a quartet of ladies I didn't know came in—drat, I'd forgotten to lock that door after Dylan—asked for coffee and Danish, and settled happily at the front table by the window.

"Anyway, you two keep your wits about you tonight," Lizzie said, as if after all that had already happened we wouldn't both have eyes practically sprouting out the backs of our heads. And with that they exited into the bright autumn morning, Dylan's arm snugged warmly around Lizzie's shoulder as they went.

"Aren't they a darling couple?" said one of the coffee-and-Danish ladies to the other one.

Yeah, I thought. Until she changes her mind or he changes his tune, or both . . .

Just darling.

Four

"Yikes," said Ellie when they were gone. The ladies at the front table chatted animatedly amongst themselves, not paying us any attention.

"You don't suppose *now* he'll cancel the party?" she asked. "Maybe we should call him?"

I looked up from what I'd been thinking: that I didn't want to go to Stone House again at all, for a party or anything else. But then I thought of enough income to carry the Moose through the winter *and* buy a new compressor; it was what we would have if we just managed to complete this one job.

"No," I said, "we don't need to call." I'd put Rafferty's enormous check into the bank's night deposit box on my way home; if he canceled now we'd still have half the fee, and rightly so. "I was just thinking that if things today go okay," I lied, "we've got just enough time to put the silver sugar-bobbles in the eyeholes of the white chocolate ghost cookies and manage to get the rest of the witches' hats baked."

And put them between parchment layers, then into the large plastic totes we used for carrying fragile stuff, finally into the back seat of Ellie's car right along with the pumpkin-shaped orange plastic platters and the black napkins with bats flapping across them, I thought but didn't add.

Just getting the baked items—we'd decided to add a few cookies, gratis; man cannot live by muffins alone, after all—to Stone House and onto the platters would be a lot of work, and there was always some socializing involved, too, though we tried to minimize it.

By the time we were done and back home again at last, we'd be feeling like the walking dead. Still, we were getting it over with now, weren't we? And I thought what we'd managed so far on short notice was pretty impressive.

The "witches' hats" were peanut butter blossoms, each with a sweet chocolate kiss pressed into its center, and the ghost cookies came from Bella's sugar cookie recipe, painted with white-chocolate buttercream and sprinkled with sanding sugar.

"He'll call us," I said, "if he wants to cancel." I doubted he would, though, with just half a day until the appointed hour; probably some of the guests were already on their way here.

Besides, at this point I meant to deliver, get paid, and dust my hands of Hank Rafferty and Stone House, and everything connected with them. As far as I was concerned, we'd earned our pay just for the amount of unpleasantness we'd had to deal with.

So we finished up with the eyes and hats, and then more customers came in: doughnuts, cannoli. But there weren't many, emphasizing how slim the pickings would be once winter arrived.

When they'd gone, Ellie slid a tray of cookie-press cookies into the oven and started mixing pfeffernuesse: flour, sugar, butter, aniseed, cloves, nutmeg, allspice, mace, cardamom . . .

My father always said you could blast off a rocket ship with those pepper cookies, so spicy they would also clear your sinuses and fix your digestion. Ellie rolled them in powdered sugar, then dipped them in melted chocolate with instant coffee stirred into it.

While she worked on those, I cleaned up, washed dishes, and generally kept things shipshape. We'd planned to close early, finish prepping and eat dinner, and arrive around 7:15. By the time three o'clock rolled around in ye olde Chocolate Moose, I thought our plan might actually work.

Plastic totes filled and ready to be loaded into Ellie's car, check. I grabbed up aprons and hairnets, and then the telephone—not one of our cell phones but the one on the wall behind the counter, which I'd almost forgotten about—rang.

Ellie and I paused, each in the middle of doing something fairly urgent and neither of us wanting to pick up. But at last Ellie gave in and did, and when she heard who it was she put her hand over the receiver and motioned me to get onto the kitchen extension.

"It's Arlene's mom," Ellie mouthed. Cautiously I put the receiver to my ear.

"... why you would even *suggest* such a stupid thing," the woman on the phone was demanding to know. Her voice had more scratches than an old vinyl record, and I thought it might be a little slurred.

"*My daughter* doesn't need to be exposed to any *Hollywood heathens* throwing *depraved parties* in a place where none of them have any business being anyway!" it went on indignantly.

I stifled a giggle. For one thing, I happened to know that *her daughter* had been exposed to a lot worse. According to Lee, her friend Arlene might seem quiet but she ran with a way faster crowd than Lee ever had, then told Lee about her exploits.

And Lee told Ellie, and Ellie told me. "So no, thank you," Arlene's mom said sourly, "but I won't be needing my little girl introduced to anyone, especially not this slimy Rafferty person, whoever *he* is."

She hung up hard, which is still one of the great pleasures of having a landline at all, but it hurt my ear.

"Ow," I said, rubbing it. But as soon as the pain stopped, I didn't think much more about the phone call at all. Clearly the woman was not 100 percent capable of having a conversation, or at least not right now, and anyway when we were this close to zero hour on a catering assignment, anything that wasn't actively bleeding or on fire got shoved aside until the job was finished.

I picked up the stacked plastic totes with the muffins in them. Ellie held the door for me, then came out and locked it. Dusk filled the street, a daily reminder now of winter to come.

"Poor Arlene," Ellie said as we were getting into her car.

"There's that," I conceded. Lee said Arlene was funny and smart, just not so much when her mom or dad were around.

"Here, give me those." Ellie took the stacked totes from me and shoved them into the back seat with the cookies; then we got in and took off for my house. Closed inside the car, the air was fragrant with chocolate, spices, and the pine air freshener that her husband, George, had picked up in some gas station somewhere and hung up as a joke, several years earlier.

She'd tossed it at once, but the car never lost the smell. "Do you and Lee want to stay and eat?" I asked as we turned onto Key Street.

I still had to shower and change clothes but unless I found time for dinner, I'd be a zombie later.

"No, thanks. Lee has plans." The porch door of my big old house opened and the girl came out to the curb as we drove up.

"Kids still down for their naps and the great-grandparents are, too," she reported as I got out of the car and she got in. "I don't know where Mika and Sam are, though, or your husband."

"Are the kids by any chance upstairs in their rooms and not in the annex?"

Lee looked regretful. "Sorry, no. Mom said you wanted Bella and your dad to have their own space, but . . ."

What I'd said was I wanted the little hellions kept out of the area that I'd built strictly and specifically for—

". . . but Bella took them with her when she went to lie down, and after that, I couldn't . . ."

"Yeah," I sighed, "I get it." I put the totes down and dug in my bag for the pair of hundred-dollar bills I'd put aside for her; if Rafferty could pay what a thing was worth, I could, too, I'd decided.

"Thanks, Jake." She turned to Ellie. "Mom? We'd better—"

"Yep," Ellie said, and drove off down the street while I went inside where the dogs waited, prancing and yipping.

I crouched, rubbing noggins and scratching ears. The German shepherd's eyes narrowed sweetly; the God-forbid Irish wolfhound grinned, his wiry coat like Brillo as he wriggled in delight.

Everything else was quiet; no TV, no serenades from any toy musical instruments. So I did what any sensible person would do: let the dogs out into their fenced yard, moved Bella's comfy old rocking chair closer to the still-warm stove, and sat.

Just for a minute, I thought, and that's where I was when Bella woke me an hour later by putting a tray with my dinner on it in my lap and shaking my shoulder. My eyes opened to the sight of baked meat loaf, mashed potatoes, and some of the baby green peas that Bella had grown and frozen last spring.

There was plenty of butter on the potatoes and ketchup on the meat loaf, and I tucked in gratefully while the rest of the family gathered. Soon the old kitchen was full of us; Sam and Mika had come home, and they and their kids filled up one side and both ends of the table; my dad and Bella sat across from them with the serving dishes that Ephraim would certainly reach for otherwise.

"Meat woaf," said little Nadine cheerily, and pressed a generous ketchup-smeared handful of it into the vicinity of her wide-open mouth.

She was a good eater, but her accuracy needed work; Mika wiped the child's hands and tomatoey face with the damp cloth she kept ready.

"Po-ta-toes, po-ta-toes," chanted Ephraim, pounding the table by his plate with one hand while stabbing a fork into his pile of mashed spuds with the other.

His father paused with a spoonful of gravy hovering over his plate to glance pleasantly down at his son; seeming to know what was good for him, Ephraim quieted. But then from upstairs the baby began to wail, sounding like he meant it.

Mika got up. She had not, I noticed, touched her own plate, and Sam had said something about her leaving the ball game early last night on account of not feeling well.

I got up, too, and rinsed my plate at the sink. It was later than I'd planned, and getting chaotic again in the house: baby howling, Ephraim riding Bella's broom like a horsie, and Nadine trying yet again to climb onto the "woof-hound," as she called him.

Luckily, the woof-hound was a lamb in woof's clothing. "Thanks," I told Bella, leaning in to kiss her papery cheek. She moved her shoulders impatiently, but I knew she was pleased. "I expect I'll be back by eleven," I said. "If not, I'll give you a call."

She'd be up waiting, otherwise. Just then Ephraim and his horsie galloped into the annex; almost at once I heard him begin making loud, atonal wheezing sounds on the harmonica.

I was about to say something when Mika came downstairs with a squalling bundle of infant fury in her arms. Wade once said that if you mounted the kid on a car roof you could use him for crowd control.

Meanwhile, Nadine had also gone into the annex, and now a ringingly loud series of xylophone arpeggios erupted from out there, sounding almost exactly like a garbage truck backing into a plate-glass window.

"Maybe you should be wearing ear protection," I added. The metallic cloud of ear-splitting sound now being produced by my granddaughter was surely above allowed EPA levels.

Bella smiled and nodded as if agreeing, but I was sure she couldn't hear me through the metallic cloud, so loud now that it was nearly visible, so I left her rinsing the plates with water as hot as what they use to sterilize surgical implements.

In the hall I found the wolfhound curled up in a pile of coats that had fallen from their hooks. In the parlor, Mika rocked the baby, who seemed mollified by this; as I went by Mika put a finger to her lips and smiled, but not very convincingly.

It was past time for me to get seriously into my pre-event routine: brush teeth, wash face, change clothes, check personal supply kit: Advil, Band-Aid, dental floss, eye drops, 22-caliber short-barreled semiautomatic pistol . . . What can I say, Wade gave it to me as a wedding present. He'd taught me to shoot, out at the range where he still spent time regularly, so it made sense. The gun wasn't a regular part of my life, though. I even thought about leaving it home, but decided against.

There'd already been one person found dead up there at Stone House, and I doubted that the guy got those bullets in his head by mistake.

Because one bullet may be accidental. Or deliberate: sad, but people do it. Two, though . . . Well, let's put it this way: it's hard enough to shoot yourself in the head once. But twice?

Nah. I closed and locked the gun safe, flipped the gun open and found it loaded, made sure yet again that there wasn't one in the chamber, and snapped it shut. Burnt sheds with dead guys in them made me nervous, the more so if they had bullets in them, and if this little popgun made me feel more secure, so be it.

Downstairs in the kitchen I smelled Comet cleanser; if Bella ever retires for the evening without first scrubbing the kitchen sink, I'll know I should call the doctor. Then just as I laid my phone on the table, Ephraim came in and spied it, and made a beeline for it.

"Pokemon!" he yelled delightedly. Grabbing it up, he raced away from me with the device.

I'd known it was a bad idea to play Pokemon with him on my phone, but I hadn't been able to resist.

"Ephraim," I called after him. "I need that, please."

"Poke-poke-Pokemon!" he crowed, sprinting off down the hall with me in pursuit, and by now the dogs had gotten interested as well, so they galumphed after us.

Finally Sam emerged from the front room where he had been watching the ball game on TV to scoop Ephraim up off the floor.

"What's going on out here?" he mock-growled, hoisting his son up over his head.

Ephraim gasped, then giggled in nervous pleasure, still waving my phone; luckily, we had high ceilings. Unluckily, though, surprise had loosened the child's grip. I watched the phone fly from his small fingers, up and away—

Two old red runner rugs carpeted the hall. But the bare space between the rugs was . . . yeah, it was hard, as evidenced by the sharp *crack!* of the cell phone's landing.

Ephraim looked horrified. "Uh-oh," he whispered.

"Ma, I'm sorry," Sam began. "I'll get you a new—"

The cell phone rang. I scrambled to it and picked it up.

". . . hello? Is this Mrs. Tiptree?"

I'm not Mrs. Tiptree anymore; I'm Mrs. Sorenson. But never mind: "Who is this?" I asked. "What's wrong?"

It was a girl's voice. Loud music filled the background, dance music, I thought. Something made of glass smashed.

"Can you come and get me, please?" A sob escaped the girl. Whoever she was, she was clearly scared.

How she had my number or even knew who I was, I had no

idea. Still: "Yes, I'll come." Because of course I would, for heaven's sake. "Just tell me where you are."

Meanwhile, somehow it had gotten to be 7:25, so of course I was also thinking about the party I was preparing to supply with dessert, about how much we were getting paid, about how much time I had left before Ellie would get here to pick me up, and—

And then I found out who my mystery caller was and why she'd reached out to me.

"It's Arlene Cunningham. Lee's friend? I'm at Stone House."

Arlene, who had wanted so badly to meet Hank Rafferty and whose mom had forbidden it—well, it sounded as if she'd done it, anyway. And now—

Something fell over at the party Arlene had crashed, a table or a chair. The music's volume went way up, then cut off.

Ellie's car horn beeped outside my house. "Is Hank there? Can I talk to him?" I said into the phone.

I could tell him that we were on our way and that we'd take charge of the girl when we arrived. But:

"No," Arlene sobbed. "He's . . . please get me out of here!"

Fifteen minutes later we were at Stone House, on the high turret's balcony looking down at Hank's body. I'd already called Lizzie, told her the problem, and let her know that most of the guests had already taken off or were doing so, the new driveway bumper to bumper with hastily departing cars.

"I guess they didn't want to be at a party whose host just went splat on the veranda," I said. "Bad publicity."

"Mm," she'd said. "Guest book?"

I told her I'd try to find one and she said she was on her way. It was starting to hit me that we'd walked into a murder scene; I mean, that balcony railing was waist-high. You'd have to work pretty hard to fall over it accidentally.

"Drat," said Ellie, still looking down. A couple of party guests paused to stare at the body on their way to their cars.

"I wonder if he'd written our final check yet," I said.

Ellie chuckled bleakly. "Think he jumped?"

I turned to her. "No, do you?"

Ellie made a sound of derision. "Pushed. I think somebody snuck up behind him and—"

"You girls got a good view?" interrupted someone behind us.

I whirled as Melissa Rafferty came out onto the balcony beside us, wearing a long clingy dress in fire-engine red with a neckline that plunged to her belly button. With that platinum hair and fake lashes so long you could've swept the floor with them, she looked . . .

Well, I couldn't decide if she looked more like Marilyn Monroe or Jessica Rabbit, and I didn't understand how a young woman like her could be so fashion-clueless.

"I'm so sorry about your husband," I said automatically. "Can we do anything? Have you called anyone?"

To help her, I meant; a relative or a friend. A harsh bark of a laugh came out of her.

"Why, you think anything can be done for him now?" She put her fingertips to her forehead. "I was out in the driveway greeting a guest when I . . . heard him."

Hit the flagstones, she meant. She seemed stunned, still in shock, probably.

"I don't know if you've looked closely," she went on.

I had. Even from up here, the motionless body with its neck twisted so wrongly and the blood glistening around it were way too visible.

"He's dead," she went on. "Dead, departed, defunct . . ."

As she spoke, she sank toward the balcony's stone floor until she sat cross-legged, staring blankly; she was very intoxicated. We got her downstairs where she passed out on a sofa; then I recalled why we'd come here in the first place.

"Arlene," I said, and we turned to start looking for her. Ellie first peered out the front door in case she was in the courtyard somewhere, or on the terrace.

"Jake." She'd opened the big door, then closed it partway again, waving me over to where she stood.

I peered past her out to the white stone fountain, its spray reflecting the multicolored lights strung from tree to green-house-grown potted tree on the terrace.

Seated miserably on the pool's edge was Arlene, peeking through her fingers at Rafferty's corpse. A cell phone lay by her feet. On the way out to her, I spotted an open guest book on a stand by the door and shoved it into my jacket front.

"I'm not going back in there," Arlene said when we tried to move her indoors where it was warmer. Her short, choppily cut brown hair was probably styled somehow when she started out for the evening, but now it looked like a buzz saw had been at it.

"Come on. It'll be okay," I coaxed, but it wouldn't be, and she shot me a pitying glance for saying it.

Finally she got up. "You look very interesting," was all I could think of to say when I saw her outfit: a mid-thigh-length black velvet dress tightly belted with a green satin sash, black leggings, and black ballet slippers. Her makeup was too smeared to know what it had been like at the start, but she'd worn lots of it, plus a musky cologne I couldn't identify.

And she meant it about not going inside, so we put her in Ellie's car with a blanket and some hot coffee from the kitchen, where the finished-and-cleaned-up dinner caterers waited to be told they could go.

So I told them, and if anyone didn't like it, too bad, I thought as they trundled out. When I got back, Ellie had started the car, turned on the heat, and was trying to extract Arlene's promise to call her mom on the cell phone I'd retrieved for her.

"She's not there," Arlene muttered, sniffling. "Can't you just take me home and not call her? Please?"

Of course; Arlene's mom didn't know she was out. "Big no to that one, kiddo," I told her, beginning to be annoyed.

Even with makeup smeared and hair ruined, she looked way older than fifteen; alone at an adult party, she was lucky just seeing something bad was the worst that had happened to her.

A few minutes later Lizzie Snow pulled up into the circle drive with Hudson beside her. Hopping out of the squad car, she shot us a wave and went directly to examine Rafferty's body.

Looking irked, Hudson got out of the car, too, and walked over to Ellie and me.

"Sorry if I spoiled something," I said as he approached.

One dark eyebrow rose. "Oh no," he replied, "your timing couldn't have been better."

Sarcasm was his superpower. I angled my head at Rafferty's body. "He didn't exactly make an appointment."

Hudson nodded thoughtfully. With his tousled dark hair and brooding, angular face, he cut quite the striking figure standing there in the moonlight he looked like the hero in a romantic suspense novel. He was smart, too, and on top of all that he'd saved my life and my grandson's once.

So I probably was biased. He squinted down at Rafferty. "It must've happened right after I left," he said.

"You were here?" But then I realized. "Working security?"

That had to be it; Hudson rarely even went to the parties of the few people he liked, much less ones he didn't know. But the ex-cop did provide hired security on the rare occasions when someone in Eastport or nearby needed it.

"But I don't get it," I went on, "you were working but you left early?"

He shrugged, looking boyishly guilty. "Yeah, after I came close to punching the host in the mouth, I figured it was time."

Hoo, boy. Hudson was lovely, he played chess with my dad, and he adored Lizzie; overall Dylan was a peach, if an annoying one on occasion. But his legendary temper went from zero to a zillion in a flash if you pushed the wrong button.

I decided not to probe further. "We were coming out here to cater dessert, anyway, when we got a call from a young friend who needed a ride home," I said instead.

In the house, lights went on in the room behind the balcony from which Rafferty had descended.

"I'd like to get her home now, in fact," I added, "before it really gets crazy around here." Lizzie's was just the first, minor wave of attention this situation was going to get from Maine law enforcement, starting real soon, now.

Hudson frowned, gesturing at Ellie's car with Arlene's face visible inside. "She was here when it happened? Did she see it?"

Had she witnessed Rafferty's fall, Hudson meant. "I hadn't thought of that," I said. "But I guess she could have."

From the passenger-side window Arlene's pale, tear-streaked face peered back out at me.

"What, she crashed the party?" Hudson asked astutely.

"Yeah." Then Ellie and Lizzie came back out and started across the driveway toward us.

"How'd she get by me, though?" he wondered aloud. "I was right there by the front door until the, uh, unfortunate thing with Rafferty."

Which, I noticed, he did not describe in detail; probably his own behavior hadn't been stellar, either, once he'd been provoked.

"Kitchen door, maybe?" I said. Then Arlene tapped the horn impatiently and I shot her the same kind of look I'd have given an eight-year-old, and she subsided.

"Lord knows what might've happened to her if she'd actually succeeded in attracting Rafferty's interest," I told Hudson.

The TV personality had seemed like a nice enough fellow, but lots of guys do, and this one had married a twenty-year-old.

Rapping hard on the car window, Arlene mouthed, "Let's

go!" and if looks could've killed, she'd have joined the other ghosts on this property.

If any. "You know, though," Dylan said thoughtfully, "I'm not so sure she didn't. Attract him, that is."

Headlights down at the road entered the long driveway, vanished around the first curve, then reappeared as the car emerged and kept coming uphill toward us.

"No," Dylan said, watching them, "I'm not sure of that at all."

"Wash that crap off your face!"

Arlene's mother, Dot Cunningham, was home when we got there—and she was livid. Once she'd marched Arlene off to the shower, she proceeded to deliver a red-hot tongue-lashing to Ellie and me, a tirade that didn't stop until I interrupted her.

"We didn't take her there," I said. "We just went and got her. She sounded upset."

The Cunninghams' small two-story bungalow stood on a cleared quarter-acre on a dead-end street near the high school, its expansive yard backed by a thickly wooded area that made it feel remote and rural.

Dot Cunningham's mouth tightened. "Hmph. So she must have hitchhiked. Yet another thing she's not supposed to do."

Arlene was in trouble, all right. "Go to your room," Dot hissed furiously when the girl reappeared minutes later in the cluttered kitchen, a 1970s redo in varnished knotty pine, gold appliances, and redbrick-patterned linoleum.

Overhead a purplish fluorescent fixture flickered. "Mom," Arlene began, "you don't understand, I only went because—"

"Oh, I understand, all right," Dot snapped. "Just get out of my sight."

Arlene's scrubbed face crumpled and she ran sobbing from the room. When she was gone, her mother turned back to us.

"And you two," she began, and have I mentioned how much I like having an index finger stabbing at me while someone harangues me?

"Look, Mrs. Cunningham," Ellie began; so far, Dot hadn't exactly charmed Ellie's socks off, either.

"She called you," Dot interrupted, meaning me. "Why did she even have your number? And you"—she stabbed the air in front of Ellie's face—"you're Leonora's mother, aren't you?" Her eyes narrowed meanly. "I'll bet they cooked this up. I always did say Lee was a sly little vixen. Too darned smart for her own good, that one."

Ellie's face smoothed dangerously. "Unlike you," she said mildly. "Oh, and you're welcome."

By now we were at the door, which in the short time I'd been here I'd already come to regard as the passageway to a better world. Ellie turned and went out, shaking her head.

I turned to Dot. "Good question, though," I said. "About why she called me instead of you when she got scared. I mean, instead of her mother."

It took her a second, but she figured it out, and when she did she began shouting angry curses and didn't stop until I got to Ellie's car.

"Get in," said Ellie urgently. In the house all the lights went on upstairs. I felt sorry for Arlene, although I also wanted badly to swat the teenager with a rolled-up newspaper.

Ellie drove us toward my house. "Do you suppose the police will question Arlene?" she wondered aloud.

"Sure. They'll want to talk to everyone who was there."

Which reminded me, I still had that guest book. The cops could use it to track down the guests who'd skedaddled when the party started featuring a dead guy.

"Right," said Ellie. "She's a possible witness, isn't she?"

I took a deep breath and said it out loud. "At least. It's the least that Arlene could be."

We'd reached the Coast Guard station and the entrance to the breakwater, empty and still under the dock lights except for the fishing boats shifting on the rising tide.

"For all we know, Arlene could've been up on that terrace with him," I said.

We'd both been thinking it. The cops would, too, once they knew she'd been there and why.

"Maybe he made a pass at her." The big plate-glass windows of the storefronts on Water Street reflected the street lamps' yellowish glow as we went by. "A more serious one than she wanted, maybe." Whereupon certainty of her girlish dreams would shatter pretty abruptly, wouldn't they? "She could've shoved him reflexively, or maybe to defend herself," I went on.

"Have to shove him pretty hard."

Yeah. Rafferty was of average height, so the balcony wall would've stopped him from going over otherwise.

All of which Arlene's mother, Dot Cunningham, was going to learn about soon, because Arlene, poor foolish little girl that she was, had signed the guest book.

I'd have to get the book to Lizzie in the morning. I told Ellie about it as we drove past the Frontier Bank building, the Happy Crab, and Peavey Library, then turned up Key Street. At the top of the hill my big old house came into view, its gables and chimneys and shutters all bathed in blue-white moonlight.

Which was fine. What was not fine was that every single window in the place was lit up, as if some sort of uproar was going on in there.

"Now what?" Ellie said, pulling to the curb; she'd seen the lights, too.

"Take me to the airport. There's got to be a flight leaving for Timbuktu sometime soon, wouldn't you think?"

I didn't know what was going on in there, but I doubted it had much to do with the calm, peaceful rest-of-the-evening I'd been envisioning.

Ellie smiled. "You wouldn't like Timbuktu. Anyway, I meant what about Arlene."

"Oh." I thought about this. But I didn't know what else we could do for the girl.

"Jake, they're going to suspect her, you know they are. She might not be the only one, but—"

Oh. Darn. "Yeah, you're right. Young girl, emotional about Rafferty, way out of her element and maybe a little drunk . . ." Getting weird about him, Lee had said of Arlene. "And I suppose you'd like to try helping her out, is that it?"

Inside my house a great deal of running was occurring, both dogs were barking, and a toy piano banged out a fractured tune, over and over.

I looked around the car interior. "You wouldn't happen to have anything to drink in this jalopy, would you?"

Ellie's husband, George, had been known to carry an unopened pint of Fireball in the glove compartment in case of emergency.

"Sorry," Ellie said. She could hear all the commotion going on inside, too. "He moved it to the pickup truck."

That made sense. Inside my house, either a bomb went off or someone dropped a piano. A real one.

"About Arlene, though," Ellie went on. "I get it, Jake. I don't feel like getting involved, either. But Arlene and Lee have been friends since preschool." She made a rueful face. "I don't understand the friendship but I do know it's real. So I don't think I can just ignore this whole thing and let whatever happens, happen. For one thing—"

"I understand," I cut in. I did, too. Ellie and I both knew plenty about growing up alone, even though her folks were alive while I'd had one dead, one (my dad, on the run) gone. "Hey, we've had worse reasons," I said.

We kept saying we would never do it again, but then we did. On the other hand, maybe they'd arrested someone else already, and we wouldn't need to.

"Okay, look," I said, and Ellie glanced hopefully at me. "I've got to give the guest book to Lizzie anyway. I can at least try getting the lay of the land."

She brightened momentarily, but then her face fell again. "You'll have to tell Lizzie about Arlene, though, won't you?"

"Right." That she was there, that she'd called us... "But probably she already knows," I said. "Dylan would've told her."

As I got out of the car, from the house came the howl of a toy fire engine's siren, the thumpity-thump of feet, and Sam's voice, patient but sounding a little frayed.

I closed the car door, its faint thud drowned out by a blast of toy-piano crescendos not followed, unfortunately, by any diminuendos. Then I leaned in the passenger-side window.

"Are you going to find Lizzie right now?" Ellie asked.

Another onslaught of tone deafness erupted from the house behind me. I'd never known there were so many devil's intervals on a toy piano.

"Oh, you'd better believe I am," I said.

When I got back to Stone House, the courtyard with the fountain spurting in it looked like a disco ballroom, flashing with red and blue lights of squad cars parked at odd angles.

I pulled in behind one of the white pickup trucks that the Eastport Police Department bought instead of riot gear; Lizzie had said if people started rioting in Eastport they'd have a reason, and running an army tank down Water Street wouldn't fix it.

As I crossed the terrace, Dylan Hudson, sitting alone at one of the glass-topped tables, looked up and saw me.

"Hey," he greeted me. "Lizzie's gone back into town," he added.

He was eyeing me curiously; the man had cop instincts and knew more was wrong than just the lump still motionless on the terrace, now at least covered by a blue tarp.

So I pulled out the guest book and told him how I'd gotten it. And when I finished, he was properly apoplectic.

"You're telling me you and Ellie were here, on the balcony, soon after it happened. And this Arlene girl was up there, too?"

"No. When we arrived she was sitting over there on the edge of the fountain, staring at the body," I said.

He looked severe, which he could do very effectively. "So you didn't tell me the whole story before?"

I blew out through pursed lips. "No. I'm sorry. But listen, Dylan, Arlene and her mother aren't going anywhere, no one has to go pound on their door in the middle of the—"

"Not my call." Tucking the guest book into his jacket, he caught the eye of one of the officers at the scene, a tall, fit-looking woman in a tan state police uniform.

"She's in charge," Dylan told me. "I don't work with those folks anymore, remember?"

That was an understatement. From some of the stories he'd told I gathered Dylan was practically radioactive to quite a few of his old colleagues.

"But you know her," I pressed. "You could put in a word for Arlene, remind them that she's a child, so if they could just remember that when they talk to her . . ." It was the slimmest of threads, and I grabbed on to it like it was steel cable. "Come on, Dylan, Arlene's just a kid."

Behind him, the state cops were setting up bright-white floodlights. In their sudden glare, Hank Rafferty's body under the tarp looked sad and small.

"Yeah," he said finally, "I could do that." Then he flashed me that smile, the sweet, sly one that you could fall right into and never complain, and dropped an arm onto my shoulder.

"So okay, now, you've done your duty. Go on home. I'll be leaving, too, right after I hand this over."

When he said he would do something, you could take it to the bank; I figured I might as well follow his advice. Maybe I'd get home and find them all sound asleep, not laughing, sobbing, burping, running, squalling, fighting, or toy piano–playing.

Especially no toy piano–playing, and no kazoos. But just then the coroner's van pulled in.

"Wow," said the tech who jumped out from behind the wheel, "two calls here in one day?"

Hard to believe that the shed blaze had happened just last night. I continued toward my car, then saw the other tech bend to the body, pull back a tarp corner, and look a question toward the tan-uniformed woman whom Hudson had said was in charge.

From where I stood, I could only see Rafferty's head. The size of the blackish-looking pool on the flagstones beneath it was no surprise; we all know what head wounds do. What the tech said next, though, was a new wrinkle.

"Somebody called this in as a DBU?" he queried.

Death by Unknown Cause, he meant, but it sure looked clear to me: splat. The tan-uniformed woman strode over; Hudson, too.

The tech squinted up at them. Hudson aimed a flashlight, already nodding tight-lipped when the tech spoke again.

"Because hey, I'm no doctor," he said, as I moved closer to see where the tech was pointing: Rafferty's forehead. "But even with these cuts and abrasions disguising it . . ."

Yeah. I saw it now, too: small, round, reddish black. It was the exit wound that had bled so much.

". . . I mean, doesn't that look like a bullet hole to you?"

It did.

Five

Heading back toward Eastport in the Fiat, all that I'd seen and heard felt like a bunch of metal pots and pans clattering around in my head. Home might be as silent when I got there, but I'd be bringing my own mental noise with me.

So instead I just drove. Across the water, the moon was setting behind pointed firs with tops like sharp black teeth. The tide was falling, the rivulet-channeled mud flats shining in the last gleams of moonlight.

At the top of the hill where the land sloped to pasture on the right and rose sharply to a gravel pit entrance on the left—the pit wasn't dug much anymore, guys mostly just stored lobster traps in the off season—I took a right turn into the jumbled warren of twisty, confusing streets that made up Quoddy Village, and in the dark I got lost almost at once.

The little wooden houses built to shelter Army engineers during World War II sank into vacancy afterward, then came alive again years later as new young families moved in. Now I drove slowly among postage-stamp yards and newly installed picket fences around neat bungalows, most dark for the night.

And while I drove, I thought about murder . . . or at least about unnatural death. Two of them had occurred in as many days at Stone House, and if that was a coincidence, I thought, I'm Ferdinand the Bull. But if it wasn't, then the deaths were connected, and so far, only Stone House connected them.

Mulling this while peering ahead into the darkness, I turned left onto a small, rutted road that I was fairly sure I hadn't ever been on before. In fact, I didn't think it had even existed the last time I was in Quoddy Village.

Which seemed odd, but then I realized: it wasn't a road at all. The bits of gravel on it dwindled rapidly to dirt, and the deeply gouged ruts, large, sticking-up rocks, and a washboardlike surface that rattled the fillings in my teeth began manifesting themselves.

Then water began running down it straight toward me, filling the ruts and sparkling in the Fiat's headlights. Maybe from a small spring or a burst pipe somewhere uphill? Also, the soil here was the kind that got slick the minute it got wet; suddenly the tires were spinning in slop.

I tried to reverse. The tires spun uselessly again, just in the other direction. I rocked forward and backward; no luck. I was stuck, and of course now my phone couldn't be found; it was in Ellie's car, probably, on the floor or between the seats.

Unless Ephraim had filched it out of my bag after I put it in; he'd done it before. But that didn't matter; where it wasn't was right here, where I could call for help with it.

Finally I turned the engine off and sat back, suddenly feeling that the utter silence I'd been yearning for wasn't so good after all. Also, I tried to come up with an exit strategy that didn't involve getting pulled out of here by a tow truck.

Calling Wade was out of the question, even if I'd had a phone; my husband would not be pleased to get out of his nice, warm bed to go out and rescue his wife's vintage Italian sports car from a mudhole she never even had to get into in the first place.

So I racked my brain for a plan B. The only other person I could call at this hour was Ellie, and since George was home tonight—the job he'd expected to start on tomorrow was delayed—that meant him finding out, too.

And I so much did not want a major production made of this. Questions, objections, skeptical comments; how would I explain wandering around all alone late at night, driving up and down unknown driveways by accident and getting stuck in them?

Much less visiting a murder scene, which was what I'd been doing before that. I could've walked home but I didn't want to leave the Fiat here, so I was about to get out and slog back down the old lane or driveway or whatever it was, find one of the little houses that still had its lights on, and knock on the door; probably they'd let me use a phone.

Just as I put my hand on the car door, though, I heard sounds from outside, coming closer. *Schwuck. Schwuck.*

If a zombie just happened to be shambling through a swamp straight toward you, it would make precisely that sound. Then someone rapped on the passenger-side window and peered in.

All I saw were two eyes as big and round as soda-bottle bottoms. With a faint, startled *eep!* I shrank back against the driver's-side door, trying to melt into it.

But then whatever it was rapped again, and the fingers looked human. Also they ended in manicured nails, and I thought hardly any zombies had those.

Heart hammering, I leaned over and rolled the window down. The face that peered in was gray-headed, pink-cheeked, and wore thick-lensed glasses that magnified its already large blue eyes.

"Are you all right, dear?" The woman standing outside the car shone her flashlight in at me.

I put my hands up to shield my eyes. "No! I mean, yes, I will be if you'd please stop shining that light in my face."

The light went out. "Oh! Of course. Sorry." A brief pause, then: "Now, how exactly were you planning to get out of here?"

Yeah, *exactly* was the problem, all right. A sigh escaped me; here I was, in difficulties of my own making, having to get help from an elderly lady who from what I could see was probably a lot more fragile than I was.

Good going, Jacobia. Still, she probably had a phone, maybe even right here with her now. So I asked her.

She nodded approvingly; so I *did* have a plan. "Yes. Phone. Right. Come along with me, then, it's back at the house."

Personally, if I'd been going out at night to find out what the heck was going on in my neighborhood, I'd have brought my phone with me. But when she'd gotten me down the drive-way—more *schwuck! schwuck!*—and after that down the narrow, curving lane to her house, I understood.

The phone was a landline. "It's in the kitchen," she called over her shoulder, going in ahead of me while I stood on the doorstep, standing first on one foot and then on the other, peeling off my muck-soaked shoes and sodden socks.

The house was one of the old wood-framed bungalows I mentioned, once home to a corpsman engineer and a young family, probably: door center front, windows on either side, gables at the ends. Someone had put a new foundation under it and energy-efficient windows into it, and the gables were newly vented.

So: money. Not lots of it, but some; I'd owned an old house myself, so I knew. But then I went inside in my cold, bare feet and changed my tune the moment my toes touched the heated tile floor.

Yeah, definitely money. "Go ahead and use the phone," my rescuer called from deeper in the house. "I'll be out directly."

The front door led directly into the living room, where a green-enameled woodstove flickered on a brick hearth. Orchids in pots clustered on a table below the picture window, and a row of prisms hung in front of the window glass.

An incense cone smoldered in an onyx burner. A Burmese cat peered narrow-eyed at me from atop the stuffed-full bookshelves covering most of one wall.

Music played: gongs and a theremin. For a minute I feared I might start chanting "OM" and not stop.

Yeah, not really. But it was a lot to take in, and the cat's stare made me feel like the creature was mentally dividing me into cat-sized portions.

Finally the woman who'd brought me here reappeared. I was examining the books on the shelves.

"Sorry, I didn't mean to snoop," I said, but she didn't seem bothered. She also didn't look like the little old lady I'd thought she was.

That hair wasn't gray, it was blond, thick and beautifully cut. Also, she looked different without the glasses: younger and less fragile, somehow.

Much less fragile. She saw me assessing her and smiled. "I'm Maggie Davies," she said with the air of someone used to introducing herself. "And you must be Jacobia Tiptree."

The small, snug room glowed by the light of a dozen potted candles burning on tables and in wall niches.

"How did you know my name?" I asked. I was certain I'd never encountered the woman—Maggie Davies, she'd said her name was—before.

She wore ankle-length black leggings and a moss-green wool shift; a few thin, gold bangles; and a necklace of wooden beads.

"My mother has mentioned you," she replied, still not solving the mystery of how a complete stranger could address me by name.

She waved me to a low chair that looked like, but of course could not be, vintage Eames; the one with the leather upholstery and rosewood frame, no less. Hesitantly I sat, and the wonderful old chair seemed to gather me in.

"And Ellie," she continued, reaching to coax the cat down from the shelf onto her shoulder and from there to the floor. Its legs made frantic scrambling motions before its paws touched hardwood; then it shot from the room.

So much for any rapport with animals that I might've been kidding myself about. Maggie opened the little stove to poke the fire and lay another chunk of wood on it.

"Your mother?" I asked, still puzzled, but the stove door clanking shut must have drowned out my voice. And it didn't matter anyway. "I'd better phone home," I said. The later it got, the worse it would be. Besides, the only way through this was to do this, as Bella would've put it.

I got up before I could fall sound asleep in that amazing chair. But Maggie stopped me. "I might have a better idea. I've got this friend who—look, let me just make a call."

Fatigue made me obey; that and wanting to take care of all this without fanfare. Her voice from the next room was faint but clear:

"Hi, Dot, is Chad there?" A pause. "He's in the truck? Great. Listen, Dot, could you call him and ask him to stop over here on his way home? Little towing job, only take a minute." Another pause. "Yes, I'm sure he has heard that one before. Thanks, Dot, tell him I owe him."

Listening, I couldn't believe it. If I wasn't mistaken, I was being thrown a lifeline. Maybe I'd could even get home and inside with no one the wiser.

But the lifeline was being thrown to me by Chad Cunningham, stepfather of Arlene and husband of the ferociously dislikable Dot.

Maggie returned in minutes with tea and a plate of cookies. They were not Chocolate Moose cookies, but they were decent and I was hungry.

"Sorry I took so long," Maggie said. "This isn't my house, it's my mother's, and I don't know where anything in it is."

My eyebrows must've gone up.

"Mrs. Boyd?" Maggie said. "Used to have a bakery . . . ?"

"Oh, of course! Oh, I'm so sorry she's fallen ill." I looked around again. Lil had made a lovely place for herself.

"Yes, I came up from Boston after I couldn't get her on the phone," Maggie explained. "She'd been so active and healthy all along, but when I got here . . ."

"Oh dear." It was among my greatest fears, that Bella or my dad might fall or suffer some other sudden catastrophe.

"Anyway, I've found her a wonderful spot in a great place in Boston, close to me."

Maggie glanced around at the many small, charming objects in the room. Plants, candles, crystals, books . . . and the cat, of course.

"Dealing with all this is going to be a project," said Maggie with a helpless little shrug. "Right now, though, I'm just here to pick up a few things for her."

"I'm so glad it worked out as well as it did," I said. "I'll be holding a good thought for her. Boston, you said?"

A small frown tightened the skin around those amazing blue eyes of hers, the color of opals. But then her face cleared.

"Yes, and I'm lucky I didn't hit any radar on the way here, or I'd probably be in jail now." She poured the tea. "Anyway, my friend is coming with his tow truck in fifteen minutes or so."

Relief washed through me. Also, on second thought, why would Chad Cunningham care whose car he hauled, as long as he got paid? He likely didn't even know yet about Arlene's exploits tonight.

"Thank you," I told Maggie sincerely, and sipped the tea, which was hot, strong, and loaded with lemon and honey.

"You're most welcome. What brought you out here, anyway?"

By tomorrow, what had happened at Stone House would be all over town. So I wasn't telling secrets when I sat there and told her why I was out tonight at all, and how if I didn't find out what was going on, fast, then a young girl was headed for a very unpleasant interaction with the criminal justice system.

I hoped that was the worst that could happen. "Right now, though, it all still remains to be seen," I finished, and just then lights from the road arced across the front window.

But it wasn't a tow truck, and it didn't stop. "I'm taking up too much of your time," I said. "I could wait in the car, I'll be fine." Then I realized something else. "I've got fifty dollars with me, d'you think that's enough?"

Maggie was also on her feet. "Let's both go," she said, and moments later we'd pulled on our jackets and I'd reluctantly put on my wet, squishy sneakers again, and we were off.

A distant streetlight twinkled faintly, blocks away. Stars prickled overhead, and the night was silent.

Maggie strode briskly ahead of me. "Are you always so wide-awake this late?" I joked quietly.

"Yes," her voice came from the darkness ahead of me. "I've never mastered the early-to-bed trick."

It wasn't far to the Fiat. Water still streamed along its tires, turning everything to muck. No tow truck was in evidence, nor was there any sound of one approaching.

"He'll be here," Maggie assured me. "I've got my phone with me now, he'd message me otherwise." Frowning, she looked around with the flashlight. "Where's this water coming from, I wonder?"

It could be traveling overland from Niagara Falls, for all I cared. All I wanted now was that truck.

"I'm sure he'll show up soon," I said, trying to sound confident. But now that I was out here in the chilly darkness, I didn't feel that way, and the silence around us felt suddenly intense, like someone else was in it with us.

Maggie didn't seem to notice, and then without warning the feeling was gone, vanished as if it had never been there.

"Funny they called it Stone House," Maggie's voice came back to me out of the gloom. "Where you were tonight, I mean," she went on. "Don't people usually give new houses a different name from their first ones? And with such bad luck in the original place . . ."

I leaned on the Fiat's front fender. "Really? The Stone House people had an earlier house here in Eastport?"

Over the years, mostly through Ellie, I'd acquired bits of knowledge about almost all the old houses in town. A few still even had descendants of the original families in them.

But I'd never heard about this one. "Is it still standing?"

An amused-sounding laugh came back to me. "You could say that. Try right up there."

In the side glow from her flashlight her face appeared, a strong, determined visage. She pointed the light up the driveway. "There it is, ye olde home place."

I looked where she indicated. Between clumps of trees and ancient stumps, old walls had stood: long humps in the earth, covered in leaves and leaf mold, too straight to be natural.

A small house. "Who were they, does anyone know?"

She was already nodding. "My mother looked into it. The Hallowells were a Boston family. He was a doctor and a maker of medicines, but after they came here on holiday once and saw the bay, he got more into the import-export business."

Smuggling, she meant. Canada was very nearby, and every dollar you didn't pay in taxes was a dollar in profit, then as now. And then of course there was Prohibition, when Canadian whiskey got sneaked in by anyone with a boat and some nerve.

Meanwhile, still no tow truck. If this went on much longer I'd have to call home. Then all at once I became aware that the night had gone silent once more; like, *extra* silent.

I glanced over at Maggie, who didn't seem to have noticed anything unusual, then past her and uphill to where the first of the Hallowells' homes had stood a long time ago.

And of course what I saw then was an illusion, the pine board walls and the stone-built well with the hand crank and wooden bucket. The long, wide porch was a figment, as were the windows reflecting pale moonlight from two centuries ago.

I gave myself a shake. When I looked again, the house was gone; then Maggie pointed past me. "Here he comes."

Cock-eyed headlights jounced toward us. Then the truck pulled up alongside us, and the driver leaned out. "This it?"

"Yep. Just haul 'er out," Maggie replied, "and thank you very much, Chad." She gestured at me. "This lady will pay you."

"And I," I told her, "will repay you, somehow." I had no idea how Maggie Davies knew Chad Cunningham well enough to ask favors of him, but she'd completely saved my bacon.

Or she had so far; I still needed to get the rest of the way home. But the out-of-the-mud portion of the program was now underway, and could my own driveway be far behind?

Surely it could not, I thought as burly, bearded Chad Cunningham hooked a chain to the Fiat's rear axle, then got back into his truck. The winch started up, the car's rear end rose, and the rest of the vehicle followed until it was free and out on the pavement once more.

Then he took the fifty I offered, muttered thanks, and took off with the truck's cherry-red taillights dangling from the back end like cartoon eyeballs.

Once he was gone I stuck the key in the ignition and turned

it, put the transmission in gear, and let out the clutch, feeling like I might be okay. All I had to do was get home, get into the house, and . . .

The engine died. I started it again; this time a sort of low grinding sound came from it.

Not a good sound. A smell rose from somewhere below, like hot wires or possibly burning transmission fluid. But the Fiat did run now, occasionally bucking like a mule and smelling like an electrical fire was about to break out any moment.

As I nursed the little car along, anxiety prodded me; no one at home had heard from me in quite a while and now it was—I glanced at the dashboard clock—nearly midnight.

Wade would be worrying, and when he got worried, he got mad; Bella, too. I pressed harder on the gas pedal but backed off as the car shuddered, threatening another seizure.

Half a mile, half a mile, half a mile onward . . .

Oh, Lord, was I ever in for it.

"Okay now," Bella pronounced the next morning when she'd heard the whole story, "*that* is *weird.*"

"Deeply," Ellie agreed. "And then what happened?"

We were at the Moose, around the front table by the window.

"I came home," I said. "In fits and starts, but I made it."

After I'd seen the ancient house site in Quoddy Village, I meant; that was what we all agreed was so unusual. The Fiat was already down at Spinney's Garage on Washington Street. I'd left it there the night before and walked home, in case it didn't start at all the next time I tried.

"I still say," Bella grumbled, "you should have called."

Tiptoeing into the dark house, I'd heard only silence. The dogs had blinked drowsily up from their dog beds and I'd thought I'd gotten lucky, that everyone was asleep.

Then Bella's frizzy head had poked out from the annex. I

could tell she was about to start in on me, so I fled to the hall where I encountered my thoroughly unhappy husband.

Meanwhile, Mika was upstairs being violently ill in the bathroom she and Sam shared—don't ask me how I knew this, okay?—and of course now the kids were beginning to stir: first Nadine, then Ephraim with a xylophone.

And after that the whole coming-home-late scene went about the way I had expected. In the end, though, seeing me alive and well had improved Wade's mood swiftly; ten minutes later he was back in bed, asleep.

But eight hours later, Bella was still miffed. "Yes," Ellie told my elderly stepmother-slash-housekeeper, "it would've been better if she'd had her phone." As I'd suspected, Ephraim had pilfered it. "But listen," Ellie went on, "what do we do about the money Rafferty didn't get to pay us? He was going to do it last night, but . . ."

Ah, yes, last night. "We did the job we said we'd do," I pointed out. "So it's true we deserve it."

I squinted out the window. Across the blue sky over the bay Canada geese arrowed south. "But do you really want to find Melissa and say something like, 'Sorry about your husband, where's my money?' "

"I'd rather go to the poorhouse than say any such thing," Bella declared, echoing my feeling. Then I got up; it was almost time to open the shop.

Chocolate doughnuts were the treat for today, and it was time to start frying them, so I got the batter bowl out and turned the electric frying kettle to high. Then I rolled the dough from the bowl onto a parchment sheet floured with sweetened cocoa and cut out the doughnut shapes.

With a doughnut cutter, of course, which I do enjoy pressing into the cold, firm batter, then giving the cutter a hard twist against the parchment paper to make sure the dough is cut all the way through, all the way around.

Finally I put the cutouts into the fryer, using a spatula. The smell of the sweet stuff suddenly sizzling in fresh oil rose up like a promise of glory, perfuming the shop. I could almost see the tendrils of sweet, fresh doughnut aroma snaking out the front door, hooking unsuspecting pedestrians by their nostrils and drawing them irresistibly in.

Then Lizzie Snow did come in, shaking off the early morning chill, peering around for coffee, and not looking talkative.

Silently I handed her a mug; she poured and sat, still without speaking, in the booth by the counter. I left her there while I took care of the doughnuts some more, and when they were done, drained and powdered-sugared, I brought her two of them.

"Watch it, they're hot," I warned, sitting across from her with my own coffee.

The rich, cakey circles of fried chocolate dough would be even better with chocolate frosting, but they weren't half bad now and she looked as if she could use one.

"Thanks." She reached out, then drew back hesitantly. "They don't have bombs in them, do they? Because everything else I've touched so far this morning has blown up in my face."

"I know the feeling." I'd managed to avoid many questions last night when I got home, but this morning at the breakfast table had been exasperating. "What's going on?"

She drained her cup, set it down with a clink. "I just left the Cunninghams' place. State cops have been there all night."

Poor Arlene, I thought. Her dad must not have known about it yet when he pulled me out of the mud. But when he found out, I doubted his reaction was calm and fatherly; Lee said the guy blew a gasket if you looked at him wrong.

"They took her phone, her computer, some notebooks," Lizzie went on. "They got the judge who'd signed the search warrant—"

Oh, good heavens. I'd had one of these served on me back in the bad old days, when my then-husband suspected me of having an affair (I wasn't). It's like having a rhinoceros snoop through your cabinets and your underwear drawer.

"—to put her on house arrest," Lizzie finished, sounding disgusted. "I mean, come on, if you suspect her, why not let her loose and surveil? See what she does and with whom."

My first thought about Arlene's confinement to home was *Good, then Arlene can't get into even more trouble.* But in principle I agreed with Lizzie: no risk it, no biscuit.

Still, none of this justified the bleakly resigned look on Lizzie's face as she sat watching the boats go out. Finally:

"Arlene's mom did a bed check a few minutes ago."

Ellie had come to the kitchen door with the doughnut frying spatula in her hand. "Oh no," she said.

"Oh, yes." Lizzie laughed humorlessly. "Got out through a window, like no one should've been expecting that." She shook her head. "And this time when they find her, they're taking her into custody. The DA is talking to the judge right now."

Great, I thought, now the charming and brilliant Arlene Cunningham had revealed herself to be a serious flight risk in the most direct way possible: by fleeing. I wanted to take her and shake her, not that it would've put a lick of sense into her; for that thick skull of hers, you'd need a brickbat.

"So ask Lee, will you? If Arlene's been in touch. Better I should find her first than those guys, you know?" Lizzie said.

"Aren't the state cops being kind of hasty about all this?" Ellie asked. "Why are they already so sure it even was murder?"

Rafferty could've shot himself, she meant.

Lizzie sighed. "Bullet wound but no weapon found, and no gunshot residue on the vic's hands. That say anything to you?"

Yeah, it said that either Rafferty got shot by a ghost gun that now had vanished back into the spirit realm, or some live person—not Rafferty—had fired a real gun.

With a real bullet in it. But how the hell—?

"And the thing is," Lizzie went on, "the gun's been found."

I waited.

"Under Arlene's mattress."

And there it was, the stinger in the tale. I said nothing, knowing what that last revelation meant, and it was Ellie who ended up putting it all into words for the three of us:

"Arlene Cunningham," she intoned gravely, "is in deep and serious trouble."

Later that day we learned more about Arlene Cunningham's flight path.

"She called me," Lee said. "Around six this morning, she wanted me to give her a ride out to Perry Corners."

It was where a bus to Bangor stopped each morning at 7:15. Obviously, Arlene had intended to be on it.

"Did she say where she wanted you to pick her up?" Ellie asked. And on second thought: "You didn't take her, did you?"

We sat at the soda fountain in Fickett's Pharmacy, on High Street next to St. Rita's church. The place smelled sweetly of aspirin and malted milk powder; the mirror-backed shelves behind the soda-fountain counter displayed vintage glass medicine jars: codeine, arnica, sarsaparilla.

"God no." Lee was drinking a root beer float. But then she took in our faces: worried, questioning. "Why, what's happened?"

So we told her pretty much all that had gone on the night before; Arlene, apparently, hadn't filled her in.

"You didn't take her there last night, did you?" I asked. "To Rafferty's place, to the party he was throwing?"

"I was cramming for my Latin test," she replied, looking me in the eye.

"Well, now she's run away," Ellie finished. "The police are looking for her."

"Holy criminy," Lee breathed, putting aside the rest of her sweet, creamy drink. "What's going to happen now?"

"That depends," Ellie said, "on how quickly she's found."

Lizzie had told us that Arlene's prompt return, plus an apology to the court and the explanation that she'd panicked and wouldn't do it again, would all help a lot.

But at this Lee grimaced. "Fat chance. If she's in trouble, the last place she'll go is anywhere near her mother."

"Yeah," I sympathized, thinking *that poor kid*. "Dot's the last person I want to get near, too. But she's got to, Lee."

"That's right," said Ellie. "This is serious. So if you see her, or she calls you again . . ."

Lee slid off her stool, nodding agreement. "Okay. I get it."

She turned toward the door, then faced us again, walking backward on Fickett's vintage black-and-white tiled floor.

"You believe me, though, right? About driving her this morning?"

Ellie nodded until the girl was gone, then turned to me. "She drove Arlene to Rafferty's last night, though, didn't she?"

It was a pretty good bet that she had. I sighed, thinking about how smart I'd been at that age, which was not very.

"Yeah, probably," I replied. "What can I say? Can't live with 'em, can't sell 'em for parts." I finished the rest of Lee's root beer float. "Now what?"

Ellie shrugged. "Go back to work, I guess. I'm not about to serve Lee up to the cops on a platter."

At the very least they'd put her through the wringer on the topic of Arlene's current whereabouts; at worst, depending on what she actually knew or had done, Lee could be an accessory to Arlene's crimes.

If, that is, Arlene had really committed any; despite the gun they'd found, I still wasn't sure.

"Fine," I said, sliding off my stool at the counter. The antique codeine bottle on the soda fountain's back shelf said it was for HEADACHE AND TOOTHACHE, THE ARNICA FOR SORE MUSCLES.

I wondered what got taken back then for Irritated Beyond Belief. "Maybe we should just let Arlene run."

"The girl's fifteen," Ellie reminded me, and with that, of course, she knew she had me back on the hook.

She knew that at fifteen, I'd been alone in the big city, earning my way by taking stapled-shut paper bags to addresses that I'd had to memorize, since if they were in writing they could be used as evidence.

Now Ellie and I paid for our sodas and made our way toward the door. "What I really wish is that we'd never taken the Stone House job."

"You and me both," Ellie sighed as we passed the magazine rack. The sweet, old-fashioned aroma of colored ink on thick, glossy paper drifted from it.

Or maybe that was just my imagination, too. Outside the Moose, we stopped beneath the cutout wooden silhouette of a moose head with large antlers, googly eyes, and a goofy grin.

"By the way," she said casually, "did I mention we got an order in yesterday for four dozen chocolate fruitcake cookies?"

I looked at Ellie the way you might look at someone who's just made a root canal appointment for you. Fruitcake cookies weren't as much work as actual fruitcake, but they were a big project, and I disliked handling the sticky candied fruit.

Through the front window I could see Bella inside the shop, behind the counter looking like she wanted badly to give someone a piece of her mind.

I didn't know why, and that was okay with me. "You know," I said slowly, "maybe I shouldn't come in right now."

Ellie tipped her head. "Because?"

"Because I need to take the Fiat out for a test drive. Spinney could be done with it by now."

Ellie looked unfooled. "Okay, and if by any chance you happen to spot Arlene while you're test-driving . . ."

"Yeah, yeah," I said, waving her off with a smile. She knew the real reason I was going out. "Don't worry," I told her, "you bake the cookies and I'll go do the other thing that we do best."

Which was snooping, of course.

Spinney's Garage was a cavernous concrete-block structure painted white on the outside and stained black inside by decades of car exhaust, engine smoke, and radiator spew plus dabs of spray paint here and there. Two stumps where the gas pumps used to be stood out front near the air pump; a car-wash device dispensed hot or cold water from a metered hose.

The Fiat sat outside, looking spiffy. I ducked under the half-open garage door and found Alf Spinney tinkering with the restored Model T he'd brought back to mint condition over the course of ten Maine winters. He was wearing ear protectors so I just shook the Fiat keys at him to let him know I was taking it.

Outside, I settled behind the wheel, popped on a pair of sunglasses, smiled at the satisfying growl of twin carburetors, and pulled out of the lot. Then, even though the car's top speed was bat-out-of-hell, I drove sedately all the way up Washington Street and out of town.

For one thing, nobody needed to know that if it had to, this car could catch them and eat them; also, the speed limit here was enforced now that Lizzie ran the cop shop.

But when I got to the old textile mill and the fifty-five-mph zone, I stomped on the gas and the feisty little vehicle leapt forward with an eager snarl.

Five minutes later I pulled in among trees and saplings alongside Route 190. The flat waters of the cove sparkled gaily in the autumn sunshine; to my right, a sandy cliff rose pretty much straight up.

I parked the car so it would look like I'd simply gotten out and crossed the road to the water's edge. A narrow beach, sandy and studded with granite outcroppings, was busy now with small seabirds devouring what the last high tide had delivered.

It was easy to believe that I might've decided on impulse to walk on that beach; maybe even past the farthest tall chunk of granite jutting out into the cove. It wasn't that far, it was the kind of thing I might do, and people knew it.

But the last place on earth I meant to go was to the beach. No, I was going . . .

I craned my neck to squint at the cliff's crumbly looking top. Back out of sight from its edge, I knew, stood Stone House. Taking a deep breath, I approached the foot of the cliff where it met the shore.

Arlene Cunningham might know something about how Rafferty died. She might even have killed him. But what if she didn't and hadn't? Then someone else must have, and killed the shed man, probably, too; anything else was just too much of a coincidence.

That one of the party guests might be guilty was a nonstarter; the cops would talk to them, but none of them had been here when the shed man died, as far as I knew.

As for other possible suspects . . . well, that's what I was here to start finding out. Thinking this, I turned reluctantly to my planned ascent route.

The first part wasn't sand but steep shale slope, nearly as bad, partly concealed by a granite outcropping on one side and large fallen rocks on the other.

Not completely hidden; still, it was the best way up that I could see. Driving up the driveway, by contrast, was sure to get me noticed before I ever got to the top.

So I began: the flat, sharp-edged shale pieces slid when I put my weight on them; right away it was less like climbing and more like swimming uphill. Ten minutes later I was only half-way to the top, scrabbling with my hands, pushing with my feet, and swearing with my mouth.

And then I got stuck. Under the sliding layers of shale I'd hit sand, soft and slippery as silk; my feet paddled uselessly. Gritty dust clotted in my mouth and my fingertips were bloodied ruins of what had been a halfway decent manicure.

I flung my arm up again as far as I could; ouch. But I only touched more of the talcum-powder soil. Nothing to grab on to, dammit, not a rock, root, or . . .

Damn. This was supposed to be a quick reconnoiter, not an all-day affair. Probably I should back off now, try a different route later. I put my hand out to start clambering down.

Then . . . wait a minute . . . I felt something. *"Ngyah!"* It *moved.* Like a snake, which was unlikely, or a lizard, even more so.

Or like . . . it wiggled at me again . . . like a rope?

But that was the silliest thought of all, because there was absolutely no reason why a rope of any kind, and especially one with such a convenient loop handle, should be—

"Jacobia," Ellie's voice came impatiently from above, "will you just grab the darned thing?"

We hurried along the massive stone side of the house, seeing no one. Ellie's car was parked by the shed ruins, still blackened and now strung with yellow tape.

"How did you know I was there?" As we drove downhill on the new driveway, I took the water bottle she handed me and guzzled.

If she hadn't known, sooner or later I'd have had to call her, and I didn't want to; it was embarrassing, getting stuck hallway up a cliff.

She pulled onto the highway. "Wanda Wilkins was coming home from Calais and saw you pulling off, across from the beach."

If Ellie and I hadn't already been the town busybodies, Wanda would've been.

"She came into the Moose wanting to know if I'd heard from you, that you might be having car trouble."

Good old Eastport, where keeping an eye out has developed into an art form of which gossip is the performance aspect.

Ellie pulled over onto the gravel shoulder near where I'd parked the Fiat. I got out of Ellie's car, got into my own, and followed her back into town . . .

The Fiat, by the way, ran like it was brand-new—

. . . where I learned that Arlene Cunningham hadn't returned, and now there was a warrant issued for her arrest.

"Ayuh," said Magda Devine, slapping my change down on the counter at the Bay City Mobil station.

Magda's shoulder-length hair was an interesting shade of fuchsia, held back by two Betty Boop barrettes.

"Got troopers coming in and out. They think she's still here on the island somewhere."

She wore a brown flannel shirt over a T-shirt whose logo read I'M NOT YOUR MOMMY, plus brown corduroy pants, and the thing about Magda was, you never saw her anywhere but here. I wondered if at night they just leaned her against an interior wall and turned the lights out, and she'd stay that way until morning.

"Crawlin' all over the place," said Magda, dropping the cash register receipt on top of my change, and what I saw on the rest of my way downtown confirmed this.

Everywhere I looked there were state and county squad cars, blue-jacketed officers, supervisors in topcoats and shoes too good for the conditions, two K-9 units, and a woman—upswept gray hair, blue wool suit, sensible footwear—who was either a child psychologist or played one on TV.

Out in front of the Moose, a few tourists strolled on Water Street, shoulders touching, their faces turned happily up to the day's sunshine. The little bell over the door jingled as I went in with Ellie behind me.

"How," I asked, "did you know I was on the cliff?"

The tables were empty, Bella was gone, and Ellie was already in the kitchen. On the sound system, Elaine Stritch was singing about ladies who lunch, absolutely belting it out.

It made me feel better, a little. "Well," Ellie called back to me, "you know all that sand and shale you were busy kicking down behind you?"

She'd pulled on an apron, stuffed her hair up into a paper cap, and was at the sink washing her hands.

"I mean, d'you know where it went?" she added, scrubbing, and when I still didn't answer she went on. "It went down to the foot of the cliff, right next to the road." She grabbed a clean towel. "By the time I got there, the dust cloud looked like cartoon smoke signals," she finished.

"Oh," I said. Damn. "I, uh, didn't think of that. Thanks for saving me."

"You're welcome. Good effort, though, I hadn't thought of just climbing up the damned cliff."

Because of course she knew as well as I did that we needed a fact-finding trip. What we knew wasn't even enough to point us toward finding out more about Rafferty's unplanned demise.

Unplanned by him, anyway. Right now, though, Ellie was getting out the ingredients for chocolate fruitcake cookies, which despite me disliking the fruit-handling part so intensely are still divinely scrumptious once they've been made.

"I had to come up with a good reason to go to Stone House

at all, though," Ellie added. "Because of course someone would see me in the driveway and wonder why."

Gosh, I loved that woman; a pretext, she meant. And now that she'd begun cutting equal parts butter and lard into a mixture of flour, salt, and sugar plus twelve drops of almond extract, I had a bad feeling that I knew what that pretext was.

"And?" I asked, but the sound of pieces falling into place in my head was deafening. Darn.

"I went right up to the door and asked Melissa Rafferty if she had any people coming to the house, and if she needed help feeding them, and it turns out she does and she does," Ellie said as she worked the pastry cutter through the pastry mixture.

"And what did you promise her?" I asked apprehensively.

But at the sight of plastic containers full of brightly colored candied fruit coming out of the refrigerator one after the other, of course I knew:

"Just the fruitcake cookies."

She said it casually, as if these were not a delicate four-stage operation that had to be managed every step of the way so the filling didn't scorch, the pastry didn't burn, and the sugar sprinkles stuck onto their tops.

"A batch of cookies," she added, scraping the cookie dough from the sides of the bowl. "And two platters of jitterbugs."

"Oh," I said slowly, and have I mentioned that Ellie can be the sneakiest, slyest, most devious little . . .

She smiled sweetly at me. "We need a way to get in there, don't we? I mean," she added with a crooked grin, "unless you really do want to climb sand mountain again."

Her eyes widened innocently. She'd cooked this all up on her own while I was flinging myself bass-ackwards at a doomed cliff-climbing attempt.

"And at what time tonight are we to deliver all this sweet, chocolatey goodness?" I asked, unable to keep from smiling.

We wouldn't have to sneak out or make any excuses as to

where we were going. Or sneak into Stone House, either. It was just another catering job, totally aboveboard.

Of course it was. "I'll pick you up tonight at eight," she said. "We're only delivering, not serving, so we should be home again by ten at the latest, I expect."

Want to bet? I thought, and oh, was I ever right.

Six

After dinner that night, I asked Bella to come into the parlor, a small room behind the family living room and separated from it by a set of French doors.

"Sit down," I said, waving her to the chintz-covered settee by what used to be a delft-tiled fireplace; that is, before it caught the chimney on fire and nearly burned down the house.

Bella sat calmly, folding her liver-spotted hands in her lap. Except for her frizzy red hair in its purple hairnet, her big, grape-green eyes, and her jutting jawline full of various colors of aimed-every-which-way teeth—

Except for all that, she looked like a schoolgirl expecting to be reprimanded.

"Bella, I'm not mad about anything," I hurried to let her know. She brightened at once, tipping her head curiously at me.

"We're in the parlor with the door closed because it's such a circus in the rest of the house, even in your rooms."

Right now, my father was playing with the children while Sam took a shower and Wade waited to be next; Mika was upstairs with the baby, trying not to be sick—when asked, she said she must have eaten something that disagreed with her—and the dogs were outside digging holes in the garden while they pretended to be guarding the house.

"The thing is, Bella . . ." Somewhere outside the little room a small object crashed, shattering. Toddler wails followed.

"The thing is, everything is so hectic while the kids are still so little. So I thought a place where you and Dad could go and get some privacy, some peace and quiet, would be—"

Another crash and a quick series of thuds made me wonder if maybe the house was being demolished; a wrecking ball couldn't have made more commotion.

". . . good," I finished in the moment of silence that came next. But only a moment:

"No!" shouted Nadine. Next came the sound of her small, sneakered foot stomping angrily. "No, no, no!"

She owned her feelings, that was for sure. But her "no!" was brushed aside like a mosquito; in this house, bedtime was a sacred hour not subject to negotiation.

"See, out in this part of the house is one thing," I said. "Kids make noise, sometimes lots of it, but they live here, and we love them. So it's no big deal." A small smile curved Bella's thin lips. "But when they act like your place is their own special playground," I went on.

The smile vanished. Bella would step between those kids and a freight train, and any criticism of them had better stand up to some rigid scrutiny, her glance said clearly.

She was listening, though, and this seemed like a good sign until I realized: not to me. The baby was crying, and she'd tuned out as soon as he started. There'd be no talking to her now, not about the kids rowdying around in the annex or anything else.

"Is that it, then?" she asked. Nicely; it was just that she wanted to go upstairs and move mountains, if necessary, to stop the baby's huge, hitching wails.

"Yes," I said. "That's it. I just wanted you to know that if you or my dad ever feel you need my help in getting some—"

Privacy around here, I meant to finish, but she was gone, her footsteps already hurrying up the hall stairs.

"Okay," I said after a moment during which little Ephraim, for no particular reason that I could discern, began singing the Baby Shark song. At the top of his lungs, naturally.

"That went reasonably well," I said to myself, drawing the French doors apart. Instantly the TV's din plus the noise of Nadine playing on Sam's phone joined Ephraim's bellows.

Singing, rather. *Positive words create positive outcomes,* I reminded myself as I turned off the TV, sent Ephraim upstairs to get ready for his bath (now that Wade was out of the shower), and took Sam's phone from Nadine's sticky grasp, replacing it with her own pink toy device, which she eyed scornfully.

Finally when Ellie's car pulled up outside, I grabbed my jacket, hat, flashlight, and gloves, and of course the gun. That Wade had given it to me made having it now feel even more reassuring. Also, perhaps this may help answer any questions about what my husband thought of my snooping expeditions. Mind you, he climbed swaying ladders over cold, rolling seas every day of the week; it was how he got onto the big container ships that he piloted in through our bay's deadly currents, huge and powerful tides, and deadly granite ledges.

So he could hardly object very strongly to my activities. But even back then when my snooping tendencies were still in their infancy, Wade caught my drift, and I still thought his gift was a touching gesture of support, beyond the call, really, and useful sometimes, too. After all, just because I hadn't needed a weapon last night didn't mean I wouldn't tonight.

Finally with Ellie outside waiting I hurriedly grabbed my stuff, then went on out into the chilly evening to snoop around in a haunted house.

Outside, I found Ellie behind the wheel of her Toyota. In an orange hoodie, a black turtleneck, and an orange plaid skirt that ended mid-knee, plus black ankle boots—

"You look like a cheerleader for Halloween High," I said as I slammed the passenger-side door and she pulled away from the curb.

I'd worn blue jeans and a sweater, so now we knew who'd do any dirty work that might be required, I supposed.

Her answering smile was good-humored, almost as if there hadn't been two murders recently and her own daughter might be involved in one of them. Unwittingly, but still.

That's the way the cops would see it, anyway. "Some people respond to dressing up, others to dressing down," she replied perceptively. "So some will talk more freely to you, some to . . ."

"I get it." We were heading out of town; in the sodium glare of the parking lot lights at the bank and the IGA, the trees' leafless branches splayed thin, pale fingers across an indigo sky.

"But do you really think they'll talk about what happened?" I wondered aloud.

The people visiting Hank Rafferty's widow tonight, I meant, whom we'd baked cookies and made sandwiches for; that is, Lee made the sandwiches, but still.

Ellie shrugged, her eyes on the road and her face calmly purposeful in the dashboard lights. With her wavy, strawberry-blond hair, heart-shaped face, and eyes the deep, dark blue of forest violets, she was slim and delicate-looking and about as fragile as a bull moose. "What else would they want to talk about? I mean, maybe not right away, but they'll loosen up," she said.

Hashing over the details wouldn't bring much comfort to the new widow, though, which was what I had thought this gathering was for. On the other hand, my sense of this particular widow was that to affect her feelings one way or the other you'd need a water cannon.

We turned onto the new driveway. Ahead, lights flickered

through the freshly planted trees and shrubberies that Rafferty had paid to have planted.

At least they'd make good, if very expensive, firewood. The camelias, especially, were a bonehead idea.

Just as we swung around into the circle drive in front of Stone House, my phone jangled out the first few notes of the Baby Shark song. Ephraim must've reset the ringtone during some brief stretch when he'd had it in his hands, unsupervised; at five, my grandson knew more about the device than I ever would.

It was Lizzie Snow calling. "Hello, Miz Police Chief," I answered, "what can we do for you?"

"Okay, now, listen to me," her voice came crisply through the phone. In the background I heard people, plates and glasses clinking, a server's voice cutting through it all.

"I just got word that Arlene Cunningham's been found."

Ellie kept glancing urgently at me. I waved at her to just let me listen, would she, please?

"Jake, the girl's in bad shape. It looks like someone tried to—"

Ellie parked the car alongside half a dozen others near the burned-down shed.

"—kill her. Meanwhile, it turns out the gun we found under her mattress is definitely not the weapon that killed Rafferty. Wrong caliber."

"Holy criminy," I breathed. This changed everything, since the gun was Arlene's main problem, incrimination-wise.

"So does that mean she's in the clear?"

Lizzie answered regretfully. "Unfortunately, no. Bullets bounced around a lot inside Rafferty, got too deformed to match them to a specific weapon."

"So?"

"Arlene's dad owns quite a few handguns, and over the years he's lost track of a few, too."

How you lost a handgun has always been a mystery to me.

Stolen, sure, or lent but never returned. Misplaced, though? You, what, forgot where you put your deadly weapon?

Anyway: "She could've taken one of those to Rafferty's," I said, "and it hasn't been found, yet. If," I added cautiously—I was looking at it from the cops' point of view, not my own, "she did it at all."

"If," Lizzie agreed. "But you haven't asked about gunshot residue."

My spidey-senses tingled warningly. "Okay," I said. "What?"

"Of the party guests who hadn't yet flown home to wherever they were from—"

A mental picture of people hurrying out of Stone House and away into the night flashed through my mind.

"—only one of them had fired a handgun recently, and it wasn't Arlene."

"Oh! Well, that's not such bad news, why . . . ?"

Still with the phone to my ear, I got out of the car. Since yesterday someone had put up yard lights so bright, they could probably see them on the moon. Inside the house, either a string quartet was playing or somebody had put in a decent sound system since yesterday.

"Jake?" Lizzie's voice on the phone was impatient. "Are you still—"

"Yes, I'm here." I'd been getting the fruitcake cookies out of the car's back seat while being distracted by a dark-haired girl in a silver lamé dress, tottering across the flagstone veranda toward the fountain with a champagne glass in her hand.

Oh dear; so it was that kind of gathering. "Sorry," I said into the phone. "But you said someone had fired a gun recently?"

Ellie made impatient faces at me, twisting the *wrap it up* sign in the air with her finger; I mimed that I would, and didn't.

"The positive for gunshot residue was Dylan," Lizzie said.

Whoa. "There was some kind of big upset between Dylan and Rafferty at the party," Lizzie went on, "and you know Dylan's temper isn't exactly a secret."

Right, and since the state cops were his former colleagues, they knew about it, too.

Big-time, probably. "He was there, he was armed, and there's some talk of Hank Rafferty saying something about me that Dylan didn't like," Lizzie went on.

Oh, Lord, so that's what it had been about. "So he was supposed to be defending your honor?"

"Yeah." We paused, contemplating this notion. Next, he'd be flinging his jacket over puddles for her to walk on.

"As for the residue, he still shoots every day, so—"

Dylan kept his firearms skills polished to a shine at the Eastport Gun Club, knocking down targets each morning while racking up high marks on the clubhouse scoreboard.

"His hands probably always have residue on them," I said.

"You got it. Also, some of those state cops aren't fans of his."

Again, no surprise: Hudson was not the most diplomatic man, and when he got his dander up—Bella's phrase, but you knew that—his sarcastic remarks were always barbed, poison-dipped, and true enough to pierce deeply. Also, he wasn't automatically on the cop's side of the shooting whenever one occurred.

"Have they talked to you and Ellie yet?" Lizzie asked.

Across the floodlit driveway inside Stone House, the string quartet started playing something bouncy and bright. After slamming the car door and locking it, Ellie turned to me again, raising her eyebrows and dusting her hands together in a way I found intensely communicative.

"Lizzie, I've got to go," I said into the phone. "Was there something you wanted us to—?"

"Yeah. Let's go on keeping the celebrity aspect of this on the down-low for as long as possible, okay?" She took a breath. "Because believe it or not, an autumn birdwatching event starts in Eastport tomorrow, and I don't think flocks of grieving Rafferty fans are what they're coming to watch."

"You got it. Ut-up-shay." *No problem,* I thought as we hung up and I put away my phone.

"Here I come," I called to Ellie, who'd already crossed the driveway carrying the container of jitterbugs. I'd filched one of them as we left the Moose, and it was delicious.

The girl in the long silver dress sat forlornly on the fountain's edge. When I went by, she appeared to be weeping.

Inside, the cavernous front hall was full of flowers: roses in tall, cut-crystal vases, colorful mixed spring blossoms that must've been sent in at great expense, and a display of the palest green orchid blooms with their stems in foam blocks.

In the music room behind the parlor to the left, a real string quartet was indeed playing. The silver-dress girl came back in, not weeping after all but simply befuddled; I gathered she must've emptied that champagne glass she was carrying a few times already.

"Honey, are you okay?" Ellie called to her while balancing two of our plastic totes in her arms. I held the other two, praying not to drop one and scatter fruitcake cookies all over that gleaming mosaic-tiled floor.

The girl flashed a wan smile. "I'm fine, thank you," she said. "Or I will be, once I get out of here."

Then she went back into the parlor with the other guests; maybe a dozen of them, it sounded like, and they were talking about money and investments, not eulogizing Rafferty.

Still, I guessed everyone grieves differently. I didn't see Melissa anywhere, so we took our cargo out to the kitchen on our own.

"Wow," said Ellie, staring around. Another cook had been here earlier, clearly, leaving a baked ham in a Crock-Pot and the side dishes in the oven.

But that wasn't the surprising part. Ellie put her totes down on the marble-topped kitchen island and crossed to the double sink. It was stainless steel with a pot-washing faucet, a garbage disposal, and a dishwasher big enough to service a banquet hall built in underneath it.

In other words, it was a completely new kitchen, no longer the moldy old relic with the cracked yellow window shades and age-dulled paint. Melissa, it seemed, hadn't wasted much time making the place more to her liking.

"It must've cost a fortune, getting it done so fast," I said, and I confess I was the tiniest bit envious. In my old house, if you opened a pipe to install a dishwasher you'd start a chain reaction, a sort of old-plumbing apocalypse that eventually took down every pipe in the place. And don't even talk to me about what a hot water radiator will do for revenge.

"Custom cabinetry," Ellie said admiringly. "Two ovens and a warming drawer, five burners plus a griddle. And these windows."

She gestured at the diamond-paned sashes over the sink, each with its brand-new crank for easy opening and closing, then peered into the restaurant-sized refrigerator with the ice maker and cold-water dispenser in the door.

Its shelves were full of the kinds of specialty foods people buy at fancy stores and have delivered: caviar, mangoes, artichokes, cheeses, and under a sheet of plastic wrap a pair of tenderloin steaks so fresh you could practically still hear them mooing.

A sudden transformation in two days was possible, I knew; when my ex-husband Victor came home for the last time, I turned a guest room into hospice quarters complete with a hospital bed, piped-in oxygen, and a call button in a day and a half.

Now the cookies and jitterbug sandwiches waited in their totes on the white-marble-topped island with the three green-enameled lamps hung over it. "If no one's going to tell us anything," said Ellie finally, "we might as well just—"

Right, find platters to arrange the goodies on, take them to the guests, then fade into the shadows. If anyone questioned us while we explored the house, we'd say we were so enthralled by the old place's beauty that we just couldn't help ourselves.

We got the cookies onto some nice cut-crystal-looking plastic platters that Ellie found in the cabinet by the brand-new refrigerator and carried them to the parlor.

"Here goes nothing," breathed Ellie in the doorway, but then we stopped. The room was lit by tall brass floor lamps and miniature electric candelabras on the windowsills.

Six people were there, seated on chairs pulled up to a low, round table; six others looked on. A candlestand lit the table and the thing on it, which they all studied so intently.

"Oh dear," Ellie breathed, and I let out a sigh as well. Why, I wondered, would you do such a thing here?

It was a Ouija board glimmering eerily in the candlelight, and yes, I do know it's just a game. Someone else can play it, though, not me, thanks ever so much.

In the gloom I finally spotted Melissa Rafferty standing behind one of the chairs. Her pale, clipped hair reflected the candlelight, turning it orangey red; her lips, painted the color of blood, pursed troubledly.

Seeing us, she made her way over. "Put them in the dining hall," she said, then led us to a room whose windows faced the water between blue floor-length drapes tied back with gold cord.

"Should we set them all out?" Ellie inquired tactfully. Because we'd brought enough cookies for a banquet and there were only a dozen guests.

Melissa shook her head. "No. I thought if I invited his family and some of his old friends, a few of them might come." She bit her lip. "But the only people from his private life who showed up are his housekeeper from before we were married, his personal assistant, and his pool boy."

"I'm sorry," I said inadequately. I'll admit I hadn't felt very warm and fuzzy toward Melissa; she'd seemed like a shallow brat. But now she just looked like the loneliest kid on the block to me, and I felt sorry for her.

From behind us a cultured male voice in the parlor rose breathlessly over the rest. "Look! Did it twitch? Didn't it just twitch a tiny bit?"

"Somebody's got the shakes," Melissa diagnosed acidly, "and now he thinks the spirit world's trying to spell out a message to him. Like B-O-O or something, I guess." She made a wry face. "I swear, who believes that crap, anyway? And even if it's real, who says dead people only tell the truth?"

Well, she wasn't stupid. Because look, let's assume the planchette-mover is a dead person; that doesn't mean it's *your* dead person, even if they say they are.

You can't really know, can you? So what if it's someone—or some *thing*—else? Thinking this, I heard myself speak.

"Melissa, who do you think killed Hank?"

She turned those big baby blues on me. "Arlene Cunningham, of course. Why?"

Well, maybe a little stupid. That, or smart.

Really smart.

It took a few more hours for the guests to go back to their motel rooms, none of them looking bereaved or anything like it, and for the Widow Rafferty to go to bed, also not seeming grief-struck. By then it was 10:30, and I'd begun yawning. To stay out of sight, we'd ducked into a linen closet nearly filled with white cotton sheets and coverlets, freshly laundered and interleaved with lavender sachets.

We'd meant to do most of our Stone House snooping when everyone was still here, the better to weasel ourselves out of any little difficulties that might arise, should we be caught. But we hadn't been out of Melissa's sight all evening.

Ellie did manage to slip out and move her car down the driveway and out of view, so it would look like we'd gone home. And that awful Ouija board got put away, finally. So now it was time to come out and start looking around for—what?

Straightening painfully in the dark, I realized I didn't know. Outside the closet, the grand staircase curved to a landing that stretched left and right at the top of the wide stairs.

Stretching to loosen up, I felt a pop in my spine, some gritty-feeling pain in my left shoulder, and a loose, off-its-hinge sensation in my right knee that was just like the time when a horse stepped on it.

Multiple closed doors ranged down both sides of the second-floor hall. It was dim here; I pulled out my penlight, and Ellie produced one just like it.

"You go that way, I'll go—" She pointed, I nodded, and we each went up and down the hallway, quietly trying doors. All of them opened, and behind each it was the same: nothing there.

Nothing in any of the rooms, no carpets, no furniture. It made sense, actually. The place was immense, after all, and the Raffertys had just moved in.

At the corridor's end, more electric sconces burned low along another, steeper flight of stairs leading up. "How about this Dylan Hudson stuff?" I puffed.

Ahead of me, Ellie shrugged. "I don't get it," she replied, taking the steps as lightly as a bird hopping up them. "Why in the world would the police think . . ."

I filled in the backstory for her: Rafferty disrespecting Lizzie in front of Hudson.

"Oh," said Ellie. "Oh, I see." She knew Hudson's reputation for quick fury as well as I did.

Most of Eastport did, actually. Hudson once gave a trucker from the port a bent nose over a wolf whistle at Lizzie. Another time he handled a drunk at the kids' talent show by taking the beer bottle from his hands and bopping him with it.

And word gets around.

We reached the third floor of Stone House and emerged from the stairwell. "Wow," Ellie breathed.

Me too, because everything up here was entirely different from the rest of the house, which here seemed more like a good hotel than whatever those strange faux-medieval design choices downstairs were supposed to be.

I took a few steps, my feet sinking pleasantly into the new wool rug's deep pile. Fresh paint and fixtures, mild-mannered paintings, lamps that shed light instead of shadows . . .

"Look," said Ellie softly, pointing at one of the hallway doors. Unlike the others all the way up and down the hall, it stood open, so when we reached it we looked in.

And then I recognized where I was. On the room's far side, a pair of French doors opened onto the balcony where Rafferty had fallen, or been pushed, or maybe the bullet had carried him over the rail.

Grimy shoe marks in the otherwise pristine cream-colored rug told me the police had been here. So did the wastebasket by the bedside table, brimming with opened swab packets, used latex gloves, and Q-tips with the stems bent in half.

Ellie crossed to the balcony doors, yanked them open with both hands, and went out to look over the rail.

"It looks higher from up here, doesn't it?" She wasn't complaining; she liked rollercoasters, too, and those rides that take you up very high in the air and then drop you.

I peeked over. The far-below flagstone terrace didn't quite surge up and grab me by my ears, pulling me to my doom, but I felt very strongly that it would have liked to.

I straightened dizzily. Then: "I think I hear something."

Ellie listened. "Me too," she said. "A sort of . . ."

They were footsteps, dammit, coming up the carpeted stairs.

"Quick!" Ellie grabbed my sleeve and pulled me back from the balcony room's doorway just as Melissa Rafferty's pale head emerged from the stairwell.

I peeked through the crack between the door and the frame. "She's coming in here!"

Ellie dragged me toward the balcony and back out onto it, yanking the draperies closed behind us with her other hand.

The bedside lamp in the room snapped on, casting a filtered glow through the curtains. "Now what?" I mouthed silently.

Ellie eyed the drop from the balcony speculatively.

I shook my head in a way I hoped ended that foolish notion definitively. Ellie was fearless and as lithe as a cat; me, not so much.

Which ruled out just jumping off the damned balcony; also, I suddenly desired urgently to get inside and find a bathroom.

Minutes passed. It was cold out here, too, and we didn't have jackets. "I wonder if I could shimmy down the gutter pipe," I mused, by which of course I meant fall down it.

From inside we heard Melissa on the phone. "Yes," she was saying. "Of course I'm upset. I'm—yes. I've got my things together. No thanks to—wait a minute, what? Whose car?" She listened a minute. "Okay, that's it. This whole place is—I'm getting out of here. Hank's agent is coming back for me in a few minutes. I'm moving to the motel in town." More listening. Then: "Hey, guess what? You're not the boss of me anymore, so quit telling me what to do."

The call ended; by now my eyes had adjusted and I could see clearly through the curtain. Melissa checked her purse, wallet, and keys, then shouldered the duffel she'd filled and went out into the hall.

Quickly Ellie nipped up to the doorway and peered out to the right and left.

"Where is she?" I whispered. I was still on the balcony and dying to peek out over the rail, to see while not being seen by whoever came into the driveway.

"I don't know," Ellie whispered. "She was here and then . . ."

"Oh, come on, she couldn't just . . ."

She had, though. The hall was empty and there was no one in the stairwell. She'd turned the lamps out as she went, so only our penlights lit our way; the still, cool air up here smelled faintly of rug cleaner and wallpaper adhesive.

"Jake," Ellie said quietly. "How come there's no window at the end of that hallway?"

Huh. It wasn't what I'd been wondering about, but hey, she was right, and not only that—

The distant whine of some smooth-running machinery sounded loud in the silence. After a moment I recognized it.

"Criminy, I should have known. She didn't vanish. That's an elevator."

Ellie took off toward the elevator's whine; I went for the stairwell, where I was reminded yet again how much I hate running downstairs. By the time I reached the main floor of Stone House, Hank Rafferty's widow was nearly to the front door.

Ellie burst through a sliding-open pair of doors at the back of the hall; so it *was* an elevator, I thought distantly as Melissa dashed out and across the driveway to a waiting car.

It was pulling away before she got the door shut. Ellie caught up to me and stood catching her breath as headlights raked the charred shed's blackened debris pile, swung around the rest of the circle drive, and disappeared down the driveway.

"I wonder if she knew we were here?" I mused aloud. If she had, she'd done a good job of pretending not to.

"I got the feeling she might not have cared," said Ellie. "That exit she made had serious I'm-getting-out-of-here-forever vibes, didn't you think?"

"Almost like she was afraid of something," I agreed.

But of what? Not of us, I felt sure, and as for ghosts, I'd grown reasonably certain that any weird things happening here were weird people's work, not that of any lingering spirits.

"At least now we know we'll have the place all to ourselves

for a while," Ellie said. "But first let's make some coffee in that amazing new kitchen, and eat some cookies."

"Fabulous," I concurred. Snooping makes me hungry. So with a feeling that the rest of this night would be calmer—and I hoped more instructive—than the first, I went to the front door to close it and turn out the yard lights still illuminating the stone fountain.

But I must've flipped the wrong switch. Suddenly we were in darkness so complete, it was like a heavy shroud had dropped.

Then a door slammed somewhere in the house.

"Ellie?" My voice sounded loud in my ears, and my mouth was so dry that it felt like I might just swallow my own tonsils.

"Where are you?" I'd have felt around in the darkness with my hands, but my no-ghosts confidence had fled and now I was very much afraid that someone—or something—was feeling around for me.

"Stay right there," Ellie said. She'd heard that slam, too.

Her penlight came on. In my fright I'd forgotten about mine though it was still in my hand. Besides, now I wasn't sure any light was a good idea; other eyes might use it, too, after all.

We made our way back toward the house's interior, across the wide-tiled floor under the gaze of whoever might've been lurking in the shadowy gallery above. But when Ellie started up that wide, curving stairway again, I stopped her.

"Are we really sure we want to do this?" By *this* I meant snooping in a supposedly haunted house that was not only the scene of two recent murders but also where all the lights have just mysteriously gone out.

The glow of Ellie's penlight reached the top of the stairs. "You coming or not?" her voice floated back to me. So I guessed we *were* sure, then; reluctantly, I started climbing.

But, I thought suddenly, why not go up at the far end of the hall, in the elevator? That way Ellie and I would meet in the middle, trapping anyone between us before they trapped us.

So with my hands out in front of me—I still didn't like the idea of switching on that penlight—I aimed myself toward the rear of the hall where the elevator was, and began moving blindly toward it.

Quickly, too, on account of the small sounds I soon began hearing from behind me: *clickety-click. Click-click.*

My hands hit something solid: a wall. Then a door's edge was there, but no doorknob, and then . . . yes!

Elevator buttons. Pressing one, I felt a rush of stale air as the doors slid smoothly open. Inside the lights were dim; the elevator, I realized, must be running on some kind of emergency power.

Standing in the shadowy box while the doors closed in front of me, I wished I had emergency powers. I wondered what I might find when the doors opened again, too. But as the elevator kept rising and rising—surely by now I'd risen past the second floor—I changed my mind and began wondering if they would ever open.

Then with a little jolt the elevator stopped and the doors opened onto darkness. "Ellie?" No answer.

I spied a faint gleam from down the hall. Not the same hall we'd been in a little while ago, though. In the gloom it looked more like . . .

The glow at the end of the hall brightened suddenly. For an instant my concentration shifted to it and away from holding the elevator doors open, whereupon they punched me in both shoulders so hard that I tumbled out through them like I'd been spit out.

Even without ghosts, this horrid old place had plenty of unpleasantness up its sleeve, I thought; then the glow in the distance brightened once more and Ellie's face appeared.

"There you are!" she exhaled, sounding relieved.

A propane lamp in the room behind her gave off the glow; I

recognized the faint hiss and the rotten-egg smell. She waved me in, then turned it up again; walls materialized around us.

No Sheetrock, no plaster; just stone in this part of the house that seemed rarely used.

"What is this?" I asked. The faint clickety-click sound I'd heard earlier came from somewhere again, then faded. Ellie picked up the propane lamp and shone it around.

"I'd stopped on the second floor where we saw Melissa," Ellie said, "and I heard a noise above me. When I went looking for it, I found out this house has back stairs."

Oh, of course it did. Creepy old houses always had back stairs. So she'd come up to this unused and mostly unfurnished third floor, all alone.

But that's Ellie, so impossible to intimidate that even if a whole flock of ghosts showed up, wailing and rattling their chains, her first response would be "fooey," and her next one would rattle their chains a whole lot more than they expected.

"What kind of a noise?" I asked, alarmed and hoping it wasn't chains. Or wailing, either. Just because I now thought no ghosts were here didn't mean they weren't.

"A sort of click-clicking," she said. "Moving around."

Like what I'd heard, in other words; this, too, failed to calm my nerves. But this room that we'd just entered—

Ellie raised the lantern. "Go on, look."

At first, I could hardly make sense of what I was seeing: a wooden table, four straight-backed chairs, four large battery lanterns. This very old section of the house had no electricity at all, I realized now.

A large map lay unrolled on the table. Ellie snapped on the remaining three lanterns and peered at the maps with me.

"Survey maps," I said, recognizing the markings. I'd had to get them for the Key Street property when I added the annex.

I traced with my fingertip the lot lines of the property depicted. "It's maps of this property. Of the land around Stone House."

The long, rolling slopes, wild and windy and overlooking the water, the salt marshes, the rocky beach . . . there was the bay, there lay Route 190 running right along it. Beyond to the west lay Carryingplace Cove.

But those weren't the map's only features: a curving road that didn't exist yet, marks for plots of land, for grading and drainage . . .

Several pages of diagrams and legends were stapled to the map's edges. I saw notes about planned population density, green space, public utilities requirements and the right-of-ways for them.

"It's a subdivision proposal." I straightened, puzzled. "But Rafferty said he'd never divide this property. He loved it on sight, he said." I looked up. "Remember? I wonder what changed his mind."

"Who says he knew about this?" Ellie waved at the maps. "Maybe it was all Melissa's plan." She frowned, thinking. "She didn't seem like the type to care about things like nature and conservation and so on."

"Melissa cares about conserving Melissa, is my diagnosis." I riffled again through the papers stapled to the map: an attorney's letter opining that the proposed subdivisions would conform to current land restrictions as long as the nearby salt marshes weren't harmed, an estimate for the cost of putting in power and sewers, and a paving company estimate.

There were also some business cards from local building contractors, although hiring them was way down the line from just getting the permits to do the work.

"Looks as if somebody knows what they're doing, land-development-wise." I put the papers down. "In fact, I think we might've just scored some kind of a snooping triumph."

Ellie smiled wanly. "Too bad we don't know what it means."

"Right. But someone wanted to hide this stuff, so it means something sneaky, I'll bet."

"Melissa might've been plotting to make some big money on this place," said Ellie, warming to the notion.

"Getting rid of him could've been a part of the plan," I agreed.

But "could" and "maybe" weren't going to unravel anything, having a thread to pull didn't mean it would go anywhere, and meanwhile here we were in a big, old, dark house that was a) the scene of a recent murder and b) haunted . . . or was it?

Ellie jumped, looking around. "Did you hear that?"

I hadn't before, but now I did. Someone was sneaking up on us, or trying. "Footsteps," I whispered. "Out in the hall."

Getting closer, too. And of course, all our lanterns still burned, sending out a here-we-are signal so bright they could probably see it in town. The same odd clickety-clicking I'd heard earlier was back, too, almost as if—

Suddenly Dylan Hudson's face loomed in the doorway: tired, unshaven, and unhappy in the extreme.

"What the hell are you doing?" he demanded, lowering the gun he held.

"I could ask you the same," I retorted. For a minute I'd thought the little popgun I'd brought might see real action.

But instead, here was Hudson, stomping around Stone House leaving physical traces of himself everywhere, ones he might end up having to explain.

A grim smile creased his face. "Well, see, I happen to have a cop radio in my car, and I know the cop frequencies. So I hear things."

The lightbulb went on in my head. "And something you heard brought you here?"

"Yeah," he said. "All those state cops? They're coming out here again, they're on their way right now."

Gangway. I headed for the door with Ellie right behind me.

"They're having a meeting, going over the info in case they missed anything," Dylan said. "They'll confer around that big dining room table downstairs."

On the night of the murder, I'd glanced briefly into the mahogany-paneled dining room, a dim, low-ceilinged chamber on the far side of the kitchen. With its silvery-gray window treatments, black marble-topped table, and pewter-colored carpet and upholstery, it had seemed like the perfect place to throw a dinner party for ghouls.

Ellie caught on before I did. "Eavesdropping, are you?" she asked, and Hudson finally cracked a smile.

"Something like that," he said. "I hear rumors that they've gotten interested in me."

That explained the stubbly chin; he hadn't been back to his own place since yesterday. Now he glanced up at the room's small, dark windows.

"Let's go before they start showing up."

In the hall the clicking sound came again, louder. I'd have mentioned it, but instead another question came suddenly to mind.

"Dylan, how did you know *we* were here?"

"Saw the lights from outside," he explained. "From where I pulled my car off the driveway into the trees."

The elevator was smooth and fast; we rode down and got out at the rear of the big front hall.

"But," Ellie objected as we made for the front door, "the driveway is on the other side of the house from where we were."

He didn't hear, distracted by the lights now filling the driveway. Moments later men began piling out of squad cars and a couple of unmarked ones, too, out there by the fountain.

"Damn," said Dylan, turning an about-face, and suddenly we were scuttling back into the darkness.

"Kitchen," Ellie pronounced, locating it with a quick flash of her penlight; Dylan and I followed her.

"Hey," said one of the cops now entering the house behind us, "what's with that old Toyota parked out there?"

Ellie's, he meant. We looked at each other frozenly. But:

"Caterer's car," said a different voice, unconcerned. "I saw it here last night, too, but it checked out okay. They'll be back for it, I'll bet."

And that was that, crisis averted. I couldn't believe it, but before I could let relief sink in:

"Quick!" Ellie whispered, pushing us through the kitchen door ahead of her, and then we were among all those shiny new appliances, hunkered down between them and quiet as mice.

A whimper came from beyond the door. Also: that familiar clicking. The whimper came again, louder and more emphatic, as if any minute whatever was making it might start howling.

"They'll hear it," Dylan whispered tautly. "Those cops, it'll get them looking around back here, we've got to—"

The door opened a crack. A furry white head poked through. The head sported short, pointed ears, bright, black shoe-button eyes, and a cold, wet nose, as I found when the animal scrambled into my arms and burrowed its face into my neck, trembling.

This was Melissa Rafferty's dog, I realized; she must have left it behind. Real fury surged hotly through me as the animal licked my earlobe, then settled in my arms.

But this was no time for cuddles. "This way," said Dylan urgently from behind me. "Hurry."

The kitchen door leading out to the deck eased open with a creak of old hinges. To our left, glossy white propane tanks stood in a row; for hot water and heating, I supposed, although the idea of what heating this big place must cost gave me the shudders.

The lights on Campobello twinkled coldly from across the

bay at us as we crossed the deck. Above, the stars went on forever in the black sky.

"You come along in my car," Hudson said. We skirted the terrace, hustling along, and at last reached the driveway.

"We don't want Ellie's car moved now," he added as we started down it. "Those cops would notice when they came out."

No kidding, and who knew what they might think about it? So we made our way another hundred yards downhill to Hudson's vehicle, a trip that made me enjoy nighttime hiking even more than I had before. Heck, I only twisted my ankle twice and sat down hard once, so what's not to like?

Next, I said you couldn't start an automatic-transmission car like Dylan's by pushing it, but he said you could, so he did. The car was a Chevy Malibu and fortunately he'd parked it heading downhill. I steered, and when it started to roll down the driveway he ran a few steps alongside, already gaining speed, then grabbed for the door handle.

And missed.

Meanwhile, his sprint was becoming a gallop. I thought he might lose his grip and slip under the car's wheels.

"Dylan," I said, trying hard not to slam on the brake. "I think you'd better . . ."

"Hah!" His flailing hand slapped the door handle at last and closed on it. Yanking the door open while still galloping, he vaulted into the driver's seat, hip-checking me hard to shove me sideways out of it.

"Saw that in a movie one time," he gasped. "Always wanted to try it." Then he turned the ignition key and stomped on the gas.

In response I thought the car might just buck us right out through the roof, but by some miracle and after some chugging, the engine smoothed out. Soon we were at the road.

"Phew," said Ellie.

"Likewise," I panted.

Hudson pulled out onto Route 190 and hit the gas again. It

was no Crown Vic, but the Malibu turned out to have some juice. When he goosed it, it shot forward in a way I found massively reassuring; soon Stone House and its unpleasant mysteries were in the rearview.

"Yeah," said Dylan, swinging into the long, banked curve just past Carryingplace Cove, and if you haven't ever done that at high speed you should try it before you die. While it's happening, you'll probably think you might die that very minute, but it's worth it and you won't . . . probably.

Noticing my expression, Hudson lightened his foot. "So what about these lights you saw?" I asked when the car had slowed to something like only thirty miles or so over the speed limit. "The ones that told you where we were, you said?"

By the time he'd gotten there, I thought we'd probably have finished on the main floor and started upstairs.

In the dark. Just our penlights.

Dylan looked impatient. "Jake, they were all on. The fountain was running when I got there, for Pete's sake, and every light in the house was blazing."

Ellie's eyes met mine in the rearview mirror as he slowed for the twenty-five mph sign coming into Eastport. *Weird,* her look said.

Yeah, you think? A superstitious chill rippled icily up my spine at the notion of the house lights blazing uncannily from every window—

Just not on the inside. Not for us, there in the dark.

But that idea was so immensely unhelpful that I turned my mind back to the facts: dead bodies, burned sheds, secret maps.

Yeah, whoopee. "Dylan," I said finally, "why don't you just talk to the cops? I mean, you can't really be a serious suspect, and you must have some friends still on the job . . ."

I heard my voice trail off as I realized the unlikeliness of that last part. Dylan's general wise-assery took a good deal of getting used to; I couldn't imagine it had won him many pals on the job.

His sour grimace in the car's dim passenger compartment confirmed my suspicions. "Yeah, maybe not friends, you know? Like this one guy, he and I go back a ways."

I waited. Dylan rarely told war stories, and when he did, there was a reason.

"Back when I'd just met Lizzie," he said, "and this guy, I walk into the squad room, he's mouthing off about her."

Uh-oh. Talk about déjà vu. Behind me I felt Ellie sitting up straight. "And you did what about it?" I asked, knowing the likely answer.

But it was even worse than I feared. "I knocked his block off," said Dylan ruefully. "Broke his jaw, couple of other face bones, he lost the hearing in one ear."

Silence greeted this. Dylan sighed. "Yeah. He was laid up ten weeks, I got suspended, nearly fired, and he sued me."

So that's why the Malibu; he must have sold everything that was worth anything to pay the judgment against him.

Ellie spoke up. "So not only is this guy—he's on this Rafferty case now, is he?" she asked. Hudson nodded unhappily. "Not only is he on this case, he's also your personal enemy *and* you've got a history of this stuff. They can say maybe you snapped this time, too."

The little white dog sighed deeply and resettled himself in my lap. Bella would have what she called a conniption when she saw him. She thought our two dogs were already one too many, although each of them being the size of a small pony probably had something to do with that.

Hudson nodded. "Yeah, that's about the size of it. I was an ass, end of story." His phone chirped; he thumbed a button on the dashboard.

"It's me." Lizzie Snow's voice came tinnily through the dashboard speaker. "Arlene Cunningham's gotten away from MYDC somehow. They were about to release her into her mom's custody now that the gun didn't match, but now she's running again."

The Maine Youth Detention Center was the state's reform school–type facility for minors, also used for teen custody in pretrial situations.

Dylan's face tightened. "Great," he said sarcastically; it was anything but. Then he asked, "You okay?" Because nothing and no one else mattered to him as much, and that was that.

"Fine," she assured him. His devotion was touching, but it was driving her nuts, too, I happened to know. Although to be fair she also seemed quite unable to do without it; witness the way she had gotten dolled up the other night, for example.

Dylan started to speak again but she'd hung up. "O-kay," he said, tucking the phone away.

Not his usual phone, loaded with bells and whistles and more apps than your average smorgasbord; probably she was using a Walmart special, too, for communicating with Hudson.

We passed the old power plant, the new Baptist church, Bay City, and the IGA, all dark and silent. Then Ellie spoke again.

"Hey, you guys? Aren't we forgetting about someone?"

"Right, Arlene Cunningham." But I hadn't forgotten. "Where could she have gotten to by now, do you figure?"

But Ellie shook her head. "It's not where she is, it's who she's with that I'm worried about."

If any more lightbulbs went on in my head I might turn into a chandelier, I thought, because she was absolutely correct.

"See, the thing is this," Ellie went on. "If Arlene didn't kill Rafferty, then someone else did."

"O-kay," said Dylan patiently. Ahead, the bay glimmered under a high, hazy half-moon, Campobello a silvery bar on it.

"And," she said, "Arlene might know who it was. She might even have seen it happen."

Hudson pulled up in front of my house. "Then why didn't she say so?" he inquired, but to that Ellie had no answer.

None of us did. We got out of the car and started toward the porch, but he waved me back.

"What?" I was so done with this whole night that I might've been a little short with him, but he didn't seem to care.

"Hey." He stopped, considering his words. Then: "I'm not that guy anymore, Jake." He started to say something else but changed his mind. "I'm just not."

He didn't say *I hope you believe me.* He didn't have to. "I know, Dylan. I know you're not."

In the year since I'd met him, he'd blown off enough angry steam to run a power plant; he broke a porch rail slamming his fist down onto it once, and on another memorable occasion broke his foot kicking a brick.

I can't remember what the brick did to offend him. But he'd never raised a hand to anyone other than to defend one of us.

"Stay safe," I said, and he waved tiredly. Then he was gone, the car's engine sound fading away down the dark street.

"So now what?" I asked Ellie as a yawn overpowered me. I felt too jazzed up and too utterly exhausted all at once.

Ellie's hair glinted coppery under the street lamp. Her face was tired, too, but also full of concern.

"Not sure. I know one thing, though."

"Which is?" Over our heads, the branches scrawled scraggly unreadable lines on the night sky.

"I know," Ellie said, "that if Arlene is with someone tonight, that someone almost certainly intends to kill her."

We were in the bakery the next morning before dawn, so the last of the season's lobster fishermen could get coffee and pastries before going out on those chilly-looking waves.

"Let me get this straight," I said as I plunged my hands into a bowl of comfortingly warm brioche dough. Once I'd punched the whole soft, sticky mass down to a third of its original yeast-swollen volume, I turned it out onto the lightly floured work-table to knead it.

"Arlene's on the run and probably in bad trouble," I said.

"Dylan has reason to think he could become a suspect and needs to clear himself." I gave the dough a satisfying thump with my fist before shoving it around some more. "So have I covered everything?" I thumped it again.

"You didn't mention the other half of our paycheck," Ellie said, adding a huge heap of money that we would or wouldn't get to my already-long list of concerns.

"Right. But Arlene's the big problem." The one who, in the short term, could come out of this the worst; i.e., no longer among the living. "Let's talk to Dot again," I said.

Out front, the little bell over the front door jingled. Ellie went to help whoever it was—late-starting lobster guys, probably, and a glance proved me right—while I returned the dough to its bowl and covered it with a clean linen towel.

Then, after setting the bowl on the warming shelf and checking on the dreamy-looking dark chocolate and butter chunks melting in the double boiler, I took a bite of a custard-filled chocolate éclair and washed it down with a swallow of coffee.

Breakfast of champions, I thought happily, secure in the notion that persons obliged to rise so ungodly early deserved a little leeway in the proper-dietary-choices department. But then the sound of someone screaming came from the front of the shop.

I rushed out and found the fishermen gone. But Arlene's mother, Dot Cunningham, was there, spitting swear words and trying to get her hands around Ellie's throat.

"You've ruined my little girl!" she screeched, digging her grimy fingernails into Ellie's collarbones. "You let your daughter fill her head with *ideas . . .*"

Yeah, perish the thought. Just then the bell jingled again and two more lobstermen in fleece hoodies, bibbed blue jeans, and rubber boots came in—just in time to see the next thing that happened.

First, Ellie raised her arms and spread them fast, knocking

Dot's hands away from her throat. At the same time, she hooked a foot behind Dot's right leg and pulled.

Dot suddenly dropped down onto her backside, landing so hard that the cut-glass parfait dishes on the shelves behind the counter rattled. She sat for a moment as if stunned, or perhaps she was taking stock of just how badly a lot of things had been going for her lately.

Or maybe the jolt to her brain knocked some sense into her. But for whatever reason, she didn't come up fighting; instead, all the fury went out of her like air out of a balloon.

Ellie knelt by her. "Dot. Are you all right? I'm sorry, I didn't mean to hurt you."

I did. I still did. Ellie was the better one of us. "Come on, now," she said, helping Dot to a chair.

Dot sniffled, took the paper napkin that Ellie offered, and blew into it. "Thank you," she said quietly, and got up.

I handed the lobster guys their coffees and doughnuts, made change, and wished them a good day on the water while Ellie got Dot some coffee.

Like I said, the better one. Outside it was getting light, the clouds to the east reflecting the first pink hints of dawn on the horizon. After gazing at it for a moment, I grudgingly tried following my friend's example and fetched two doughnuts, one for Dot and one for myself.

She nodded thanks and bit into it hungrily. I thought of that cluttered kitchen of hers and wondered when she had last eaten an actual meal.

"Kids," I said, trying to ease the tension. "Can't live with 'em, can't sell 'em for parts."

She didn't smile, but the corners of her lips twitched.

"When my kid was eleven, he was shoplifting pints of Jack Daniel's and smoking funny cigarettes," I said.

That had been the least of it, actually, but it was enough to make my point.

"The police chief before Lizzie Snow used to haul him home in the patrol car," I said, "and help me get him upstairs."

This time she did smile slightly. Horror stories from your own kid's youth make excellent conversational fodder when you're with other moms whose offspring are also impossible.

Especially if they turned out like Sam. "Back in New York he used to ride on top of subway cars with his pals," I said, "while they took stolen pills and washed them down with tequila."

In short, he'd already been too cool for school and headed for the kind of end that didn't even rate a cursory write-up in the newspapers anymore.

Dot sighed; still not friendly, but thawing, glancing at her cigarette pack on the table and then outside.

"Why don't I get us more coffee and bring it out there," I said, "so you can smoke?"

And so I can ask questions that you might even answer, I added silently, *due to the pharmaceutical triple-whammy of chocolate, caffeine, and nicotine cruising around your system.*

Outside, Dot took a drag off her Camel unfiltered and sighed the smoke out into the cold air. On the water, crying seagulls flocked behind lobster boats motoring from buoy to buoy in the half-dawn gloom.

"Lee thinks she can do anything, so of course Arlene thinks she can, too," Dot said. "She had a crush on a grown man, so she sneaked out to try to meet him, even though I'd said no. I could have told her what would happen."

Dot sounded resentful, angry, and generally annoyed about all the upset going on. What she didn't sound was worried.

"So all this just serves her right," Dot finished flatly.

That two people were dead and Arlene might be in danger just didn't seem to have sunk in. She dragged on the cigarette, stubbed the butt out on the sidewalk by her sneakered foot and flicked it into the street, and of course I didn't stand up and smack her sideways for this. She might've warmed up to me a little, I thought, but I still didn't like her, and the feeling was clearly mutual.

I got up, retrieved the cold butt gingerly with my fingertips, and dropped it into my napkin. "Dot," I said tiredly, "I know you're under a lot of stress. But try not to be a complete jerk, okay?"

I held the napkin up, deposited it into the trash bin by the curb while she rolled her eyes. "Oh, so you're one of those save-the-planet wackos, huh?"

She lit another Camel and dragged demonstratively on it, whereupon I was about to demonstrate for Dot a level of wacko she'd never even imagined, but instead Ellie put her head out the door at us, looking concerned.

"Jake? Bella's on the phone."

That didn't sound good. I strode past Dot, still smoking and trying out various disagreeable facial expressions. From the corner of my eye, I glimpsed an Eastport squad car moving slowly down Water Street toward the docks and the boat basin.

When I got inside, though, Bella wasn't on the phone; Ephraim was, and at five he was not exactly the clearest communicator in the world.

"Bella's mad," he said worriedly.

Oh, Lord. "Why is she mad, honey? You and Nadine weren't already out there pestering her and Pops, were you?"

It couldn't be the little dog I'd brought home; entirely to my surprise, Bella had gone hook, line, and sinker for it when she saw it, and the animal had been by her side ever since.

"Ephraim, tell Bella I want to talk to her, please."

In the background, either a teakettle was whistling, or someone was playing the same breathy note over and over on a recorder.

"Nuh-uh," said Ephraim. "She went back to bed."

Which was suddenly just what I felt like doing, too. I'd

started the week baking perfectly innocent chocolate pumpkin muffins, and now two dead guys, a haunted house, a missing teen, and an ex-cop with enemies were all on my "do something about it" list.

Not to mention that still-uncollected final paycheck. On the phone, Ephraim sniffled in a way that said waterworks were imminent.

"Okay, honey," I told him, "I'm coming home." Why weren't Ephraim's parents handling whatever this upset was, was my big question?

When I went back outside, Dot Cunningham was gone. A stepped-out cigarette butt lay on the sidewalk near where she'd sat. *Good,* I thought, bending to pick it up. *Good riddance.*

But it wasn't. It wasn't good at all.

Seven

On Sunday, not much happened; we took the kids to the park, Wade went to the shooting range, the Patriots beat the Jets 14–6, and I didn't get scared by a ghost, not even once. But by Monday morning, everything was back to what we laughingly called normal.

When I came downstairs the house was quiet, only the soft crackle of the kitchen woodstove and the shower running upstairs breaking the silence. The dogs all ran to greet me, even the little white one, wagging a forest of tails in the narrow hall. In the kitchen I grabbed a rosemary biscuit that Bella must've just baked and buttered it; the result was mood-liftingly delicious.

In the hall, even more goodness: Bella had refused many times to retire from her housekeeping duties, and she'd been cleaning the day before. So now a fresh coat of homemade beeswax made the stairway's banister, balusters, and carved newel post gleam richly, while the stair rug had recently been vacuumed to such spotless softness, I practically floated up the stairs.

There all was as usual: Wade had already gone to work, Sam

was in the bathroom, shaving, and Mika was in their room, for once not being sick ("a little bug or something," she insisted it was, but I still wasn't convinced) but instead running the hair dryer, readying for work at the job she'd just gotten.

Did I mention that she'd gotten it? Well, she had. And Bella and my dad had obviously retreated back to the annex—I'd heard *Good Morning America* set at low volume on the TV out there when I came in—but where were the kids?

A suspicion hit me, growing as I hurried back downstairs with the dogs shepherding me rowdily from behind; this turned out to be exactly as much fun as it sounds, like having my heels nipped at while galloping down the side of a cliff.

But I survived intact, then crossed the still-silent house to Bella and my dad's door and knocked. After a moment, the door opened. A sweet, half-asleep smile was on Bella's bony old face. Behind her the TV was still tuned to *GMA*, and the volume was still turned way down.

She swung the door wide. "Come on in." She didn't look mad, or sound mad; stepping inside, I wondered if Ephraim might have misunderstood.

The annex's main room was a large, high-ceilinged space with pine-paneled walls, a row of tall windows, and a heated tile floor. A lemon tree grew in a half barrel by the windows; ferns and geraniums filled a shelf facing west.

"Hi, Gramma," said little Nadine, blinking sweetly up from where her great-grandfather lay propped on his elbow on the warm tiles, playing one-handed patty-cake with her.

In the early-morning light streaming in through the windows, the room popped and fizzed with bright tapestries, ink drawings, quilts, watercolors, bird carvings, and pillows covered in vivid stitchery.

"Hi," I managed. Generally, Sam or Mika had kid duty while the other got ready for work. The time was usually fraught with crying, foot-stomping, and shouts of betrayal when the news got delivered that yes, kindergarten is on today and you are going.

"Hi, Gramma," smiled Ephraim. He sat on the floor with my dad and Nadine, watching the TV.

"Hi, Ephraim," I said. The little white dog jumped up onto the sofa, fixed Bella with those bright, alert eyes, and yapped twice: first inquiringly, then commandingly.

Bella eyed the dog, then scooped it into the crook of her arm. "There, now," she told it in a tone almost like scolding.

Almost. My father looked up, his liver-spotted old face serious but his eyes still twinkling.

"In the little while since Ephraim called you," he said mildly, "I've taken the liberty of setting a few rules."

Since nobody else seemed to be able to, he might as well have added, but he didn't. He was a generous guy, my dad.

"We knock," he said, holding up an index finger, "before entering. We are quiet; quiet games, quiet music and TV." He looked at Ephraim. "Do you remember the third one?"

The little boy replied proudly. "NO MUSICAL—" he began at the top of his lungs, then caught himself.

"No musical instruments," he murmured, and went back to making funny faces at the little dog Bella still held.

"And especially no xylophones," said my father, reaching over to pat the boy's head fondly and ruffle his dark hair.

Oh, so that was what had turned out to be the last straw for my housekeeper/stepmother. On the TV, Al Roker quit doing the weather and a woman started demonstrating how to prepare fried coconut shrimp in three easy steps; step one would be making the restaurant reservations, as far as I was concerned.

Ephraim wrinkled his nose at the raw shrimp on the screen and, after a glance up at his great-grandfather, switched to a cartoon show. Then I noticed that baby Lawrence, wrapped in a blanket with blue lambs cavorting on it, lay asleep on the floor between my dad's pajama-clad legs.

Sensing my surprise (Lawrence had strict requirements for sleeping conditions; a perfect pink cloud with angels flying around it might possibly have made the cut), my dad smiled serenely, as if he hadn't just performed the biggest miracle since that whole business about the loaves and fishes.

"Well," I said, for once nearly at a loss for words, "this looks wonderful."

Actually, it wasn't merely wonderful, it was my wish come true. Ephraim's hand grabbed automatically for the remote and thumbed up the volume; suddenly a brass band in Michigan blared out at us in Maine.

In response, my dad gave Ephraim a look from under his bushy, raised eyebrows: pleasant, interested, waiting for what came next. But it was also the kind of look you could've cut steel beams with: laser-focused, not messing around.

Ephraim smiled mischievously, but his eyes clearly said *uh-oh* and he turned the volume down fast: crisis averted. I didn't know how it had been done, but he was obeying my father.

Or maybe my dad was the first one who'd explained to him what exactly was expected in the behavior department, I mused thoughtfully.

With a last glance around this sweet, peaceful scene of family harmony, I went back out to the kitchen and ate another rosemary biscuit while I thought about what I'd just seen.

And I was still thinking and chewing the last, lovely bite when the phone rang.

"I got some information I thought might interest you," said Lizzie Snow.

Five minutes after her call, I found her drinking coffee and eating a chocolate doughnut at the window table in the Moose.

On the table before her lay a sheet of paper, the printout of an email.

"Bottom line is, the cops've been in touch with everybody who was at the party," she said.

"You're kidding." From behind the counter, Ellie sounded skeptical.

"That guest book you found did the trick," Lizzie said to me. "And never underestimate the usefulness of a Zoom meeting."

Despite the early hour and the lateness of her final patrol last night—in Eastport the top cop took patrol shifts like anyone else—she looked bright as a new penny.

Noticing this, I got another chocolate doughnut for myself. Who knew, maybe that's what did it.

"Anyway," she went on, "almost all of them can alibi each other and say where they were in the house when they realized that something was wrong. And those that can't are very un-likely suspects."

She put the email down. "Seems Rafferty didn't invite many personal friends. These were almost all people he worked with or who worked for him."

I remembered him saying as much. "But there could've been business clashes, ego battles . . ."

Lizzie nodded. Her clipped-short black hair gave off bluish glints in the early morning sun through the window.

"Right. But there weren't," she said. "The only problem any of them mentioned was with Rafferty's wife."

Ah, yes, Melissa the dog-abandoner. "Lovely young woman," I said acidly.

Lizzie cast me a glance. "Several people called Melissa Raf-ferty 'fragile' or 'high-strung.' "

I pictured Melissa's china-doll look: flaxen hair, opal-blue eyes, and perfect skin the color of skim milk.

"Yeah, you could put it that way." I went on to tell her how

Ellie and I had found the bereaved widow on the third floor of Stone House, tossing things into a suitcase and saying she was moving into town, and that we'd seen her being driven away.

Which of course led to what we were doing there in the first place, and to what else we'd found: survey maps. Legal opinions. The beginnings of a plan for subdividing the land around Stone House.

Lizzie looked up. "Uh-huh. The state police asked her to stay around. She didn't like it, but she checked into Milliken House last night instead of flying home."

Outside, Eastport was waking up as the sun lifted over the evergreens across the bay on Campobello. A truck hauling lobster traps went by on Water Street, then one full of scallop-dragging gear. Out on the water, a light chop riffled the waves.

"These maps and so on, though," said Lizzie. "I wonder why the state cops didn't find them."

I put my cup in the sink behind the service counter. "It could be the maps weren't there yet."

"Huh." Lizzie finished her coffee and got up. Today she wore a black leather bomber jacket with her badge pinned to the pocket, black jeans, a white cable-knit sweater, and a pair of wine-red leather boots, beautiful and useful: pointy toes for style and kicking, stacked wooden heels with cleats to meet any clobbering needs that might arise.

Her sidearm was on her hip, and there was that look in her eye, as usual: *Don't mess with me.* But now on her way out the door she smiled, showing bright white teeth.

"I hear you ran into Dylan last night." She usually smiled when she mentioned Hudson, unless she was so furious with him that she wanted to kill him.

"Yes," I plunged right in, "and I don't think it's a good idea for you to be—"

Hiding him, I'd have finished, because clearly she was; if he wasn't at his place, where else would he be? But she stopped me before I could say so.

"Yeah, you know what?" Her eyes flashed caution. "Let's not talk about that."

I opened my mouth. Then I closed it again. Lizzie was a big girl, she could decide for herself whether she wanted to risk a variety of felony charges.

Also, she was our friend, Ellie's and mine. "Okay," I gave in. "Do what you want, but just don't come crying to me when the whole thing goes south."

She laughed, but I was right. Harboring a fugitive was not a crime that got settled in traffic court; we were talking jail time.

"When they lock you up, we'll bring you a cake with a file in it," I said. "A chocolate cake, it'll give you the energy to saw your way out of your—"

"Jake, I'm not going to be sawing my way out of anywhere. Neither is Dylan."

Her hand hung relaxed on the doorknob, her low, melodious voice pleasant. But there was steel in it, too; I thought Dylan Hudson was lucky to have such a stalwart defender.

Then Ellie spoke. "About Arlene, though. I hope she's found before anything bad happens to her."

Right. Because she might be the only witness to Rafferty's murder—and the killer would know that, probably.

Lizzie was halfway out the door. "Yeah," she told Ellie, "I'm worried about her, too."

In the doorway she squinted upward and popped on a pair of sunglasses. In the black leather jacket, red boots, and bright lipstick and with that Glock 22 on her belt, she looked like a cop out of some near-future apocalyptic movie.

"Later," she said as she went out, and when I turned back to Ellie she was already in the kitchen, shutting things down.

"Don't start," she warned, grabbing her hat.

"I wasn't going to." Closing up shop so we could snoop was a rare event, but today Lee was on a school field trip to Maine Maritime Academy and Mika had that job, so neither of them could cover for us. Plus Bella and my dad were on babysitting duty with the littles until Lee's school-day ended.

"You thinking what I'm thinking?" Ellie asked as she got into the Fiat. I'd been dragging my feet about garaging it for the winter—it was an Italian car, after all, it didn't like Maine's cold—and now I was glad.

"You bet," I answered Ellie as I settled behind the wheel. The Fiat's size, speed, and general pizazz made it perfect for a mission whose outcome was uncertain and whose methods would be reckless, maybe even dangerous, if history was any guide.

At any rate, we'd never nabbed any Eastport killers by sane and sensible methods, that I could recall, and I doubted we'd be starting anytime soon. Also, the Fiat's twin carburetors made it sound like it could catch you and eat you, an effect I quite liked.

Meanwhile, it was time for an event that had become a tradition in our standard snooping procedure: the brainstorm ride. I backed the Fiat growlingly into the street.

"Seat belts," I said, fastening my own. I'd gone for the racing-style cross-body model when I installed them, since the Fiat was as vulnerable among bigger cars—and, dear God, big trucks—as a fly among swatters.

We headed out past the Arts Center and the old Methodist church. "I talked to Lee again," said Ellie.

"And?" At the airport a two-seater floatplane was being taxied out of a hangar.

Ellie shrugged. "Either she really didn't take Arlene out to Stone House or she's a better liar than I hoped." She rummaged in her bag for her phone. "And I kind of don't think I'm kidding myself when I say she's not. A liar, that is."

I agreed. This driving-around-while-brainstorming stuff worked well; that is, when we found time to do it.

And when I didn't end up needing a tow truck afterward.

"I don't think so either," I said. "And if Lee's telling the truth, maybe we should try to find whoever did take Arlene. Maybe she said something to them then that could help us now."

Crossing the causeway, we slowed behind a flatbed pickup truck stacked high with lobster traps, then a few minutes later turned north onto Route 1 over the Machias River bridge. The Blue Star Highway, as it is called, consisted of narrow, two-lane blacktop winding through old evergreen forests, mown hayfields, blueberry barrens, and small clusters of houses.

"What do you say we blow the carbon out of this thing?" I asked, meaning the Fiat, and in answer Ellie let her head fall back against the headrest and closed her eyes.

In the pine-bough-filtered sunlight, the chilly air smelled like leaf mold, balsam sap, and fallen apples fermenting where they'd dropped from the gnarled old trees. I put my foot on the gas and the car *shot* forward; soon *fast* fell away and *oh, holy criminy* took its place.

The trees flew by, the fenceposts likewise, and in the harvested blueberry fields the low shrubs spread their autumn-red leaves like a wine-colored carpet over the hills. I just drove, powering around the turns, letting the dappled sunshine and forest-scented cool air rush over and through me until I felt clearheaded again.

Ellie shot me a glance and I backed off on the speed; her nervous system enjoys it for only so long, and I respect that. Slowing even more for the sharp, twisty downhill near the end of the Shore Road, we headed back toward Eastport again.

"Someone should be on her side," Ellie said as the bay went by on our left, small rail-fenced farms with pastures, woodlots, and hay barns on our right. Laundry billowed out from wash lines strung on pulleys from porches and poles behind the farmhouses.

"Arlene's side, you mean? Guilty or innocent, regardless?" Yard dogs slept in the driveways or stood on porches, barking.

"Uh-huh." Now the shoreline crept nearer to the road and steep, sandy bluffs on our right dropped sharply to a rock-strewn beach.

"Lizzie's got Hudson's back no matter what," Ellie pointed out.

"That's different." Beyond the pointed firs, the bay's blue water looked deceptively summery, sparkling in the sun.

"Somebody," Ellie said, ignoring me, "should have Arlene's. I'd want it for Lee if she were in trouble."

Which she might still be. Just because we believed the girl didn't mean the cops would. "Good point."

The road swooped dizzily through a last set of long, downhill curves and around sharp hairpins, past fast-changing views of trees, water, sky. The Fiat zoomed through it all with gusto and a responsiveness that made it feel almost alive.

I let out a big breath. "Okay, then, not much about any of this is making much sense, so far, so how about if we just try to find Arlene, get her out of harm's way if we can, and let the rest go."

Hey, maybe we still didn't know what exactly to do, but at least we knew what we were doing it about. The Fiat made low, guttural rumbling sounds as we reached the foot of Shore Road and turned back toward Eastport, past the sadly closed and shuttered New Friendly Restaurant (not connected with the chain eateries), the tiny white-clapboarded post office, and the Farmer's Union general store.

"While keeping an eye on her," I added, "in case by some freak development—there are other guns in the world, after all—it turns out that she did really shoot Hank Rafferty in the head and heart."

Approaching the store, I downshifted to slow for the car in front of me. "Anyway, text Lee, will you? Ask her if Arlene had other friends we could talk to."

Because if it wasn't Lee, then somebody else must have helped Arlene get to Stone House. The outfit she'd been wearing, for one thing, wouldn't have held up to a long walk. And if she trusted someone enough to ask for a ride, then she might've told them things, too.

Things that might lead us to her. Ellie tapped her phone keyboard. A reply pinged back almost at once.

"She says Arlene had a boyfriend," Ellie reported. She swiped through more text. "Ex-boyfriend now, but they still talk. Lee says he's strange, kind of a loner, but okay."

"Uh-huh. Well, there's a recommendation for the ages. And where does this strange but okay ex-boyfriend live?" It wasn't much, but we had to start somewhere. "And has he got a name?" I added.

"Steven Clute," said Ellie, "He lives . . . oh."

She pointed to the right, up South Meadow Road as we approached it on our way to the Route 190 turnoff. "Up there."

I turned the wheel and the Fiat swung nimbly around the turn, uphill and along the river, then around two sharp turns past the old railroad trestle, now standing alone with its feet in a salt marsh.

Next came hayfields carpeted in gold stubble, a boat launch down to the water, and finally a straight shot through massive old-growth pines with high canopies and rough burled trunks.

"Here," Ellie announced as a smoothly graveled driveway appeared between the trees.

I pulled in and stopped. The silence around us was so thick that I felt like my hearing had been turned off suddenly. High overhead, a squadron of starlings screamed and flapped, driving off a hawk.

Finally, when I was about to drive on, a small gray squirrel scampered out into the middle of the driveway, got a look at the car, and ran first one way and then the other before sitting up and chittering at me.

"Make up your mind," I said, but its indecision persisted and honking the horn at it would've felt vile, here in all this silence. I was just about to try driving slowly around it when suddenly something big sailed through my field of vision, almost too fast for me to see.

When it was gone, so was the squirrel. "That hawk," Ellie said.

"Yeah." I hoped there weren't larger ones up there, seeing as with our car top down, we were sitting ducks.

Also, we were here at the back end of beyond, with no other cars behind us on the road and no people in evidence. A small wooden sign at the road's edge read CLUTE, though, in jagged painted letters.

Beyond the sign a narrow, less-well-graveled track through the impenetrable-looking undergrowth could not possibly be, but apparently was, the way in.

So we started along it, me cringing every time a twig or branch touched the Fiat's paint job, until the brush thinned and I glimpsed a pair of chickens in a dusty yard.

Then we were in the yard, too, along with an old yellow tractor, a flatbed trailer whose tires were all flat, a boxy little VW sedan painted gunmetal gray—with a paintbrush, I mean—and a new-looking white Toyota Highlander with current Maine plates.

We pulled up behind the VW. Everything looked fine. Only the clucking chickens broke the silence until we got out. But when the Fiat's door slammed like some automotive version of Pavlov's bell, big dogs began showing up from every direction, converging on us.

"Um, Ellie?" From behind the barn, under the tractor, down

from the porch, out from several sheds . . . It was like one of those movie scenes where snakes start oozing from every crack and crevice of the building that the heroine is trapped in.

More urgently: "Ellie?"

First, one dog—a Doberman with *try me* written all over it—dropped to his haunches as if to say I should come nearer, he'd really enjoy it. Then a big pit bull terrier with a notch out of his ear charged me, slavering and snarling, and stopped a few feet from me. He was the type who liked eating his dinner straight off the carcass, I reflected as he eyed me.

Woodsmoke twirled sweetly from the farmhouse chimney for several long moments before anyone appeared. Then a teenage boy in denim coveralls and a sweatshirt burst barefoot out onto the porch.

"Scout! Radar! Gus! Get in your kennel!"

The dogs turned and trooped off toward the barn. I wondered how much the kid would charge to train my grandchildren.

"My mom's busy, if she's who you're here for." He angled his head toward the parked Highlander. The more I saw of it, the more it looked like a social services vehicle.

Ellie approached the porch, shading her eyes with her hand. Here in the clearing with the sun nearly straight overhead, what little heat there was in the air stayed trapped.

"Are you Steven?"

He nodded, his dark, curly head tipped skeptically, as she explained who we were, what we wanted to know, and why.

"But your parents should probably—" I began.

Meet us first, I'd have finished, but before I could, he jumped over the porch rail and landed on both feet, right in front of me.

"Dad's out back somewhere. Mom's, ah, she's got her hands full. Come on, though, my room's out here."

He led us through the pine-scented sunshine to an old red barn with iron hinges and iron latches on its doors. An old but serviceable-looking bicycle leaned against the faded red wall.

An ancient bathtub turned into a water trough and a blocky white salt lick on a short length of iron rebar furnished the wire-fenced animal pen, which was empty just now.

The barn held stalls, milking apparatus, some shelves full of animal remedies, human first aid stuff, and a large glass jar of assorted jellybeans. I took one, and it was fresh.

"This way," said Steven, leading us around stacked bushel baskets and a row of galvanized buckets hanging on hooks. His calm, adult manner was less awkward than teenage angst would have been. It made me wonder, though, what kind of trouble in his young life had forced this kid to grow up fast.

A hollow-core wooden door led into a small room made by drywalling off a corner of the building. In it, a desk with a gooseneck lamp, a small bookcase, a laptop computer open on the bedside table, and the bed itself—green chenille bedspread, oversized pillow—were the only furniture.

There was a nice-looking target pistol lying on the chest of drawers. He smiled embarrassedly when he saw me noticing it and the target-shooting booklet from the local gun club.

"I fool around," he allowed, although the scores in the booklet said Steven could shoot the eye out of a sparrow.

No posters, though, no trinkets or photographs. No music-playing gear. Just books with titles like *Introduction to String Theory* (which I gathered did not have to do with guitars) and *Essays on the Nature of Being*.

Being what? I wondered. He waved us to the bed while he took the chair.

"So, don't worry, my mom's not going to mind me talking to you," he said with a sad kind of worldly knowledge that he was much too young for. "Dad's another story, but I haven't seen him since I got up. I talked to the cops already, too, by the way."

Of course he would have; he hadn't been hard to find. Now he sat with his hands on his knees, leaning forward a little, seeming eager to help.

All the while lying like a rug. "All I can say is what I told them," he said, "that Arlene was so crazy about that TV handyman guy, more all the time, and I hated him and worried about her, and we broke up over it."

Ellie tipped her head interestedly. "Why'd you hate him?" she asked. "You weren't jealous of him, by any chance?"

He laughed in reply. "Yeah, no. Arlene and I weren't all mushy and stuff. I'd only seen him on TV—Arlene, too, by the way, it's not like they were pals—but that was enough." His lip curled scornfully. "He was slick. I didn't even have to look hard to know it. Twinkle in his eye and a worm in his heart, you know?"

He looked up, a skinny, acne-spotted teenager with glasses on a nose his face hadn't yet grown into, braces that looked like a roll of steel wire had won an argument with his teeth, and an apparent gift for vivid phraseology in his hormone-addled head.

"And now look at all the trouble she's in," he added. "All because that creep showed up in Eastport and got himself shot."

The three of us sat contemplating this idea for a few silent moments until the boy spoke again. "Also, Arlene's mom is flaky as hell and her dad's a jerk. I don't know if they'll be able to . . ." He broke off with a sigh. "People's parents are supposed to help them, you know?" he finished.

Yeah, maybe not quite so grown-up after all; I felt sorry for the kid, suddenly.

"We're going to try to help," Ellie said, and he glanced up gratefully, but didn't look convinced.

"Right," he said with another short laugh. "Sure."

"So, Steven," I said as he led us back outside. I got the feeling that despite his protests otherwise, he'd just as soon not be seen talking to us by either of his parents; thus, the visit to his room.

"So you didn't drive Arlene out to Rafferty's that night?" I laid it out for him. "We really need to know, Steven."

Yet another dog ambled across the yard and started walking

up to Ellie, grinning and wagging its whippy tail. Next came a bunch of chickens, clucking and scratching, and then a goat with part of a burlap sack in its mouth, its jaws making energetic grinding motions as it stepped herky-jerkily through the dust.

"Are you kidding me?" Steven went over and got the bag from the goat's mouth, stroking its neck and speaking to it quietly as he did so.

"The cops wanted to know that, too," he said, looking right at me with the burlap piece in his hands. "Okay, I'll tell you what I told them. No, I didn't. Not in a million years. End of story."

"Okay." He was starting to get impatient, so I offered another question, the adult-to-kid kind. Changing the mood—the vibe, Sam would've called it—felt like my only chance to pry anything more out of him: get him talking, see where it goes.

"Didn't feel well this morning? Because last time I looked this was a school day, you know?"

He shrugged minutely, this time not meeting my eye. "Didn't feel like getting asked about Arlene a million times, is all."

"Uh-huh. And your mom . . ." But before I could probe further, the farmhouse's front door swung open with a bit more force than I thought was strictly necessary, and a woman carrying a large canvas satchel came stomping across what little the chickens had left of the front lawn.

"Social services lady," Steven explained quietly. "See, my folks are breaking up and my dad's trying to get custody of me. It's all a mess."

The white vehicle departed in the speedy, emphatic way that means the driver would like to peel out in a spray of gravel but can't, on account of having to behave like a professional person.

Once she was gone, the boy seemed to lose interest in us. I tried to get him talking again but brief, polite answers were his only response. Finally we gave up.

"Thanks, Steven," I said as we got into the Fiat. Hey, we were probably lucky we got anything out of him; Sam at that age would've told a couple of nosy strangers where they could stick it, with step-by-step instructions.

The chickens squawked, scattering when I turned the key, and at the Fiat's snarly grumble Steven's interest revived.

"Awesome car," he said, almost cracking a smile. I might have offered him a ride around the lake in it, if I hadn't begun sensing that we were running out of time, even though I didn't know for what.

And if Steven's dad hadn't appeared from behind the barn at just that moment, scowling and marching toward us with his head down, his shoulders bunched, and his fists clenched.

And if we hadn't recognized him.

It was the same big, bluff, whiskery guy that we'd seen at Rafferty's, wearing the same red-and-black-checked flannel shirt. Same big meaty hands, thick neck, mess of dark salt-and-pepper hair . . . no bear-trap grin, though.

He stood with his hamlike forearms crossed over his broad chest and looked down at us skeptically from beneath thick, dark eyebrows.

"Hell d'you want? More social workin'?"

I have never in my life been so glad to be able to deny being a social worker. "No," I croaked.

Glancing over to where Steven had stood only a moment ago, I found that skedaddling without being noticed was a talent of his. I wanted to do the same, but it was too late.

Steven's dad worked a blade of dry grass around the corner of his mouth while he waited for us to account for ourselves.

Right, and I was waiting for an apology regarding my nearly mashed kneecaps and his truck's front bumper, but that wasn't going to happen, either.

"We asked Steven about Arlene Cunningham," I said. "She's

missing. We're trying to find her." That was all this guy needed to know.

"Good." He pulled the grass blade from between his lips, shooting a stern sideways glance at his son while he did it. "Girl was trouble. So's her parents. He don't need that. He don't need any of 'em."

He glared down at me, but now I saw a flicker of amusement behind his fierce look. There was, I can report without fear of exaggerating, no amusement in my own. This guy had just ticked me off royally, and not only about my knees.

"Didn't I see you at Stone House?" I asked. "How do you know Hank?"

Surprise and a flicker of unease appeared on his face. "Wait a minute," he said, and peered more closely at us. "You two are those snoopy town women, ain't you? Yeah, you were in the newspaper."

The *Quoddy Tides* had run a feature on the Chocolate Moose and had mentioned our side gig. RECIPE FOR MURDER had been the (unfortunate) headline for the piece, which had also included our photographs.

Clute looked even less happy. "Stick your noses in every-where, do you? Now you're out here rootin' around?"

I let a happy smile spread across my face. "That's right! Wow, good on you for figuring that out!"

He squinted puzzledly, decided to let it go. "And you want to know what I know about Hank Rafferty, is that it?"

Nope. But gift horse, et cetera; I nodded eagerly.

"Or you think you want to." He turned toward the house. "Come on, then."

Dust puffs rose from beneath his boots as he strode away from us among dogs, goats, chickens, junk farm machinery, old cars, and more dust.

"But I'm warning you," he called back to us from the porch steps, lined with bedraggled clay pots of dead or dying plants.

"You stick your nose in that guy's business," he went on with his hand on the screen door, "it might get bitten off."

That wasn't the impression I'd gotten, and besides . . .

"Hank Rafferty's dead," I reminded Clute as we followed him inside.

"Yeah. So what?" he said.

Eight

His name was Steven Clute, Sr., he told us when he got inside, and his friends called him "Shoop."

"Sit," he added, waving at a wooden kitchen table with four straight-backed wooden chairs pulled up to it.

I felt fairly confident that by "friends," he didn't mean us. I was also pretty sure that the last time any dishes got washed in here was sometime back in 1972.

Pots, pans, plates, and glasses heaped the sink; on the counter lay the remnants of snacks and sandwiches long past, surrounded by soda cans and a multitude of empty beer bottles.

An inch of black ink stewed in the coffeemaker's carafe. Clute didn't offer any, to my relief. Instead he stood at the sink and looked at us like we were a couple of strange bugs he was willing—for the time being—not to swat.

"Probably I shouldn't have gone to see Rafferty," he said, "but I couldn't resist giving that little twerp the business."

He got a cola from the refrigerator, held it out to us, and when we turned it down, opened it himself and chugged.

I looked at Ellie, she looked at me, and we both kept our

mouths shut and waited. Under all the clutter—tools, more dishes, brimming ashtrays, bottles of nail polish, a gadget for pressing jewel-cut bits of colored glass into clothing—the kitchen with its red gingham curtains and woven rag rugs was cute in a way-too-much-knotty-pine kind of way.

Right now, it was sad, though. Things had been going wrong here for quite some time. Clute seemed to read my thoughts.

"Wife's sick," he said, his tone not inviting questions.

My first one would've been, *Are your arms broken?* Last time I checked, dishes weren't only a girl thing.

"She takes after me if I try," he answered my unspoken snark, and angled his head meaningfully toward the ceiling. Music floated from up there, Top 40 stuff, and a woman's voice singing tunelessly along floated down to us, then trailed off.

I didn't see any of the younger Steven's belongings in here; no books, homework material, or carelessly tossed clothing lying around. It was as if the boy lived in the barn full-time.

If I were him, I would, too, I thought. Sunlight streamed slantwise through the kitchen window, filmy with grime. A dead philodendron dangled limply from the top of the refrigerator. On the stove, old grease glistened in an unwashed skillet beside a long-ago-boiled-over pan of something.

Clute must've realized suddenly how bad it all must appear to an outsider. "I'm trying right now to get a good place for the boy," he said. "He can't stay here."

You can't, either, I wanted to say. I'd been through this with Sam. "Your wife needs help. You, too, and your son."

But from the look on his face, I thought he knew that, too, at least about the boy. Steven Sr. took another look around the shambles that was his kitchen, with the sweet reek of an un-emptied garbage pail floating through it.

"On second thought, let's go sit outside," he said.

Four old wicker chairs lined up on the porch, sporting ging-ham cushions that matched the kitchen's and looked hand-made. The marigolds in their planters—old truck tires full of loam—were shriveled, but someone had planted them; same for the window boxes full of long-gone petunias, and the little salad garden that the chickens had scratched to bits.

Someone had planted all of them. Clute saw me notice. "She was better back in spring," he said. He turned to us, his stolid, brooding expression resumed. "I'm trying to get her help," he went on. "But it's hard."

"I've done that, too," I replied sympathetically.

There was a time a few years ago when I truly expected that my son would die drunk in an alley somewhere and I wouldn't even know about it when it happened.

Those days were gone but not forgotten. "Yeah," said Clute. He set his cola can on the porch railing. "But you want to know about Hank Rafferty, right? How I knew him, and so on?" He leaned on the rail. "Mostly you want to stay away from that crowd, though," he cautioned again.

"Yeah, you said that before," I replied. "What'd you mean by it? That is, specifically."

Clute shrugged, spreading his big hands. "Yeah, that might have been a little too strong. But Hank was a driven kind of guy, you didn't get in his way even when he was a kid. I get the sense that wife of his is the same way." His eyes darkened. "Hank and I grew up in the same little town in Ohio, same age and everything."

Across the yard, one of the goats quit chewing on something and began trying to buddy up to one of the dogs, nudging and dancing around the canine, who wasn't having any.

"But Hank went to acting classes and modeling jobs from the time he was three," Clute went on. "It wasn't all his idea, his mom pushed him like a lawn mower, but he bragged about it in school, how he'd be a big TV star someday so we'd all better be nice to him."

"And were you?" I asked, still watching the dog trying to rid of the friendly goat.

Clute barked a laugh. "Yeah, for a while. He walked around like a little prince, shoving people and laughing in their faces 'cause we were all nobodies and he was special."

The dog shimmied himself into the shade under Clute's old blue pickup truck where the goat couldn't go. The goat waited hopefully but then walked away.

"That couldn't have been all of it," Ellie said. To inspire the kind of pain he seemed to be recalling, she meant.

Clute looked reflective, and when he went on his voice was level, not letting any emotion through.

"He was real chummy with me for a while when we were twelve. Made me think I was his friend and he was mine. Like I was just as special, as good as he was, you read me?" He laughed without humor. "And I was so young and dumb back then, I actually fell for it. Tree forts, swimming, bikes . . . Hank could be a lot of fun when he wasn't being a bully. Man, I was a happy kid for a while."

He smiled, remembering. But then he stopped smiling. "He had a sister, too, but I never saw much of her. Funny how that great friendship lasted just long enough for me to help him graduate eighth grade."

My turn to look up. "So he was using you?"

Clute nodded. "The whole time. That whole last semester. We'd have study sessions, flashcards, mock quizzes—and afterward of course we'd do something fun, like his mom would take us to the pool at the club they belonged to."

"So you had a good friend plus a look at a whole different world, one you felt you were being let into, and—"

He nodded ruefully. "Yep. Kept me hooked. Straight through the gills. I'd have done anything he said."

"And then what happened?" Ellie asked softly.

Clute made a noise of bitter amusement. "Next day after graduation, his whole family's gone. California, the big-time entertainment business. Never even said goodbye. Thirty years passed, not a word." He got up. "And that's it, my big complaint. Probably I shouldn't've, but when I heard he was at Stone House I couldn't resist. Just to rattle his cage a little, you know?"

"And he understood?" Ellie asked. "Why, I mean?"

Clute stepped off the porch. The dog crept from beneath the truck. "Oh yeah. I made sure he understood that I was there for an apology and the thanks he owed me. I didn't get 'em, but he knew, all right."

Ellie and I followed him across the dusty yard. "But that's all I did," he said when we reached the Fiat again. "Shoved him around a little, like he used to shove me. Just in fun."

He began limping across the driveway, still talking. I hadn't noticed what Bella would've called the hitch in his git-along before.

" 'Give 'em the old razzmatazz,' Hank used to say, and then he'd push you hard and fast. Snap your neck back so sudden, you saw stars."

"And what'd he have to say now?" Ellie asked perceptively. "When you went to Stone House?"

Clute's lips pursed. "That's the worst part of it. He didn't remember. Is that a kick in the head, or what? Studying together, yes. But about me dragging him kicking and screaming over the eighth-grade finish line?" Clute shook his head. "Nah. Or that it hurt my feelings, him leaving that way? Never occurred to him."

"And that's why you didn't confront him about it?" I asked, knowing the answer. You could tell Victor (again) that he'd hurt your feelings badly and he'd just look at you (again) like you were speaking Urdu.

"Yeah. That's why. What's the point?" Clute walked toward the Fiat, saw me noticing his bad leg.

"Nerve in my spine," he explained. "Doctor says it's from some injury I must've gotten as a kid. Repeated trauma, he says. Got me on pain drugs but those messed me up . . . ah, hell."

He turned with a dismissive wave and no farewell, just kept

walking away; not until he'd disappeared behind the barn did Steven Junior show up again.

"Uh, listen," he said, glancing around furtively and not seeing his father. "Thanks for coming. If you can help Arlene at all, that would be great."

I gathered Steven's having a girlfriend wasn't a father-approved activity. "We think so, too, Steven. We do, and we're trying. So just one last question, okay?"

His thin shoulders rose and fell. "Sure."

"Steven, I know you answered this once, but I'm going to ask you again because it's important. Did you drive Arlene out to Stone House for the party, the night Rafferty was killed?"

I expected a look of guilt, or anger that his first denial hadn't been enough. What I didn't expect was laughter.

"Sorry," he said when it subsided. "But look around."

He waved to encompass the littered yard with one old car rusting under a canvas tarp, another whose possible return to the road looked even more doubtful (open hood, empty engine compartment) and finally his dad's pickup, whose bumpers had been this close to crushing my kneecaps the previous Thursday.

I raised my eyebrows at the truck. Steven made a *nuh-uh* face. "Yeah, no. Keys are on his belt, no spares." He looked around once more. "And except for that truck," he said, "there's not a vehicle on the place that'll drive anywhere ever again, except maybe to the poorhouse."

"Steven seems like a nice kid," I said a few minutes later as we pulled back out onto the paved road.

Ellie smiled, sort of. She'd been quiet all the way out the long driveway. "Yes. I swear, though, if some kids didn't have bad luck, they wouldn't have any luck at all," she said.

"True." Smart, socially awkward Steven for instance, wasn't exactly getting launched toward the stratosphere, future-life-goals-wise, and he was obviously lonely. "Maybe we can at least get him his friend back," I said, meaning Arlene. But at this point I wasn't hopeful about it; she could be anywhere by now. Or she could be dead, a thought both Ellie and I were trying hard not to think.

Going home we were quiet, speeding along the straight parts of Route 190 and swinging through the curves. Passamaquoddy Bay glittered fiercely on one side of the causeway; on the other, the cove lay bright and flat as a mirror.

And I'm not sure if it was the cold, fresh air or the car growling with mechanical happiness after its trip to Spinney's, but as we sped past the WELCOME TO EASTPORT sign, my brain burped abruptly and a memory popped out:

That goat, eating . . . a burlap sack.

"He's hiding her. Bringing her food and so on," I said ten minutes later when we were rumbling in low gear down Washington Street into Eastport.

I'd gone over my thinking on this, looking for flies in the logical ointment, as it were. But I couldn't find any.

"He still likes her, he has very little supervision, and he can easily take her anything she needs in the way of supplies."

On the breakwater, Rosie's Hot Dog Stand was closed for the season but a trailered pizza oven was doing a brisk business.

"Ipso fatso," I said, imitating Sam, but Ellie didn't crack a smile.

Down in the boat basin, Coast Guard fellows polished the brightwork on a tubby gray vessel with tiny barred windows, enough bristling weaponry for an armory, and about as much charm as a live hand grenade.

Completing the cheery theme, a shivery breeze swept briskly off the water at us when I parked near the gangway leading down to the finger piers and we got out.

Two personal-sized pizzas with artichokes, feta cheese, and plenty of pepperoni helped lift our mood at least temporarily.

Opening the hot, fragrant pizza boxes in the Fiat's tiny passenger compartment was a trick, even with the top down, but we managed, and I had two ginger beers behind the passenger-side seat, so pretty soon we were all set.

Bite, swoon, drink, repeat; for the next few minutes we concentrated on refueling and rehydrating. Then:

"He reminded me so much of Sam," I said. Out on the water the Campobello ferry bounced on a light chop. "At that age."

Ellie nodded, chewing. "All fine on the outside, mixed up on the inside?"

"Yup." Although in Sam's case, the chaos hadn't all stayed on the inside, possibly due to all the 100-proof lubrication it got. "Trouble is, nothing about Steven is any of my business."

Ellie dug through her bag for more napkins. I handed her a packet of wet wipes.

"We'll see about that," she said, scrubbing her hands. "If your suspicion is right about him hiding Arlene, he's going to be in a world of difficulty when people find out."

She was right; aiding and abetting, conspiracy after the fact, oh, the list went on and on.

"Arlene's going to need help, too, though," Ellie added.

"If we find her." I used a wipe on my own hands, grabbed our trash, and got out to put it in the barrel next to Rosie's, first shooing away the couple of enterprising seagulls who were raiding it.

The breeze smelled like salt water, seaweed, and the kind of fresh air that's never been breathed before. This intoxicating combo pinged my brain cells yet again. If they pinged any more, I thought as I stood there, I was going to start sounding like Ephraim's piano.

But: something about Steven, then something else about him. And that burlap.

Down on the dock, a guy hoisted a bag from his boat up onto the pier; clams, probably. Watching, I searched my mind for whatever kept making me feel I'd forgotten something important. The guy hopped nimbly from the boat onto the pier with the bag over his shoulder.

A burlap bag, I saw, and then it came to me, where I'd seen more of those bags recently. I got into the car, where Ellie eyed me questioningly.

"The bag," I said, backing out of the parking spot, "that the goat was eating out at the Clutes' place? I think I know where I've seen other ones like it, recently."

We turned onto Water Street; it was time to get back to the Moose. But now that I'd thought it, I couldn't stand not knowing for sure.

At the post office building I turned right and hit the gas. Ellie looked sideways at me but didn't comment. At the blanket factory on Route 190 we turned left into Quoddy Village; the old house ruins were right where I remembered them.

I pulled up into the rutted driveway and we got out.

"This?" Ellie said, gesturing uphill.

"Yeah." The place was a dark jumble of fallen clapboards, caved-in roof, ragged holes where the windows used to be, as if blown out from the inside.

A collapsing rectangle of doorway gaped darkly above an ancient stone step. Beyond, dim afternoon light slanted through the roof's gaps, showing splintered floorboards, fallen ceilings, and crumbled walls.

A jumble of antique pipes poked up between the whippy birch saplings and decades-old mats of fallen leaves in the abandoned yard, and the deep dirt ruts leading up to the place were barely dry where I'd excavated them with the Fiat's spinning tires.

"Well," said Ellie, confronting the sad wreckage of what was once someone's home, "as long as we're here, I suppose we might as well . . ."

She turned and strode determinedly up the dirt track. But now that I'd brought us here, what she always called my gumption suddenly departed. Sitting there smugly silent in the chilly autumn sunshine, the ruins seemed to be issuing an invitation.

And I didn't want to accept. Instead, after climbing the hill without me, Ellie mounted the massive old granite front doorstep and peeked inside while I stood below and watched.

My heart was in my throat, I was suddenly so frightened of what might happen next. Finally I took a step, and then another, while a cutting breeze made my eyes water and whipped dry weed stalks against my legs.

The driveway ruts twisted my ankles and loose stones slid treacherously beneath my feet as I struggled uphill under the gaze of those dark, torn-out window holes. If Bella were there she'd have dragged me away, but she wasn't.

As I climbed, I kept glancing at the raggedy-edged vacant spaces where glass used to be, watching for something to appear in one of them.

Nothing did. Then Ellie's voice came echoingly from inside, startling me; I hadn't seen her go in.

"Ellie?" I whispered into the silence. I was still twenty yards from the house.

Someone whispered back. Or something. "*Get out.*"

A flicker of movement at one of the second-floor window holes caught my eye, but it was gone by the time I could focus on it, and when I called Ellie's name there was no reply.

Luckily, my feet knew what to do even if I didn't. Charging uphill through tangled weeds toward the old dwelling's ruins, I vaulted the granite doorstep and landed on the floor inside.

It was just like I'd seen it when Maggie Davies brought me here, the sagging structure half collapsed and the other half just barely hanging together, only now in the daylight the ruination showed more clearly.

"Ellie!" I shouted. "You in here?"

No answer. Still, she could've fallen through a floorboard or down a cellar hole or something, unable to cry out.

Or something could have gotten her. But as the thought

crossed my mind, I snatched it and flung it away from me as far as I could; this was serious, now, no time for superstition.

"Ellie!" The burlap sacks I'd seen before still lay by the crumbling stone hearth, and a couple of blankets had been added. Also, and very unwisely due to the chimney's condition, there'd been a fire in the fireplace.

Still no sound from Ellie, though I kept calling for her. In what had been the kitchen, soda cans and food wrappers filled the rusted-out sink; in the hall, what was left of the stairs had pulled treacherously away from the remains of a wall, then partially collapsed.

Those stairs looked risky as hell, but I could imagine Ellie climbing curiously up there, quick as a little monkey. The woman was so agile that the fire department called her to get cats out of trees—you should've seen what she did one time to catch an escaped parrot—and she was fearless, too.

Thoughtfully, I approached the steps, which had a sort of surreal twistiness to them, first higher on the left and then on the right. I put a foot on the bottom one; no sense being hasty about these things. Then, after uttering some words too profane to be shared here, I began climbing.

The first step went fine, so I put my weight firmly on the second one, whereupon the entire stairway unit—newel post, risers, treads, banister, balusters and all—let out a scream of tortured wood and twisted nails that could've woken the dead, sagging abruptly another three feet.

Suddenly I clung for dear life to a stairway that had mostly ceased utterly to be one. Getting up there now would be like climbing the upside-down part of the roller coaster, and those give me the willies even when they're right side up.

"Ellie!" I called again, clambering to a slightly less uncomfortable spot and managing to sit. Now I could see that the only remaining way up was via the banister.

Shimmying up it, that is. And the thing is, Ellie would never not shimmy up a banister if the missing person were me. She'd be on it like one of those sticky-footed lizards, scamper-scamper and she'd be there.

On top of which, there was the little matter of splinters; this was not your well-kept, beeswax-polished wood, smooth as satin. This was gray, dry-rotted stuff, with splinters so long and sharp they could puncture an artery.

"Ellie?" I reached for the banister, twisted like ribbon candy. My heart hammered, my palms sweated, and a little voice in my head kept crying *Don't do this!* in tones that sounded very convincing.

And yet. Ellie was with me when Victor died, and when Wade got knocked off a ladder he was climbing and landed in the water between the freighter he was boarding and the pilot boat that brought him there. We didn't hear for over an hour if he'd been rescued.

Remembering this, I raised my leg over the banister and hauled myself, wincing, astride the thing. Then I began pulling with my hands and sliding upward on my butt, and you know those splinters I mentioned? But mine was not to wonder why, mine was just to—

"Jake?" It was Ellie, above me on the stairway landing. She looked dusty and mussed, probably from poking around up here, but otherwise she was fine.

I was so relieved I nearly fell off the banister. "What took you so long?" she asked, and of course I didn't tell her I'd been about to save her. Heck, at this point I was the one who needed saving.

Briefly, she assessed her best route down, then decided and jumped. After hopping sideways to the banister, then forward onto the stairs, leapfrogging over the newel post and dancing off the bottom step, she landed solidly on both feet with a satisfying thump.

Gosh, it was fun to watch. But on its heels came the sudden

bang! of a door slam. We jumped, turning, to find that the front door had swung shut and latched all by itself.

"Probably," Ellie ventured into the silence that followed, "it was the wind."

I looked through one of the window holes. Outside, the trees' bare branches hung motionless.

"No wind," I reported unhappily. Lengthening shadows were marching through the dried weeds and saplings at us, though; it had gotten to be late afternoon somehow.

"Ah," said Ellie, looking a little pale. "Jake, what do you say we get out of here just as swiftly and efficiently as . . ." Her face changed as she looked past me. "Um, Jake?"

I turned to see what had her staring in vexed disbelief. As it turned out, I didn't believe it, either.

But it was true. The door was gone. Just . . . missing, the wall simply continuing unbroken where the door opening had been.

"Sheesh." I sank down onto the bottom step of the twisted stairway. We'd left Ellie's satchel and my canvas tote in the car, and our phones were in them; we hadn't meant to stay.

Or to get trapped. The vanished door turned out to be the only one leading to the outside (no fire regulations back then, I guessed) and the jagged-edged window holes blatantly promised complete skin removal.

Also, I was pretty sure I wouldn't fit through one of them. In the old days, windows were much smaller; come to think of it, so was I. Anyway, the windows were a no-go.

"We're hallucinating," said Ellie. "We've breathed in some kind of toxic fungus in here or something, and . . ."

This was not actually so far-fetched. Black mold toxins can make you see, hear, and feel things that aren't there, as I learned when I tore out an old shower stall in the house on Key Street. For about an hour I thought small green lizards in top hats were tap-dancing up out of the drain, singing "Danny Boy."

The shadows creeping rapidly toward us now, however, were not illusions. They signaled dusk coming, and a night in a house that wanted to scare me to death wasn't on my bucket list.

"Let's just knock all the sharp stuff out of one of those window holes," Ellie said, rubbing her hands together.

"With . . . what?"

No need to mention the window-to-backside size mismatch yet, since there wasn't a solid knocking tool anywhere in sight. Even the floorboards felt spongy, and when I pulled on a loose one, a damp chunk of it came up in my hand.

"Hmm," said Ellie. Then she scurried over to the stairs and kicked her sneakered foot at it, whereupon two of the balusters in the stairway's balustrade broke out cleanly and bounced down the steps.

She picked them up. "One for me, and one for . . ."

Yeah. The baluster felt pleasantly clublike in my grip, and we spent the next ten minutes bashing anything that could slice out our giblets—rusty nail ends dripping tetanus, glass shards with my vital organs' names etched on them, tin weatherstripping whose razorlike edges promised quick exsanguination.

"There," said Ellie, stepping back to admire our work. Outside, blue shadows filled the rutted dirt track leading back down to the road; it was getting late. But at least our exit was no longer blocked by tools for carving us into lunchmeat.

I'd thought that Arlene's geeky-but-okay boyfriend, Steven Clute, might be helping her hide here, and based on what we'd found, that seemed likely. But now it seemed we'd also gotten ourselves stuck in some kind of ghostly flypaper: *The living get in, but they can't get out!*

Or something like that. Honestly, I didn't really know what to think. All I knew was that we *were* getting out of here and it was also all I cared about.

"Jake," Ellie said as I prepared to hoist myself onto the lower edge of the window hole we'd cleared. *This won't be hard,* I told myself, and for a moment I really believed it.

"Jake, you don't have to—"

Up, big girl, I urged myself; for once I didn't intend to need rescuing by Ellie from some dumb-bunny mistake.

Up . . . I settled my backside on the sill's edge and paused there, flush with my own success so far. My hands were already pretty scraped up, but now I could —

"*Jake!*" Ellie said from behind me. "*Look.*"

I didn't, at first, not wanting to see anything even the least bit creepy; my hair-raising-events quota was full for the day and for all days in the future, I'd resolved. But:

"Jake," Ellie repeated insistently. So I finally turned my head. Then:

"Oh," I said softly. The doorway opening was back. Then I lost my precarious balance on the windowsill, slid backward out of the window hole, and landed very hard on my backside.

But I didn't care. Slowly I got up off the floor, still staring at the door, willing it not to vanish once more before I could hurl myself through it.

Or, heaven forbid, *while* I was hurling myself. "Okay," I said, approaching the warped, graying rectangle of wood with the old glass doorknob glinting in it.

"Okay, so what do you say we get out of this awful place, pronto?" I was already creeping stealthily to the door, just in case it got any ideas.

About not being there when I got there, for instance.

"Okay," Ellie said from behind me, "when you get to it, just . . ."

Yeah. Yank it open, exit screaming, and run like hell; I felt like a cartoon mouse sneaking away from a cartoon cat. Finally I reached out for the old doorknob, and —

It twitched. I yanked my hand back. "What?" Ellie demanded.

"Someone's out there. Go look out the window and see if . . ."

The doorknob rattled hard. "What was that?" Ellie whispered.

But I seemed to have lost the power of speech, as if this new fright had reached right down my throat and seized something important.

An agonized creak like the hood of an old car being lifted cut through the gloom. As Ellie's frightened eyes met mine, the door swung open.

A fortyish blond-haired woman in a tan puffy jacket and black pants stood on the doorstep in the thin autumn sunshine. Relief flooded through me.

"Maggie Davies," I told Ellie, "is who saved me the other night when I got—"

Stuck out here, I meant to say but before I could, Maggie stepped past me into the old house.

"Good heavens," she laughed, looking around by the light of the large flashlight she carried, "what in the world are you two doing?"

The leaning staircase, fallen plaster, jagged window holes, and rotted floorboards all looked like part of the stage set for an opera about dead people.

"We're looking for a lost cat," Ellie improvised with a glance at me. "Someone out this way said they'd seen him."

"Oh," said Maggie sympathetically, "any luck yet?"

"No," I put in quickly. I wasn't sure why Maggie shouldn't know what we were really up to, but over time I've found that it's best to just shut up and stick with the cover story.

"Damn cat," I said, stepping outside into the cold, clear afternoon with a feeling of having been let out of jail.

Ellie and Maggie came out behind me. "At least your car's not stuck this time," said Maggie, pulling the raddled old door shut behind us.

Through the leafless trees, sunshine as pale as champagne slanted down. I basked gratefully in it, still shaken by the inexplicable things that had just happened.

"But come on over for a cup of tea anyway," she went on

pleasantly as we made our way through evening shadows down the dirt track to the road.

"Thanks, but we really have to get back to the Moose. Those cookies won't bake themselves, you know," said Ellie, and I nodded along with her. "Another time, maybe?"

Maggie looked disappointed. "I won't be here much longer. I want to get back to Mom, I don't want her all alone down there in Boston. Clearing the house is such a big project, though."

I didn't ask why the rush on that; it was none of my business and all I really wanted was to go. Home, preferably, but anywhere was better than here.

"You know what, though?" Maggie went on. "Before I do go, there are things of hers that should probably stay in Eastport. Pictures, genealogy records—"

I felt Ellie's ears prick up and I grabbed her arm, but it was too late. "I can take them off your hands," she said.

Wave antique Eastport stuff under Ellie's nose and she goes all historical preservationist on you. But I didn't want to spend any more time here at all; behind me I could still feel the house sort of breathing in and out at me, as if it might be getting ready to suck me back inside.

"We really do have to go," I told Ellie, giving her arm a squeeze, and she caught on at once. But there was a catch.

"I'll come later for any historical stuff you're not taking with you," she told Maggie. "How about right after dinner? And Jake will come, too, would that work?"

"Great," Maggie agreed at once. "Those things are important to someone, and before I go I want them off my conscience."

Which was decent of her; she could've just thrown them in the trash. So Maggie strode off happily downhill toward her own house and I fell into the waiting Fiat like a sack of potatoes.

Chills shook me, my head ached miserably, and my heart pulsed with lingering fright-pangs. "What the hell just happened in there?" I asked, but Ellie only shrugged: *no idea.*

The house hunkered darkly, seeming to loom over us as we backed down the driveway. For several moments, managing the car occupied me completely; the Grand Canyon was a stick-dug ditch compared to those ruts.

At the bottom, I glanced back uphill for what I hoped was my last-ever look at the old place . . . and then I looked again.

A woman stood in the doorway of the very old house we'd just departed. Or—and this was my sense of it—escaped.

Tall, slim, with dark hair pulled up and back from a shadow-blurred face, she wore a long dark dress with a long white bibbed apron tied over it.

I could almost see the ruffles on the apron, and "bat out of hell" doesn't even come close to describing how fast I got out of there.

"You want to drive later?" I asked Ellie as we sped back toward Eastport. The Fiat didn't have much cargo space.

"Sure, why not?" she replied, but nothing more.

Neither of us wanted to talk about what had or hadn't just happened, at least not right away; I didn't even know if she'd seen the woman on the doorstep.

"You sure you want to come along?" she asked me.

"Sure," I echoed her despite my misgivings, "why not?"

We didn't have to go anywhere near the old house again, after all, and one more trip to Quoddy Village wasn't going to kill me—I hoped.

"You're really letting Maggie Davies dump her mom's old papers on you, though?"

I imagined the mildew-smelling boxes full of photographs too faded to see and early Xerox copies of newspaper articles, now too faint to read.

"Somebody might be very glad to get old pictures," she defended her planned errand, "and the genealogy records, too."

As far as I was concerned, if Maggie's mother could walk on water and offered to show me how, I still wouldn't have visited that neighborhood again for a long, long time.

But: "You're probably right," I conceded. If Ellie could bounce back from the scare we'd just had, so could I.

I turned right at the foot of Washington Street toward the googly-eyed moose sign hanging over our shop door, and parked out front. Up and down Water Street the storefront windows shone gold in the warm afternoon light; out on the water I heard bell buoys clanking and seagulls crying.

"Seven thirty?" I asked as we got out. I had afternoon duty in the shop today; Ellie was on her way home.

She nodded, got into her own car, and backed out, pulling away down Water Street while I let myself into the Moose.

And that's where I got the real scare of the evening.

Nine

The moment I stepped into the Chocolate Moose, I knew I wasn't alone. As my eyes adjusted I made out the dark figure in the gloom away from the window, and being in the mood I was in, I did the only two things possible:

I flipped on the light switch just inside the door, then swiftly put my head down and charged whoever this damned fool turned out to be, like I didn't have enough problems already.

A second later I was seized in the kind of grip generally provided only by steel cables, and one of my elbows was twisting in a direction that it usually didn't.

"Oh," I gasped faintly, after which I was pulled, pushed, and finally released in quick succession, which gave the whole maneuver a whiplash effect that I also didn't appreciate.

"Nice try," said a familiar voice.

Oh, for Pete's sake. After a few moments during which I stood bent over and gasping, trying to control my heart rate and my temper, I got a few words out.

"Criminy, Dylan, what if someone saw you come in?"

Because of course it was him. He smiled that outlaw smile of his, the one that always got him back on my good side.

But not this time. "I got in through the alley window, so that would've been unlikely," he said.

Great, so now we'd have to fix the window. "I'm serious, Dylan. What the hell were you even thinking, coming here?"

Now that Arlene wasn't much of a suspect anymore, he'd have become more interesting to the police, I assumed. And this was definitely among his usual haunts.

"Cop radio, remember?" he said, then confirmed what I already thought. "Man, you'd think I was public enemy number one."

Looking at him again, I realized he couldn't be staying at Lizzie's anymore. He'd managed to stay clean-shaven, and when he'd grabbed me, he'd smelled like shampoo; probably he'd used the washroom at the Port Authority building, open and skeleton-staffed but otherwise empty late at night.

Food, though. It seemed he'd already have lost a pound or two, his hawkish features sharper, the dark eyes deeper set. Meanwhile, Bella had mentioned something this morning about beef stew, that she was making a batch. With those rosemary biscuits that she'd baked, no doubt, and he really did look hungry.

"Look," I said, "you wait here while I go start the car."

He opened his mouth. I put my hand up: *Talk to this.* He looked surprised. "Who, me? I should shut up?"

"Unless you want a mouthful of knuckles, oh, you betcha." I opened the door, looked up and down the sidewalk. Eastport's relative vacancy in autumn was suddenly a good thing: no one.

Then I grabbed Hudson's sleeve, dragged him out, slammed the shop door without bothering to lock it (see *vacancy,* above) and hustled him to the Fiat.

"Get down," I said, opening the passenger-side door and pushing him in. "Put your hat over your face to cover it, like you were sleeping."

He was wearing a blue knitted cap, not the kind of hat used in the old movies for this purpose, but it would have to do. I wrestled the Fiat's top up and latched it, then got into the car and turned the key. The pleasure of not having been attacked by a lurking evildoer was fading, but so was the fright-fueled adrenaline surge of finding Hudson in the shop, not to mention the day's earlier hair-raising events.

Which I was still processing; i.e., *What the hell?* Thus expecting cheerfulness from me now was entirely unrealistic, and Hudson caught on fast. Only once on our way to my place did he try speaking:

"This is very nice of you, Jake, I didn't expect—"

"Shut up," I explained pleasantly as we pulled into the driveway of the big old house on Key Street. We got out of the car and crossed the yard with the maples' bare branches rattling over our heads. On the porch, he waited while I opened the door.

"Let's not talk about it in front of the family, okay?" I said.

He nodded, grimacing. "Wouldn't dream of it."

Under the porch light he looked older, more burdened than I was used to seeing. But the moment we went in, his expression brightened as Ephraim raced toward him and clasped himself to the tall man's leg while little Nadine hung back, smiling shyly. In the kitchen, even the baby stopped fussing and began gurgling happily, ensconced in his playpen.

"Oh, good," Bella said, looking up from the pot she was stirring as we pulled off our jackets. "You'll help eat up some of this, won't you?"

Nodding weakly, Dylan looked as if he might faint from the delicious aromas wafting from the stew pot. Meanwhile, my dad went to set chairs opposite one another across the chessboard. Soon Wade came in from work and shot Dylan a salute before heading into the shower. Sam and Mika were out for the evening.

Then we gathered at the table, and for a wonder, there was nobody crying, fighting, or playing any toy musical instruments. It was perfect, really, except for one small thing: getting rid of the dinner guest.

Otherwise later tonight when Ellie and I went to Quoddy Village, Dylan would want to know to who, what, where, and so on, and maybe even insist on coming along.

So after dinner, I brought him one of two large whiskies I'd poured. He was in the parlor with the bigger kids, one on each side while he read to them about sharks' teeth: how many, how large, and so on. Hearing about chomping power put glee on Nadine's pixie face, but Ephraim was beginning to seem worried.

Dylan looked beatific; it was as if when he walked into this house his worries all flew away. That's how I felt about it, too, except of course for the roof that needed patching, the clapboards that urgently required painting, and the foundation, a corner of which needed rebuilding before the whole place fell into the cellar.

Anyway: "Scoot, you two," I told the kids as I gave Dylan his drink, and they scampered off to the kitchen where moments later I heard them asking for juice.

I downed half my own drink. Dylan did the same.

"Rough day?" he inquired, raising a dark eyebrow.

"Not as bad as yours, I bet." I set my glass on a coaster to avoid Bella's wrath later. "Hey, I'm not being hunted by the cops, so, you know, I've got that going for me."

He nodded gravely. "Very true."

"So, what's new? Are the state cops getting anywhere? I mean, besides on your nerves?"

I was trying to be sociable but all I could really think of—other than getting Dylan out of here, somehow—was the woman on the doorstep earlier, and the other things Ellie and I had experienced.

Or had we? The woman in the long dress and apron had been there, and then *poof!* she wasn't. The door had been there, then not, then back again, not just for me but for Ellie, too.

A prickly little shiver went up my arms as I remembered; then I realized that Dylan had been talking to me for a while.

"Sorry, what?" I interrupted.

"Arlene," he repeated patiently. "I said she's still around here, or at least I think so. In or near Eastport."

"Why?" She seemed pretty gone to me, the burlap-sack bed in the crazy old house notwithstanding. That she'd been there at one time didn't mean she'd be back.

"Her mother's house was broken into," Dylan said. "Food taken, some of the girl's clothes. And a jar of loose change."

"And?" I asked, realizing that my assumption was wrong; Arlene wasn't out from under the cops' suspicion after all. And clearly there was more; I could see it in Dylan's face.

"The murder cops are there now, examining the scene for clues," he answered tiredly, "like that's going to help."

Find the girl, he meant. He sat up straight. "So, any plans for the evening?" His tone was casual. The question wasn't.

"Nope. None whatsoever." If you're going to lie, do it with gusto, I always say. "I think I'll just hang around here and relax for once," I said, yawning to emphasize this.

If I didn't get him off our trail, he'd drive us crazy by picking our brains for recent info about Lizzie and about how we thought he might finally win her over for good.

Personally I thought if she were any more won over they'd be joined at the hip. It was the intensity of her emotions that bugged her, she'd told me once; she couldn't reason with them, or pull a gun on them.

I changed the subject. "So did the state guys get to talk to Missy Rafferty again before she left town?"

Her haste to get out of Stone House rose in memory; she'd want to get out of Eastport fast, too, I imagined. But before

Hudson could answer, Bella appeared in the parlor doorway with the little white dog dancing by her feet.

"Pie's ready," she announced with a smile for Dylan, whom she regarded as a sort of adopted son since he'd befriended my father. At the table, the old man was filling glasses with the sparkling dandelion wine he'd begun making the previous spring.

Pale green, sweetly effervescent, and clear as springwater in thin crystal flutes, the stuff went down like pale fire and was so full of alcohol, you could burn it in a lamp.

"Wow," I said faintly, and sat. The afterglow from the wine made my slice of Bella's apricot pie shimmer juicily under the scoop of vanilla ice cream melting on it.

Across the table, Wade poured a first glassful down his throat, grinned, and held his emptied glass out across the table. "Hit me again, old man."

The old man raised an eyebrow. "Sure you can handle it?"

But he was pouring as he spoke. Bella sipped nervously as if her drink was dynamite, which in my opinion it very nearly was. Hudson looked on, smiling tiredly and not, I noticed, drinking any dandelion wine.

At last, when the kids were getting antsy and none of the adults could eat even one more delicious bite, Dylan got up and began clearing dishes.

"Oh, now," Bella admonished him, "you don't have to—"

He turned, setting stacked dessert plates on the table. "But what if I want to, hey? What then?"

Reaching for her hands, he danced her right up out of her chair and twirled her around.

"Stop!" Bella demanded as he twirled her again, and she was laughing so hard when she said it that finally he let her back down. Then Wade got up and lifted a kid under each arm, and bore them away; the baby was now sleeping soundly in his playpen, but Bella started warming a bottle for him anyway since soon we'd hear howls, while in the kitchen Dylan started on the dishes and my dad kept him company.

All of which gave me—miracle of miracles—five minutes peace. I called Ellie and said I'd be outside waiting in an hour. By then I thought Hudson would be deep in a chess game: losing a knight, sacrificing a rook, or already in checkmate and demanding a rematch.

"It's not like there's anything sneaky about this," I told Ellie, explaining why I didn't want his company on our errand.

"I just don't want to hear about Lizzie again all evening," I said. "Or get grilled some more on her feelings about him."

Like had she said anything about him, and if so, what? And how did she say it? Amused, annoyed, what? Whenever he got Ellie and me to himself, it just went on and on.

"Agreed," said Ellie, who didn't enjoy his constant taking of Lizzie's emotional temperature any more than I did.

So it was settled, and I hung up, hoping it all worked out. On top of everything, Hudson was the type who would have his feelings hurt if he found out we'd sneaked out without him.

Half an hour later, though, already solidly whomped two games out of three and with only a draw in the third one, Dylan got up.

"Gotta go, old man," he said, glancing up at the clock on the kitchen wall.

My dad peered wisely up at him. "It's funny how when you're losing, you suddenly need to leave."

Dylan reached down and grabbed my dad's head in the crook of his arm and pressed it to his side. "Yeah. Maybe if I ever beat you, it'll be different." He let go and headed for the door. "Hey, tell Bella I said thanks," he said, stepping out onto the porch.

It was almost seven, pitch-dark and damply chilly. "Where are you going?" I asked him through the screen door.

He wouldn't stay the night even if invited, I knew; too proud.

A fist bump later he was striding away with his head held high and his shoulders squared, out into the night.

I hurried into the house to change clothes, wash my face, and drag a brush through my hair; it was short, wavy brown stuff that took to styling the way a wild horse takes to a saddle. By then Ellie's car was out front.

"I hope you put the hand truck in the trunk," I said as I got in. The last time I'd helped Ellie with a genealogy-related project, we'd ended up renting a trailer.

"She did say she'd 'hand the stuff over,' " Ellie reminded me as we drove on out of town, "so I'm assuming it's a reasonably smallish haul. Oh, I hope Lillian's okay."

"She just said that so we'd let our guard down," I replied, "about 'handing' the stuff. I didn't get a good sense of whether she's recovering well or not."

It had felt good to tell Wade I was going on an errand that didn't involve murder. I just wished our history-preserving task didn't take us right past the old ruins that had scared me silly only a few hours earlier.

". . . we'll just load it all up," Ellie was saying, "and take it all back to my house. Sort through it and . . ."

"What?" I gave myself a hard mental shake. We were almost to the Quoddy Village turnoff.

"The papers. From Maggie. I'll take them—"

"Right, right." I sat up straight, took a deep breath. We'd be driving past the ruins, but not going in or near them; if I had to, I could just look the other way.

Except no, actually, I couldn't. As the road curved up and around past the old dirt driveway toward Maggie's house, what remained of the disintegrating dwelling perched in the gloom like some dark bird of prey, motionless but alert.

Then we were past it and behind us, the night swallowed it.

Ellie glanced at me. "You okay?"

The winding streets curved and twisted like tangled yarn.

Luckily, Ellie's sense of direction was better than mine; also, her heart wasn't thudding away a mile a minute.

"Fine," I said as she pulled up in front of the little house Maggie Davies was staying in.

"I know this place," she said as we got out. "There's a road that goes around behind it, leads to an old gravel pit and a pond that has eels in it."

I knew the place she meant, though I couldn't have found it alone. Wade used to take me target shooting there back when we were first getting acquainted.

The Siamese cat watched as we followed the path to the door. Then Maggie brought us into the dim, candlelit room where the aromas of herbal tea and sandalwood incense and the snapping of gnarled driftwood blazing on the hearth all eased my nerves.

"Hello, hello," Maggie greeted us warmly, stepping behind me to close the door. The cat on the windowsill made a sound of derision and leapt down to stalk from the room.

Maggie took our jackets politely, then turned and stuffed them both into the black plastic trash bag she'd been holding out of sight behind her back.

Which I thought was very odd, and then it hit me, what must be going on. "Ellie," I said warningly, about to grab whatever portion of my friend and business partner that I could reach on short notice and scram us out of this pop stand.

But an anguished little sound made me turn, a faint "eep!" that turned out to be coming from Arlene Cunningham, sitting on the floor in the room's far corner. Her zip-tied wrists and duct-taped mouth confirmed that we were in deep and serious trouble.

Then everything happened fast; Maggie grabbed me, turned me, and dropped me, then knelt on my back to slap duct tape over my mouth and zip ties around my wrists.

At some time or another she'd obviously taken lessons of

some kind, personal defense training or maybe karate. Ellie charged to rescue me but Maggie was ready for her, too, grabbing a length of clothesline she had conveniently handy.

Arlene's eyes widened as Maggie dropped Ellie with a punch, stepped on her, then tied a quick slipknot and tightened it around her prisoner's neck. Finally she ripped off another strip of tape and used it to stop Ellie's furious protests.

Heck, I didn't know Ellie knew some of those words. But they'd done no good; once Maggie had us silenced and unable to run, she moved on to the next phase of her plan: brandishing a gun.

It was a crappy little .22 pistol, the one with the pink grip and the cute little pink carrying case that was big news when it first came out. I'd fired one and found out that with luck you could hit the side of a barn at twenty paces with it.

But at close range it was still deadly. Maggie brandished it for emphasis. "Now, I'm going to wait here while you"—she meant me—"go start the car. Then I'll bring these two out." She angled her head at Arlene and Ellie. "And if any of you does anything but what I say, I'll shoot the other two. Clear?" She looked at me, her eyes cold. "Like try to use a phone, for instance, or drive off to get help," she added.

And getting Ellie and Arlene murdered wasn't how I wanted to end an already bad day, so I didn't do any of those things. Instead I followed orders. Soon I was sitting behind the wheel of Ellie's car with her beside me, Maggie and Arlene in back.

Of course with that tape on my mouth I couldn't ask *Where to?* like some seasoned Manhattan cabbie, but I didn't feel like trying to be funny, anyway.

I felt like dragging Maggie Davies by the hair for a while, then punching her in the kidneys a dozen or so times, is what I felt like. What I did was raise my eyebrows questioningly.

Maggie sighed. "Stone House, of course," she said, as if I should have known.

Which seemed simple enough. But when I got to the fork in the road we'd come in on and tried to go back the same way, she sat up and shook the back of my seat with both hands.

"Not that way!" She jabbed her finger the other direction, toward the old, mud-rutted driveway and the rot-raddled wreckage of a house at the top, crowded in by trees and with its gray sagging front still resembling a gaunt, eyeless face.

At the foot of the dirt track I glanced uphill and caught another glimpse of the old place, feeling with a shiver that it had caught a glimpse of me, too.

Nevertheless I gunned the engine uphill. Maybe once we got out of the car there'd be a chance to do something. Ellie's old Toyota was small and clunky but it took no sass from larger, fancier cars. Spitting loose dirt and small stones out behind us all the way, it charged up the slope as if sensing my desperation.

At the top: "Get out." Maggie punched the back of the seat.

She'd snipped my wrist tie so I could drive; now she urged me out and slid out behind me, sticking that wretched little gun of hers in my ribs, right off the bat.

"You too," she grated at Ellie and Arlene, and of course with a bullet just waiting to puncture my favorite internal organs, they obeyed. Moments later the four of us stood in the chilly gloom in front of the house, which aside from my other problems I was pretty sure was getting ready to devour me whole.

"Stop." Maggie gave the gun she was jabbing into my rib cage a harder shove, causing my liver and spleen to clutch their handkerchiefs and look around fearfully.

More leaves in the tangle of saplings and shrubbery had fallen in the thicket behind the house, so the odd little shed at the back of the property—or perhaps even over the property line, I didn't know—stood out clearly now. Maybe if we could get to it . . .

"And don't try to run," Maggie's voice cut through my thought. "Not to brag, but I'm a good shot."

She'd need to be with that little popgun she was holding. But everybody gets a lucky shot off sometimes, and getting .22-calibered to death wasn't in my game plan.

"Go on in." She waved the gun at the granite-slab doorstep. Beyond it gaped the doorway's black rectangle. I thought about it, but right now there was no way I'd get the weapon away from Maggie without somebody getting hurt, or worse.

Maybe in the darkness inside we'd get the jump on her, ideally before someone or something in that house got the jump on us. Or so I forced myself to think, so as not to think about other things.

Frightening things. "Come on, you guys," I told Ellie and Arlene. They followed reluctantly as I stepped first onto the granite doorstep, then over the rotting threshold and into a sudden sense of impending doom so strong, it turned my knees to water. Staggering a few steps, I found the hall stairs' ancient newel post and grabbed on, heedless of splinters.

"Jake?" Ellie called from somewhere behind me. My heart's thudding nearly drowned her voice.

"I'm fine," I managed. My eyes weren't yet adjusted to the gloom; I felt them widen, trying to catch any speck of light.

Upstairs, something scraped roughly across a floor. Then something slapped a wall, wetly; at this I pushed away from the post, ready to flee and that little gun of Maggie's be damned.

But then I stopped, because it wouldn't be me she'd shoot. "Hey, Maggie?"

She'd come inside, too, and gone to the back of the house where the kitchen had been long ago, taking Arlene along so (I supposed) she could shoot the girl if Ellie or I ran.

Yeah, she was a charmer, all right. I followed her, making my way by the glow of the flashlight she'd hung by its strap in the enormous stone hearth, from which it dimly lit the room.

Arlene found a corner and crouched there with her arms around her knees. When she glanced up with tear-swollen eyes

I wanted to comfort her, the poor beaten-up kid, but from the look on her face when our eyes met I thought she might bite me, so I didn't.

"Maggie, what the hell is this all about?" I said instead. I found her crouched in the kitchen hearth space, squinting up into the chimney and, it looked like, doing something to it.

Correction: she was stuffing something up there. Crumpled plastic bags, a chenille bedspread, those wadded-up old burlap sacks . . .

Alarm bells went off in my head; she was blocking the flue. "Maggie? Why are you—?"

She turned, smudged with centuries-old black soot that made a mask of her face; a fright mask, and a familiar one, at that.

"Maggie?" The truth dawned on me. "Who are you? I mean, who are you really?"

Because who she was not, I realized with a jolt of horror, was retired baker and Eastport historian Mrs. Boyd's dutiful daughter. Instead she was someone else entirely, and not, I felt certain, anyone good.

Definitely not good for Lillian Boyd, who I was willing to bet was not in some pleasant place in Boston. The truth was more like a hastily dug grave, I feared. Maggie saw the gist of this in my face and smiled, her eyes gleaming with triumph.

"Who am I?" She straightened. "I'm the last living direct descendant of Bernadine Hallowell," she said, "and as such— once the original will's terms are fulfilled—the new owner of Stone House."

Which of course made no sense. Stone House was on a lovely piece of property, but the dwelling itself was junk. You could give it all the furniture and brand-new appliances you wanted, but making the place truly comfortable—insulation, storm windows, a furnace that didn't rely on grates through the floors—would take another hundred grand or more.

So why commit murder for it? "And," Maggie couldn't resist adding, "all that beautiful property it sits on, just waiting to be developed."

And there it was, the motive. From behind me I could hear Ellie moving something heavy across what remained of the wood floor.

"But Maggie, couldn't you just . . ."

Buy it, I meant to finish, but suddenly it occurred to me that maybe it wasn't Ellie making noise. And Arlene was still sitting right where she'd been all this time, so it wasn't her.

"What, buy it from him? He wouldn't sell," said Maggie.

"But now he's dead and you're next in line," I realized aloud. "So you'll get it that way? You're what, a distant cousin or something?"

"Sister," she said flatly. "Fraternal twin. I should have gotten half, but he was born first."

I remembered Steven Clute, Sr. saying Hank had a sister, that she wasn't cute or talented so she got much less attention than Hank did.

Now she laughed without humor. "Died first, too. Served him right, he was such a show-off."

Being ignored in favor of her brother hadn't done her any favors psychologically, it seemed. She seized my shoulder and muscled me back out to where Arlene still crouched.

"I am six minutes younger than Hank." An annoyed snort escaped her. "All this trouble for six minutes."

Meaning, I supposed, that if only she'd been born first, she wouldn't have had to kill him. But looking at her now and seeing the sick thrill in her eyes, I wasn't convinced.

She'd have found another reason.

Ten

"You can see Stone House from here, did you know that?" Ellie asked. She stood on an old metal bucket half rusted away with age, peering out a window hole.

"No," I said, watching unhappily. We didn't need to see out of here, we needed to *get* out. "Ellie, can you please . . . ?"

The rusty bucket pancaked down on itself; leaping aside, Ellie hit the wall hard and fell with a loud thud. At once our captor came running in with the gun in one hand, flashlight in the other.

Meanwhile, Ellie got up, unhurt; I swear if she were any more agile, she'd be swinging through the trees. But my relief was short-lived, as suddenly Maggie hauled Arlene to her feet and shoved the girl at Ellie, who caught her and kept her from falling until the girl pushed Ellie away violently.

Behind me a door slammed shut. Beyond it a padlock's hasp clicked home.

And then I smelled smoke. "Oh, for Pete's sake." Only I didn't say "Pete's." I was way too mad for any little niceties about vocabulary.

Also too scared. Smoke billowed from the kitchen, so thick that I could barely glimpse the yellow flames of the fire Maggie had set. From the smell I thought she'd used kerosene to get it going, but whatever; the fire belched black smoke billows, thick and choking, and used up oxygen.

Like, the stuff we needed to breathe. Still, it didn't take long for us to get the restraints off; Ellie has teeth that can crack whole walnuts, so the plastic was nothing to her.

Escaping this aging death trap before the smoke got to us, though, was a different matter. We couldn't get upstairs where we might've found wood rotten enough to break through, because the smoke was already too thick. By now what we were breathing couldn't really even be called air, and Ellie had discovered something else that made our situation even more dire, the reason why the fire's fumes were already so near-overpowering.

"All the window holes except this one are covered with some kind of heavy black plastic," she reported. "I tried my penknife on it," she said. "When I stood on the bucket. But no dice."

Maggie must've planned for the fire to get rid of our bodies, or enough of them anyway that she'd be spared moving any messy parts. I did wonder how she would get rid of bones and so on, and Ellie's car. But then I remembered the gravel pit at the back of Mrs. Boyd's secluded quarter-acre and decided not to think about that anymore.

"Can't we cut through it with anything else?" I asked, hearing the urgency in my own voice. Right now with the fire burning merrily, some of the smoke was going up the stairs.

But sooner or later there'd be too much of it to exhaust that way, and then it would kill us. No one was likely to see the flames until they burst out through the roof and by then we'd be long gone.

"I've tried cutting it," said Ellie, showing a long dagger of tin that she'd broken out of the flattened bucket. "But it's layers of stuff, I think even some chicken wire, and—"

The fire's hot crackle had deepened to the kind of low roar that I imagined a blast furnace must make. The kerosene-tasting air burned my eyes and felt like jagged glass in my lungs. I knew carbon monoxide must be in it, too, unnoticeable and fatal.

"I know how to get out," said Arlene Cunningham suddenly from the corner where she'd retreated again; the air was better close to the floor.

She looked pale and sweaty, her eyes puffy red and her nose running, and she hadn't said a word until now since we got in here; I'd nearly forgotten about her, other than when Maggie dragged her around.

Now she climbed exhaustedly to her feet, all gangly adolescent arms and legs and a face like a stone carving, no expression on it at all.

"Come on." Still wearing the jeans and sweatshirt I'd last seen on her

Friday night at her mother's house, she turned to trudge heavily back toward the ruined stairs.

"Arlene, I've been up there," I began, "there's nothing . . ."

Nothing up there to help us. "Arlene, you don't have to go up there, I told you, I've already been . . ."

But upstairs wasn't where she was going. Instead, in the choking darkness, she somehow found her way to a small door hidden under the sagging stairs and yanked it open.

Cool air gushed from it; I nearly fainted with relief. Then Ellie aimed the flashlight past Arlene, illuminating the most dangerous-looking wooden set of stairs I'd ever seen: more like a rickety ladder than steps, emphasis on the rickety part.

Leading down. Ellie shone the flashlight around in the opening; the steps led to a cellar where cobwebs draped the walls and ancient (I hoped) hornets' nests studded the rafters. Something dark scuttled unpleasantly from the light in the far corner, its eyes glowing red in our direction before vanishing.

"Come on," Arlene said, and started down. Behind her, I hesitated; Ellie, too, as we looked down the stairs again.

"Dark," said Ellie, peering past me. "Quiet, too."

"Yeah," I said skeptically. Now that all the rustling and scrabbling sounds had stopped, it was quiet

Stopped as if waiting for us. "Arlene?" Ellie called, and then from behind me the fire exploded suddenly with a flash and a sound like thunder.

Ellie shoved her flashlight at me. Flames licked so close to us that I could feel their hot breath.

"You first," said Ellie, and what the hell, whatever was down there had to be better than burning to death so I went.

The cramped, low-ceilinged cellar hole was more of a dugout than a useful space. Arlene wasn't in sight but I spied a candy wrapper shining freshly on the ancient dirt floor, and another a little farther along.

"She's leaving us a trail," said Ellie, who'd followed me down those shaky cellar steps.

"Right. But to what?" Old nails, bits of glass, moldering wood scraps and other unidentifiable stuff studded the soil, which hadn't seen sunshine in many decades.

Great hideout for vampires, I thought, shivering. Ellie elbowed me. "Almost there," she told me encouragingly.

"Fine, but where's *that*?" I asked again, then squawked at what I sincerely hoped was a mouse running over my foot.

Next, I ducked under a low beam made from an adze-cut tree trunk, then came suddenly face-to-face with the biggest spider I'd ever seen. As I walked into its web, it ran *toward* me across the strands, then leapt springily to my shoulder and from there up the side of my face *scritchscritchscritch.*

"Gah," I said, frozen. I'd have run screaming in circles but there was no room for that down here; what little space did exist was full of what looked like wooden crates, opened and with the tops flung around.

I didn't care about them. All I cared about was that if it was in my hair, it could go down my shirt, and if it was in my shirt, it could get down my—

"Ellie?" It was in my hair, I'd known it must be, and now it was just kind of noodling around up there, filing its nails or reading a spidery little magazine while it waited for me to let my guard down.

As I thought this, my revulsion meter shot up into the red zone and pegged there. "Get it, please," I whispered; if it tried going up my nose I would lose it, I would absolutely—

"Hold still," said Ellie, peering calmly at my scalp.

A shriek crept up my throat.

"Okay, now," said Ellie. I felt a prickly sensation in my scalp. She plucked something from the spot and peered at it, then flung it away reflexively.

"Yeeks," she uttered, startled, and that's when I learned that it wasn't just your average enormous spider. It was a brown recluse, a spider with a bite so painful they give you morphine for it and with venom so powerful it rots your flesh, right down to the bone in some cases.

And they were everywhere down here; what I'd thought must be ancient gray curtains were webs, and were they *moving*? Sort of *undulating*?

The next thing I knew I was backpedaling fast, tripping over random obstacles and flinging the sticky strands away from my face. Then Ellie called out to me; I struggled back toward her, cringing and flailing at spiders and cobwebs as I went.

"There," she pointed. A dirt-walled tunnel entrance opened in the cellar wall; wide, round . . . there was no mistaking what it was. Then I saw the bit of candy wrapper lying on the earthen floor in front of the hole, like a sign reading THIS WAY OUT.

What the sign didn't say was "wiggle on your belly, breathe in some dirt, discover new and interesting forms of insects that bite, and get stuck often, once tightly enough to be worried."

But it might as well have said all of those things, because while Ellie slipped through slick as goose fat, my progress was inchwormlike. A beetle crawled up my nose, but at the last possible instant before he colonized my brain I caught him by a hind leg; when I felt him squirming as I pulled him out, I'm surprised my convulsive, whole-body shudder didn't bring the entire tunnel down on me.

Then as I crept forward again a chunk of it did fall, sour-smelling dirt showering down on me ominously, and suddenly the worm I was imitating punched his wormy little gas pedal and shot forward. Scramble, scrabble, flail, shove . . .

And I was out, sticky-fingered with leaf mold and probably with insect innards, frantically brushing at myself and hopping with horror when Ellie plucked a centipede from my hair.

Then I looked around and an unpleasant fact struck me, as if I needed any more of those. "But . . . we're not outside."

Roof, check. Walls, check. Door . . .

I hauled myself up, grabbed the doorknob, and turned it. The door opened easily; new hinges, brass bright.

The floor was fresh yellow pine and the windows were intact. The door hung square in its frame and bore a new deadbolt. Big one, too.

"We're in the shed up behind the house," said Ellie, who'd made a lamp of the flashlight by aiming it upward and propping it. Behind her, Arlene slumped on the floor looking much more ill than before. Sweat beads glistened on her forehead and as I watched, she shifted fretfully.

So this shed was somebody else's, after all, not a part of the establishment we'd just escaped. "But why is there a tunnel from the house to out here?" I wondered aloud.

Twenty yards distant—good heavens, sixty feet of it? No wonder I smelled like dirt—the old house burned merrily, its fiery orange glow flickering in the shed's glass windows. I had a sudden, vivid mental picture of what might fly up out of the old place as the flames consumed it.

But that, of course, was just my imagination. From across the small, pine-smelling room, Ellie eyed Arlene with concern. The girl's cheeks bloomed rosily now, but not with good health.

"You know," Ellie said, there's an old story about something that happened out here. In Quoddy Village, I mean, long before any military were here to build barracks and so on." She stopped. "Except in the Revolutionary War, probably. And of course in the War of 1812, when the British actually occupied Eastport, if you can imagine such a thing."

Guys in red jackets, gold braid, and white wigs . . . My old house was built just ten years later, and this stuff fascinated me. But right now I didn't want a history lesson, only one on just exactly what to do next.

"Something about a servant girl and a hired boy, maybe an indentured worker," Ellie said.

She looked up at me apologetically. "I didn't tell you this story before because I thought it might scare you. But now . . ."

Yeah, now I'd already been scared to death; no time for the dying part at the moment, though; I'd have to do that later.

Ellie bent to lay a hand on Arlene's forehead, frowning as she straightened. "They're in love, but he can't get to her and she can't get to him," she continued her story.

Arlene's chest rose and fell shudderingly with her ragged breathing.

"So what does our enterprising young Romeo do?" Ellie went on. She pulled one of the wet-wipe packets I'd given her from her pocket, opened it, and smoothed it over Arlene's fever-pink forehead. The girl's eyelids fluttered as she tried to speak, then slid closed again.

"He digs a tunnel, that's what. Maybe she even helps."

With a fresh wipe she started on Arlene's hands, tenderly cleaning each grubby, nail-bitten finger, and I just stood for a moment watching, stupidly happy that a person like Ellie could be my friend. Then:

"Ohh," I exhaled, suddenly understanding. "So if it did happen here, then maybe this piece of land belonged to the old house originally. But now it and this rebuilt shed are someone else's."

"This shed being right where the old one was, maybe," Ellie agreed, stepping back to assess her ministrations; it was the best she could do but I could see she wasn't happy about it.

"So why not fill in the tunnel when you put up the new shed?" I wondered aloud. It even had a proper trapdoor now, put there by the new owner.

"I don't know," said Ellie. "Don't know what this shed's owner does for a living, either. But if you wanted to keep a whole lot of something out of sight, where would you put it?"

A number of places came to mind, but none so good as this little bolt-hole, and with attached storage, too, for any kind of contraband you might want hidden. And there had been all those opened crates . . .

I got up and went to the window, sidestepping the opened trapdoor and the gap in the floor where I'd come up out of the tunnel. And . . . wait a minute.

"Ellie? Didn't you say you could see Stone House before?"

Now we were even higher uphill so the view was even better. But it was already dark when she'd looked, and no one was there. So how had she seen it?

She looked up from searching one of the many pockets in the cargo pants she was wearing. "Lights in the windows," she said. "So someone's there. Now, where's the Tylenol I had in here . . ."

I went back to our own window. A glow in the distance told me what the lights she'd seen had really been: the interior glow of what was now a huge fire reddening the evening sky.

Stone House. I stared at it, hating what I was thinking. But then I turned to Ellie, who'd seen the fire by now, too, and she was thinking it with me.

"Hudson," we said together. I'd told her on our way here earlier about how he'd left my house so much sooner than I'd expected, and she'd drawn the same conclusion I had, that he meant to follow us.

Because of course he would suspect we were going snooping, even though I'd said I was staying home (or maybe even especially since I had) and he had good reason to want to know everything that happened or that we learned.

Being, I mean, that after Arlene he was the cops' next-best suspect in Rafferty's murder, and probably in the death of the poor guy in Rafferty's carpentry shed, too.

"What about Arlene?" I asked, because of course we were going. But clearly we couldn't leave a sick kid alone here. She was on her feet again now but she looked awful and I doubted she'd be up for long.

"I just want to go home," she muttered as she stumbled along between us, out that nice, new shed door and into an evening still full of peril.

"Yeah, me too," I replied; it was an understatement but I was too tired and scared to say more. Mostly as we made our way down the rutted driveway I prayed that Maggie Davies hadn't yet moved our car out of sight.

She hadn't. There it sat, right where we'd left it, parked at the curb outside Maggie Davies's darkened house. We got in, and instantly Ellie and I both went for our phones.

Which were missing. "Maggie's thorough," Ellie observed disgustedly, tossing her bag to the floor.

"Yeah." I yanked the drawstrings tight on mine; no way to call Hudson, to see if he was okay; also no way to call help. Then Arlene spoke up exhaustedly again.

"Is there anything to drink?" Her weakened voice hitched into a ragged cough and she fell back once more.

I dug a bottled water from under the front seat where Ellie kept a few. "Careful," I cautioned, "it's cold."

Her puffy-eyed glance flicked gratefully at me. Then Ellie peeled out like it was the Indy 500, and after a hair-raising ride through dark Quoddy Village streets, we turned onto Route 190, where she really hit the gas.

On the horizon, an orange cloud spread. Soon we swung into the Stone House driveway, and the Toyota, clunky little rattletrap that it was, took a deep breath and shot up that incline, too, with smoke from above thickening around us all the way, until near the top a breeze cleared the air somewhat.

"Spare key in my pocket," she explained grimly. "It's always there. Don't leave home without it, you know?"

"Oh, my goodness," Ellie breathed, staring at Stone House now massively in flames, one whole side of the structure like a torch against a night sky now full of stars.

She pulled over and parked a hundred yards from the top of the driveway; if we needed the car fast, we didn't want it to be on fire when we got to it. Then Ellie and I started up, leaving Arlene in the Toyota's back seat.

By this time the firelight must've been visible all over the island; in the distance, sirens began wailing. A few yards from the circle drive in front of the house, flying sparks and exploding embers stopped our approach.

But we could already see Hudson's car parked alone on the site where the incinerated shed had been.

"Darn," said Ellie. "He's in there, isn't he?"

"Oh, of course he is," I said crossly. It's why we were here, ourselves; Dylan had probably guessed—wrongly, but still— that we might come out here to snoop some more, so he'd gotten here first, to wait for us.

To save us from something, maybe; he'd have loved that. But now the tables were turned, weren't they? Now he was the one in trouble, and I wasn't at all sure that we'd be able to return the favor.

Suddenly the wind shifted, sending flames sheeting from the roofline, and now we could see that fully half the old house was still unburnt, saved (so far, at least) by the whims of a sea breeze.

Half burnt, half standing . . . the vicious crackling from inside deepened, with flames whipping out the windows on the west side and licking through the roof. And while help was coming, it wouldn't be here in time for Dylan, trapped or dead in there.

So if anyone was going to get him out, it would have to be us. "Drat," I commented. Ellie nodded agreement. But the fact was inescapable: we couldn't leave him. So we began, our first obstacle being the portico over the porch entrance.

It now resembled a flaming hoop. Ellie took a run at it, passed cleanly between the pillars of fire that the porch posts had become, and turned encouragingly.

My turn. *The only way through this is to do this,* I told myself, and ran toward Ellie. A rush of breeze, astonishing heat, and it was over, but next I tripped on a loose flagstone and sat down painfully on my tailbone.

My backside hurt. My head spun. Then a hand reached down to help me and I took it before realizing: Ellie was way over *there,* so who . . . ?

It was Arlene, looking pale, sweaty, and sick as a dog; she must've ducked through the flaming portal right behind me.

"What're you doing here?" I demanded ungraciously. We didn't need a sidekick who was (a) very ill, (b) someone else's minor child, and (c) still a possible murder suspect.

And if that wasn't enough it turned out that even sick, she was a wiseass. "I could push you back down," she offered, "if it would make you feel better."

Zing. I brushed dust off my backside, liking her better, suddenly; I'm a sucker for a deadpan delivery.

"Yeah, no. Sorry I snapped at you."

"It's okay," she replied, sounding like she might faint. She didn't, though—girl's got guts, too, I thought in grudging approval—but she didn't, so we turned toward Ellie, who'd been waiting for us on an unburnt section of porch.

But now she was gone.

Showers of sparks and flaming embers spangled the dark sky.
"Arlene!" I shouted.

The girl was a black cutout shape moving rapidly away from me. The growing fire snapped and crackled like bones breaking. I shouted for Ellie and Dylan, too, but I was shouting into an inferno and got the results you might expect, plus a throat that felt, all of a sudden, raw as hamburger.

I'd grabbed Ellie's heavy-duty flashlight on my way out of the car; now I took off after Arlene with it, only catching her because a coughing fit had stopped her.

"Here." I caught up to her and handed her a tissue, and she handed back one of the water bottles she'd had the wit to stuff into her jacket pockets.

So all right, maybe she wasn't completely useless. Capping her bottle—she'd given me my own, I noticed, not made me share—she started off again.

When I caught up once more we were headed for the back corner of the house, where the kitchen door let out onto the deck. This was as far from the actively burning part of the house as we could get and still be inside; another good choice by Arlene.

No wonder she'd been able to stay uncaught. And that kitchen door stood partway open. Ellie must've gone inside, I realized with relief, and started after her.

"Wait." Arlene put her arm out. "We don't know who else might be in there."

She was right. What if Ellie hadn't gone inside on her own? What if someone *took* her in there?

"Okay," I said, and hoisted myself up onto the deck. "We don't have to rush."

Actually we did, but a bit of caution here was prudent; we didn't need a repeat of the walking-right-into-trouble scene we'd just had at Maggie Davies's place.

Pressing myself up tightly against the house, I sneaked across the deck and Arlene imitated me, looking impatient. So far, so fine; now came the going-in part, though, and while I was figuring out how to do that and still be stealthy, a huge beam let go somewhere, crashed thunderingly through a ceiling, and exploded in flaming shrapnel out the second-floor front windows.

I heard the beam fracture, saw the fiery glow rising and glass bits flying, and thought I needed to get out of there fast. But Dylan and Ellie were still inside, and it wouldn't be long before "inside" got turned to ash and they did, too.

So never mind who else was in there; I had to be. Heart hammering, I crept past Arlene into the Stone House kitchen and she followed. Somewhere another beam crashed down.

She stepped ahead of me through the swinging door to the front hall, now filled with smoke that the flashlight carved a solid-looking beam through. She'd been useful so far despite obviously feeling like crap, but it occurred to me then that not knowing for sure what she was really up to might end poorly for me if things went haywire.

I mean, you know, even more haywire. "Now what?" I said as she moved purposely ahead of me. She knew where she was going, I realized; we'd brought her where she wanted to be.

Then it hit me why. "Come on," she said, her voice moving away. I followed it to the elevator we'd used last time.

"If they're still here, they're upstairs," said Arlene, confirming my suspicion.

"You mean Maggie Davies? And she'll have Dylan and Ellie? Is that what you think?"

No answer. I caught her arm before she could push the button that summoned the car. "No!" I told her.

Then while she glared at me I told her that if the elevator car moved, it might signal someone that we were here.

"Which could be a bad thing," I emphasized quietly She nodded, and the mulishness had gone out of her face, so I thought we were cool, as Sam would've said, as we crossed the hall and started up the wide, curving grand staircase.

Halfway up, her racking, shuddering cough was a sound that cried out for a hospital bed. I hoped it hadn't alerted anyone.

"Arlene."

"What." Flat-voiced, flat-faced.

"You look god-awful," I said.

She answered with an expression that suggested she'd scraped me off the bottom of her shoe and regretted it.

Good, she was mad, which would help keep her moving and keep her blood pressure up. Also I got the sense that she wasn't just mad at Ellie and me, from the way she kept going despite feeling ghastly, I thought someone had really flipped this girl's *I'm pissed off* switch, maybe for the first time ever.

At the top of the stairway we hustled down the still-unburnt hallway toward the back stairs, then up to the third floor where Ellie and I had found the maps and subdivision plans. There she straightened, gathering herself, then staggered determinedly away from me once more.

The fire hadn't arrive at all up here yet; for one thing there was much less fuel on offer: no hardwood floors or fancy woodwork, not even much furniture. Arlene reached the far end of the passage and stopped outside an arched doorway.

Beyond it lay all the maps and paperwork . . . but now a candle flame cast a wild, flickering glow into the hall, and somehow that frightened me more than anything else so far.

Arlene glanced back at me and vanished into the room. From behind me, smoke wisps wafted casually up the narrow stairway just as if their big brothers weren't right behind them, coming soon.

All my alarm bells went off; we had to get out of here right now. A warm breeze pushed me, air from the fire coming up the stairs; maybe it wasn't here yet, but it soon would be.

So naturally I turned and strode away from the prudent direction, hurrying instead toward the arched doorway and then through it.

By now I was deeply and thoroughly in the mood where you punch all available noses and sort them later. That's how I wound up slugging Maggie right smack in the old kisseroonie, walking straight up to her and feeling my fist cock back; then *whammo*.

I hadn't planned the part about her head hitting the wall so hard, but I can't say it bothered me. Then I grabbed Arlene by her shoulders and whipped her around to face me.

"I don't know what's going on here, but if you do, now's a really good time to tell me. Do. You. Get it?"

Her face crumpled. "But . . . I don't know anything! I wanted to go to a party and now I'm, like, some kind of criminal."

She was crying now, big, brokenhearted sobs interspersed with deep, genuinely alarming coughs. "I don't understand any of this, why won't anyone believe . . ."

I just stood there. Yeah, yeah, I was thinking. She was sick, all right, maybe dangerously so. But she was still lying to me, and I still didn't know her true role in all this.

She stopped, saw my opinion of her amateur theatrics, and swallowed hard, then gave up suddenly.

It was like all the air had gone out of her. "They were going to take me along," she whispered. "I was going with them. To California, to maybe be in the movies."

Now, that sounded more like the kind of pure hooey a girl like Arlene might just gobble up with a spoon. Hurriedly I aimed the flashlight around the chamber. The maps and so on still lay on the table.

In the far corner, Ellie and Dylan sat side by side on the floor, zip-tied and gagged with duct tape. I bent to slice off ties with my penknife; they ripped the tape off themselves.

Maggie was still out cold, half sitting and half lying against the wall. The window above her filled swiftly with a red glow suddenly; the flames had spread across the roof.

"She's not dead, is she?" Arlene quavered. "Because," she repeated plaintively, "they were going to take me *with* them . . ."

"No, she's not dead," snapped a voice from behind us, and Melissa Rafferty appeared in the doorway.

The widow Rafferty's pale elfin face and pixie haircut made her look like a nymph from a fairy tale, even smeared with soot from somehow making it through the conflagration downstairs.

"It would take more than a wall to hurt that hard head," she observed at the sight of Maggie Davies stirring painfully.

I shot a warning look at Dylan: *Shut up. Don't antagonize either of them.*

Because I didn't want to finesse our escape from the fire only to get shot or stabbed due to someone's anger-management failure. Meanwhile, I thought the finesse could stand to arrive any minute, along with a good idea.

But in the absence of either of those, we'd have to wing it. "So okay," I said. "Here's what we need to do."

"Oh, really?" Melissa Rafferty cut in. "Thanks awfully, but I'll be the judge of what we do and don't—"

I whirled around so fast that I saw the fright flash in her eyes. My hands reached out and seized her by the shoulders and I spoke right into her face.

Softly. "It's over. You're done, get it? I know what must have happened, and when we get that paperwork sorted out—"

Dylan had already collected up all the maps and papers from the long table—

"—the district attorney will be able to prove it," I said. "Or you and your friend here can stay and burn to death, I don't care."

Crackling sounds came from the stairway landing, echoing down the passageway toward us. I grabbed Ellie's and Dylan's sleeves and pulled at them to hurry them along.

Out in the hallway I called back to Arlene. "You coming?" But she didn't answer, so I went back in to get her and found her standing over Maggie's slumped form.

"It wasn't true, was it?" she asked the unconscious woman.

"You weren't going to take me to Hollywood, get me a job, or any of that."

I could hear in her voice how stupid she felt for believing Maggie's promises. Turning to me, Arlene went on:

"They told me all I had to do was get the gun out of my dad's room and get it in here, give it to Melissa. I didn't have to worry, no one was going to use it, she said, it was only for a joke." Her voice broke. "They said afterward they'd help me, get me out of here to somewhere I could live. Without," she finished with a sob, "everyone yelling all the time."

Out in the passageway listening to this, Ellie turned a look on Melissa that should've sizzled her to a cinder.

Speaking of which: "Hey, let's get out of here, okay?" said Hudson. "We can argue about all this later."

Which suddenly sounded to everyone like a very fine idea, the more so when the first truly thick, black smoke billows found their way to the top of the back stairs.

"Damn," Hudson muttered, making his way through the smoke and fumes enveloping us. Hacking and coughing, we hustled down the passageway, Arlene stumbling along wheezing as she clung blindly to Hudson's hand.

Melissa didn't seem quite as bothered—it's smoky all the time where you're going, I thought at her—merely waving her manicured hand in front of her face.

"Pe-ew," she complained, hurrying behind me on tanned, sandaled feet, and of course I didn't swing around and make a twofer out of that nose-punching business.

But it was close. Instead I yanked her along faster while she twisted and tried to get free; even while being saved from a house fire, it seemed, she didn't like being told what to do.

Finally she wrenched loose from my grip, but came along anyway. I might've remarked on the wisdom of her decision, but by then I was too busy dodging the first sneaky licks of flame following the smoke billows up the back stairs.

Ellie, Dylan, and Arlene were already ahead of me on their

way down. The air stank of chemicals and burning wood. Tears streamed stingingly from my eyes, and now even Melissa stood bent over and hacking.

The only way through this . . . I grabbed Melissa's arm again and this time she let me. We started again, and this time made it down a whole flight, but then I missed a step and then she did, too, with predictable results: I toppled headfirst, she fell right along with me, and we landed together at the foot of the stairs on the ground floor, not liking each other any more than we had at first.

To put it mildly. Squirming away from me, she made as if to take off, but I grabbed her wrist.

"Look." The fire was above us now, licking hungrily along the ceiling. I got to my feet. "Ellie! Dylan?"

No answer. The massive wooden front door remained intact, though the fire munched steadily toward it; maybe they'd gone out that way.

Then two things happened. First, my belief that the fire was still confined mostly to the back of the building was disproven when orange flames burst through the ceiling over the front door. Two large beams, one entirely burnt through and the other resting on the first, sagged down through the fresh flames and crashed to the floor in an explosion of sparks.

And then a dog yapped somewhere in the house. A small dog, from the sound of it, like the dog I'd brought home and Bella had fallen in love with . . .

I turned to Melissa, who'd heard it, too. "You didn't."

She tried to look affronted. "It's my dog, I own it, I even have the bill of sale. I can do what I want with my own . . ."

"Oh, shut up," I said, disgusted.

After I'd left the house this evening, she must've gone there and demanded her dog back, and naturally our dear, stoic Bella had given it to her.

And now it was here, somewhere. "What, you were just going to leave it to die?" I demanded.

Finally she scrabbled together enough wit to look sorry but by then I didn't care; I could've throttled her without a qualm, and I might've if the dog hadn't yapped again, nearer.

I turned in time to glimpse the animal scampering through the half-open kitchen door, a small, bouncy clump of white fur that kept yapping and yapping.

"C'mere, you," I called, but he didn't, and there was no way I could go home without him; it would break Bella's heart. So I started after him; we'd get out through the kitchen door to the deck, I figured.

"Wait," Melissa cried, suddenly panicky. "How am I supposed to . . . ?"

I turned back. From the kitchen, the dog howled miserably.

"Maybe you should figure that out for yourself, the way you left your dog to do," I told her.

You murdering little brat, I didn't add, and made it to the kitchen just as something very heavy crashed down behind me. From the corner of my eye I saw the bright, flaming arc of its descent, then heard a chopped-off shriek.

I didn't look back to see what had fallen, though.

Or if it had hit anyone.

Eleven

"Okay, Punky, it's okay. Come on, fella, I've got a nice biscuit for you, and—damn it, Punky, where the hell are you?"

Punky the little white dog didn't answer. Also, he didn't emerge from wherever he'd found to hide. He could be under the sink, behind the refrigerator . . .

I peered into cabinets, under counters, behind the pantry door, down a laundry chute. No dog.

"Come on, pup," I called hoarsely as the sounds of the fire out there increased. A brief peek said that a front-door exit was now impossible; the stairway was full of flames and the hall pitch-black with smoke positively boiling out through it.

I was starting to think hard about that kitchen door and my soon-to-be-absolutely-necessary departure through it when I heard a whimper. Relieved, I dove again for the pantry; inside, two bright black shoe-button eyes peered frightenedly at me from above a wet, black nose.

Scooping up the trembling canine, I pushed back out of the pantry closet just as an enormous crash came from outside. In the kitchen, the smoke had thickened but I feared breaking a window now, in case its sudden draft sucked the flames out here.

Looking at it, though, reminded me of the row of propane tanks lined up underneath it. They ran the stove, the hot water, and the furnace in this place, and at the beginning of heating season—i.e., now—they'd be full of explosive gas.

Hmm, let's get away from those, I thought clearly. Then another suspicion hit me; the recent crashing sound had come from this direction. So I went to the door and it swung open easily, but just outside it . . .

"Oh, Punky," I breathed, realizing with a thud of horror that we were trapped; an enormous pile of stone that had once been the underside of a balcony now filled the doorway.

Unfortunately, in that moment of dismayed inattention the dog squirmed from my arms, leapt to the floor, and scrambled back into the pantry again. So of course I scrambled after him.

And yes, I do know how foolish this was, but if I didn't at least try I could never look Bella in the eye again. Besides, it's not like I'd planned this all out in advance, right? And have I mentioned yet that the flashlight had begun fading?

Anyway, I spotted the dog, grabbed him up under my arm, and turned hurriedly, only to trip over something small, solid, and seemingly immovable. It was, I discovered once I'd picked myself up off the floor, a vintage black cast-iron doorhandle with an old-fashioned thumb-press latch.

The handle was attached to a trapdoor that probably led to a cellar. With my heart quickening as the smell of smoke reached even in here, I bent to try the trapdoor, then leapt, startled, at the sound of determined hammering from nearby.

"Jake!" It was Dylan Hudson's voice. Doggy and I scrambled toward it only to find it was coming from outside that blocked kitchen exit.

"Jake, there's an awful lot of propane out here."

Yeah, great. Tell me something I don't know. "Don't just stand there, get me out of here!"

"Uh, that might be a problem."

My heart sank. Dylan never said something was a problem.

If it was a problem, he just got right to solving it. And if we didn't get out through the kitchen door, I thought we might not get out of here at all.

The dog coughed. Then I did. The stinging smoke burned my eyes and made my nose run uncontrollably; meanwhile the house went on burning energetically. A length of flaming clapboard helicoptered past the kitchen window, exploding on the deck.

Right next to the propane tanks, naturally, and now a flickering tongue of flame licked teasingly under the kitchen's swinging door, too.

The roar of the fire devouring the house was like a freight train barreling through it. "Stand back!" Dylan shouted over the sound, and in the next moment a car smashed into those chunks of granite blocking the exit, pushing them aside. Then the car came back, charging into and then onto the deck, straight into the kitchen door, missing those propane tanks by a couple of inches but unfortunately not breaking the door.

Or not in a helpful way; this time when I tried opening it, the knob came off in my hand. Also, now a big, heavy automobile was wedged up against it.

And then the car died. I heard Dylan trying to restart it, but nope, that car was done-zo, as Sam would've said. So I was, as he also would've said, screwed. Unless . . .

Yeah, desperate measures, and all that. Still holding on to the dog that I'd done all this nonsense for in the first place, I pushed my way yet again to the rear of that dratted pantry.

The air in the kitchen was fast becoming too thick and hot to breathe. But the dog kept returning to the trapdoor in here, and when I put my face to its edge, I knew why: fresh air. And I didn't know where it was coming from, but I wanted some.

Like, right now. Glancing around the pantry closet wildly, I spied an old fireplace poker leaning in a rear corner where someone had left it long ago. With it, I pried at the old latch until finally it broke.

I pulled the door off. Cool, damp air gushed up from the opening into my face. The dog wriggled strenuously, trying to escape again.

Below, the darkness smelled just like what it was, a hole in the ground. From behind me the fire howled triumphantly and I felt its growing warmth.

Yap! said the little dog, and with a sudden squirm he leapt from my arms, paddled the air to no avail with his fuzzy white paws, then dropped straight down through the hole in the floor.

"Punky!" No yelps or other sounds of distress came from below. The yellow and orange flickers peeping into the pantry behind me, however, were persuasive in the extreme.

Also, the fire upstairs was way too close to those propane tanks; wherever the fresh air was, I needed to get there fast.

Still, it was dark in that hole, and although my flashlight had lasted heroically, now it was really almost gone.

"Hello?" I called stupidly into the darkness.

No answer at first. Then from a distance: "Yap!"

And if the drop to the floor down there hadn't killed him, it probably wouldn't kill me, either. So I sat on the edge of the trapdoor with my feet hanging down into the inky darkness, glanced back once more at flames coming through the kitchen door by the simple method of burning it down, then scooted my butt to the opening's edge and dropped over it.

"Oof." The drop, it turned out, was only about four feet, but my landing was just awkward enough to twist the ankle on my right side and my knee on the left.

But I'd landed in . . . what? Something that felt like stones, fist-sized and jagged and . . . soft, somehow. Smelling like . . .

Coal. Of course; once upon a time, that furnace must have burned it; everyone's did before fuel oil and propane arrived. Now somehow I was in the coal chute, down which the black, smelly chunks would have been offloaded from a cart into the cellar coal bin.

Why there'd been a trapdoor to it was interesting but not pertinent, especially since now that my eyes had begun adjusting I thought I glimpsed . . .

Daylight. I scrambled toward it over a litter of old coal bits and oily-smelling dust that went directly up my nose. *Just a little farther,* I thought through a cascade of sneezes.

But then I heard it again. "Yap!"

I looked at the light coming in, I guessed from the old coal chute's outside door where the cart would've backed up. Then I glanced back at the flames ravaging the pantry closet's floor a few feet away.

Finally my eyes strayed yearningly back to that tiny needle of light again. I'd chased that dratted Punky through a house fire, for Pete's sake, trying to save him; wasn't that enough?

"Yap!" came the answer from somewhere in the darkness, and me being a complete sucker, naturally I followed it to where he and the little pink collar he was wearing were caught on a nail.

When I released him, he leapt whimpering into my arms as if he was really very sorry he'd ever left them, and of course I held him and petted him, whispering to him that everything was fine now, and that he was a good boy.

And then those propane tanks started exploding.

Twelve

The low, concussive *thump!* of exploding propane tanks focused my mind wonderfully, as a fiery fist punched into the cellar through the caved-in wall and reached for me. My next gasping breath was of air so hot, it frizzled my nose hairs.

At least there's more light down here now, a sarcastic little voice in my head remarked. Diving behind the base of one of the many stone chimneys in the house, I crouched with the dog in my arms until the initial burst of flame subsided.

Then still carrying him I sprinted through a minefield of choking dust, smoking rubble, twisted metal, fallen bricks, and who knew what else. And though I'll never get any prizes for athletics—Victor used to say I could trip on a linoleum floor, and for once in his life he was actually right—I made it to that blown-open wall very swiftly indeed, ready to vamoose.

Too bad my plan hit a snag: the hole was there, all right, and the black night sky above it, too, through the flames still flickering around the hole.

But the ladder I'd need to climb out through the hole was not. "Oh," I said stupidly, staring up at the distance between me and salvation: about eight feet.

I could no more jump that high from a standing start than I could flap my arms and fly.

"Yap!" Punky wiggled again, anxious about the fire in the pantry closet above us, crackling and licking its flaming chops. Soon it would have us both . . . wait a minute.

I looked around again: there was the coal chute down which came the coal from outside. So if I crawled *up* it—

Yep. I aimed the flashlight's dim beam at the chute's top, and there it was, the faint crack of light I'd seen before.

Gangway. Wedging the poor little dog more firmly into my armpit, I hoisted myself up onto the coal chute's slanted surface with a groan that I didn't even care if anyone heard.

Not unless they were about to rescue me, which at this point didn't seem super likely. The coal chute, a long, narrow track curved up at the sides like a waterside, passed directly under the pantry closet's trapdoor, the one with the flames now eagerly pushing down through it.

But by now there was no choice, it was do this or die, so I began climbing while the flames above me writhed, raging.

And your little dog, too! they seemed to laugh cruelly, and what I said back isn't printable. The air around me got hotter as I hauled myself upward, trying to keep as much room between me and the fire as possible.

But next I smelled burning hair, my scalp prickling as the strands caught and frizzled; hastily, I backed down out of the hot zone, then fell off the chute.

And sat there, bone-terrified, with a dog in my arms and a dagger of fresh terror in my heart. This was real, this was serious, I had to get out of here; in the next few moments that chute would be in flames and we'd be done for.

"What do you say, Punk? Is it curtains for the two of us?" I asked the little mutt.

Who I swear looked at me with those shiny black shoe-button eyes and answered: "Yap!"

What the hell, I could always wear a wig. "Come on, then," I said as I struggled up.

This time I didn't waste energy avoiding the flames, just *shot* up that chute like my hat was on fire and my tail end was catching. There was a moment of pure terror when heat and light surrounded me, roaring like the breath out of a runaway blast furnace. But then we were through; just ahead was the ancient wooden door to the coal chute, paint peeling and cobwebby as if no one had touched it in decades.

"Phew," I told Punky, but my relief was short-lived. The cobwebs, clotted with long-dead flies veiled the door. A warped, iron-barred window pierced it, and I didn't see hinges anywhere.

A cold sensation flooded me. Sometimes you can try all you want but you can't get there from here. And maybe that was me right now; I'd tried. I'd tried hard. But I couldn't get there from here, and that was just the long and the short of it.

"Sorry, buddy," I told Punky, still gazing at me with those shiny black eyes.

Holding him, I sank down to lean exhaustedly against the blown-in cellar wall's jagged chunks. They poked into my back, but who cared? It was nearly over now.

"Grr," said Punky, a syllable I'd never heard out of him before. "Yap!"

Which was when it occurred to me that although I couldn't jump out that high opening in the exploded cellar wall, maybe I could toss Punky out. Then I thought maybe if I went back down to try it, I should feel around one last time for some way to open the coal chute door, or try kicking it open. Not that either method was a sure thing.

Maybe the door doesn't even open outward, the pessimist in me suggested; *Shut up,* I suggested back, and then two things happened: the pantry closet's floor sagged suddenly down toward me with an awful cracking and creaking, and—

"Jake!" It was Hudson's voice, this time coming through the hole that the propane tanks had blasted. "I've got a rope!"

So that's why he'd vanished; I forgave him immediately as the bright beam of his flashlight came down into the cellar through the hole, followed by the knotted end of a length of ordinary household clothesline.

Not exactly the stout, braided towing rope I'd been hoping for. But I looked at the flashlight beam, at the clothesline, and finally at the coal chute's unopenable door.

Then I grabbed the clothesline, wrapped it around myself, and knotted it. With the dog stuffed firmly into my jacket front, I grabbed the rope with both hands and braced my feet against the base of the wall, thinking that Hudson and maybe Ellie, too, would help by pulling me up.

But instead the other end of the rope slithered loosely down onto the floor in front of me.

"Hudson?" The only answer was the crackle of flames and the creak of the pantry's floor sagging ominously further.

"Hudson!" I added a few epithets so he'd know the kind of mood I was in: scared, desperate, and hopping mad.

Snatching up the rope, I hurled one end at the hole in the wall. It went straight through, which amazed me considering the luck I'd been having.

Even more amazing: someone caught it. "Jake?" came a voice at first uncertain, then wobbly with relief. It was Ellie. "Jake! I thought you must be—"

The pantry closet's floor cascaded down in a massive rush of glowing red embers and sparks. A massive hot-air gust shoved me forward, and the dog gave a startled yelp.

I grabbed my end of that rope so fast, you'd have thought I was a professional climber. "Okay," I called out.

In response, the rope tightened, then lifted me. Bracing my feet again, I basically just walked right up the wall; to my surprise, the clothesline took my weight just fine.

All of which was odd. The rope pulled hard and I rose fast,

leaving the enlarging fire in the cellar snapping frustratedly at my heels. Too fast; surely I was harder to lift than this?

Finally when I was up high enough to finally see out, I understood why: it wasn't Ellie pulling me up, it was a cop.

Lots of them, actually.

Half an hour later, Ellie and I sat on the edge of the fountain in the courtyard and watched Stone House burn. Most of the outer stone walls still stood; inside them, wreckage still smoked and flickered.

The dog was still in my jacket, asleep.

"At least no one got killed," Ellie said disconsolately.

I looked up. "Maggie Davies is still alive?"

That the woman who'd tried to kill us with yet another fire had survived this one seemed impossible, but Ellie nodded.

"One of the firefighters went in where I told them she'd be, if you can imagine."

I couldn't. The hall had already been an inferno when I'd last seen it.

"But she wasn't there. He says he saw someone ahead of him, on his way back out," Ellie added. "I'll just bet it was her."

The paramedics had checked us both for injuries, smoke inhalation, all that. I got burn ointment, an eye rinse, and a tetanus booster; Ellie got a bandage for a cut finger.

"There they go," Ellie said sadly, turning her gaze on Dylan Hudson standing nearby with some state officers. Framed in the headlights of their car, he stood nodding at something one of them was telling him.

His rights, probably. Then Hudson held his hands out, the officer cuffed him and helped him into a squad car's back seat, and the car pulled away. "Oh, gosh," breathed Ellie defeatedly.

County cops, fire trucks, the ambulance, a KQDY camera guy, more state cop vehicles, and a support van from the Eastport Community Center (coffee, snacks, cold drinks, wet facecloths) crowded the circle drive.

"You're sure they're not still around here somewhere?" I asked, but I already knew the answer.

Maggie, Arlene, and Melissa Rafferty were all in the wind, as Hudson would've put it. I'd thought Melissa must've died, too, but there wasn't any burned body in the front hall where I'd last seen her.

Apparently, while I was busy trying hard not to burn to death, they'd taken off, and trying to tell the cops about them had been useless. They had their man, after all, and this whole thing was all over and done with as far as they were concerned.

Near the house, firefighters in yellow coats sprayed the blackened ruins, steam rising with an angry hiss from the hot spots when the water hit them. In the driveway the remaining police milled around uncertainly, looking I figure for someone to tell them it was okay to leave.

This was our chance to get out of here, I realized, before someone decided that we should be charged with something. I got up with the dog still tucked into my jacket asleep.

"You think they left together? All three of them?"

Maggie, Arlene, Melissa . . . Ellie nodded exasperatedly. "And they took my car."

I hadn't noticed, but now I did. "Huh. The way our luck is going, it's a wonder they haven't already run us over with it."

The Community Center ladies began packing up. The night seemed unusually quiet, chilly and bright with a sliver of moon overhead. At the foot of the long, rolling slope behind Stone House—this was where Maggie Davies had wanted to put houses—the old railroad bed was a pale, sandy trail, two miles to town.

"You up for a walk?" I asked.

"Sure." Ellie rose with a sigh, turning casually toward the house. I wandered instead toward the burnt shrubbery skeletons at the far side of the scorched terrace flagstones, spotted a cop uniform, and melted backward into some conveniently located bushes.

Too late I discovered the bushes were dwarf holly with stiff, needle-ended leaves. By the time the cop was gone and I got out of there, I must've looked as if zombies had been at me.

Then Ellie appeared out of the gloom beside me, grabbed my arm, and began running, pulling me out to the driveway and then sharply downhill on it.

"They're looking for us," she exhaled.

And if they found us, we'd spend the rest of the night answering questions instead of finding two murderous women and one teenage girl so we could clear Dylan Hudson.

A flashlight beam probed from above and stabbed around the driveway for a few moments, just missing us.

"Super," I said as well as I could, so short of breath from running that I thought I might suck myself inside out.

Also, somewhere along the way I'd stepped in a hole and twisted my ankle for the second time that night. Still, I meant to get to the trail leading into town even if I had to lie down and roll myself there.

"Jake?" Ellie peered over at me. We were still running, but the slope near the driveway's end was less steep and the slice of moon cast enough silvery light to see by.

"What?" To my surprise, the exercise felt good, and so did the cold air. I put Punky down and he quickstepped happily alongside us. Running on fumes and what little adrenaline I had remaining, I thought about how lucky I was to be alive.

Lucky, lucky. "Now what?" Ellie asked.

With her face upturned and her reddish-blond hair streaming behind her, she looked as if she might sail up into the sky.

"Good question." We slowed to a walk when we reached the trail, a narrow track with the beach on our left and more open land to our right. On the water, moonlight puddled like silver.

Finally we climbed the railroad embankment to the trail and started toward the flashing red light atop the water tower in town. The trail was level, flat and smooth except for where here and there an old railroad tie lay embedded. Then it swerved away from the beach and nearer to Route 190 for a while. As we made our way through a small forest of evergreens and mixed hardwood, we could hear a few cars going by, then see them through a stand of birches whose bark shone white when the headlights hit them.

"What we *could* do," I began, but just then a state police car came along, stopping on the far side of the birches from us.

It was also when I slipped, sat down hard, and discovered the many fat brown garden slugs sheltering beneath leaf mats on the forest floor; also beetles, worms, centipedes, spiders, and a large nest of blindly squirming white larvae, species unknown.

"Eeeyaggh," I uttered, yanking my hands back. As the squad car pulled out again, trailing the tinny squawk of radio static, I jumped up, feeling the insects move in my hair and hoping they hadn't gotten into my ears.

"Anyway," I said when I'd brushed them away and regained a few tattered shreds of composure, "what if we just go get them?"

The trail veered back toward the beach as Ellie glanced skeptically at me; the idea was silly except for one thing. But that one thing was why it might work.

Small waves slopped the beach, smelling like kelp and salt; the lights on Campobello shone beaconlike: *Here be land.*

"You think we can do it?" Ellie asked finally.

To our left in a stand of overgrown saplings and brush stood the old Eastport power plant, all right angles, sagging wires, and glass electrical insulators, looking like haunted playground equipment in the silent moonlight.

"And if you think so," she said as we went on mechanically lifting our tired feet and putting them down—we were both exhausted, of course, and my arms ached from cradling the dog—"why do you?"

Those wide, thick-lashed eyes of hers gleamed marine blue in the moonlight. "I mean, how are we going to do it?"

I bent to dig a pebble from my shoe. "See, there's this thing called the element of surprise."

She smiled. "Sure, if we can find them."

"We don't have to." It was hitting me still that I'd just escaped death by a hair's breadth.

"I know where they are," I added. "Or I think I do. So when we get there . . ."

". . . and if they are there, we'll call the police," Ellie finished for me. "And then we'll be done with this whole thing."

The water-tower lights were quite a lot nearer now; I glimpsed the Baptist church's white spire and more of the top of the water tower on Cony Hill.

"Maybe," I said. The little white dog stirred sleepily in my arms and settled again.

"But after the awful mess all the rest of this has been," I said, "I don't know why the next part should be that easy."

It wasn't.

At past one in the morning, the whole Cunningham place was lit up like an airport, with a half dozen cars including Ellie's parked in the driveway and the curtains all drawn.

We sat in the backyard in the Cunninghams' Adirondack chairs facing the bay. "Let me get this straight," Ellie said. "The cops have Dylan in custody, but Maggie and Melissa have Arlene. To silence her permanently, we think they're going to kill her, so they brought her . . . here? To her own house?"

I nodded, chewing. We'd dropped Punky at my house— Bella was up and took the little creature into her arms without questions when she saw the look on my face—and stopped at the Moose for food and coffee; now we were resting, getting ready for the moment when we slipped into the Cunningham house and grabbed the girl.

"Safest spot for them right now," I said. "Cops must've decided Arlene's not coming home so they're not sitting on the house anymore."

Ellie sipped coffee contemplatively. "Uh-huh," she said finally. "So up there behind us, that's the back deck, right? With the back door leading out to it?"

"Yep." I'd eyeballed all that as we sneaked across the lawn to the chairs.

She gazed thoughtfully at the dark bay. "Is there netting on the railings? The kind you might use to keep an animal from squeezing through?"

I squinted, keeping an eye peeled for anyone squinting back; nobody was.

"Yes. Heavy gauge netting. Looks like a double layer. Why?"

She finished her coffee and got up. "Means there's a dog they put out there sometimes, doesn't it? And that means . . ."

She stuffed our paper cups, napkins, and doughnut remnants into the white paper bakery bag we'd brought and stowed the bag under one of the chairs. Then she took off across the darkened lawn toward the deck's steps, calling back to me in a whisper that carried in the late-night hush.

"Door's probably unlocked 'cause it gets opened and closed so often to let the dog in and out."

Have I mentioned she's brilliant? I finished my snack, still starving. Reminder to self: two doughnuts, at least.

"So you go knock on the front door," Ellie said, "to distract them all, and I'll go in the back way and grab Arlene."

Short, simple . . . it was a great plan, and I set off at once to do my part of it. Around the house, onto the front porch . . .

From inside I heard Melissa Rafferty arguing and objecting to something. So she had survived the fire and gotten out somehow; like most little vermin, I thought sourly, she was hard to kill.

Then Maggie's deeper voice cut in, shutting Melissa down. Arlene's mom, Dot, provided color commentary, sounding like a cat being forcibly introduced to a bathtub full of water. And over it all some late-night huckster on TV sang the praises of a sealer so strong, you could build a boat with it.

Yeah, you could build one. You couldn't float it, or at least not for long, and the bay would just love to swallow a tender morsel like you—but you could build it.

I raised my hand to knock but before I could, the door flew open and a meaty arm shot out from it, grabbed my elbow, and yanked me inside.

"What do you want?" A face smelling of cigars and bourbon pushed itself belligerently up to mine.

It was Chad Cunningham, Arlene's stepfather, and seeing him here threw a wrench into everything I thought I knew: Maggie and the land deal, Arlene and the gun . . .

And then it dropped the final puzzle piece into place. I knew now who'd been behind the whole thing.

"I was just checking to see if Arlene's back, or if you've had any word from her," I lied.

"Oh yeah? Middle of the night? Likely story. What do you care, anyway?"

His heavy brow knit with the kind of dark menace I'd only ever seen on cartoon characters' faces before.

A dog barked somewhere at the rear of the house; quite a large dog, too, from the sound of it. Then it stopped; not, I hoped, because it was munching on Ellie.

"Come on." Gripping my arm, Chad Cunningham marched me to the kitchen and let go of me with a shove. "Stay here," he uttered threateningly, raising a fist. To show us, I supposed, that he meant business.

Right; I didn't quite yawn in his face but I'd met guys like him before. Back in the bad old days in the city, I'd collected their weekly envelopes full of the large sums of money they'd extorted, highjacked, robbed, or got in other seriously illegal ways over the past seven days.

Sometimes they gave me some backchat along with the money, or especially if they didn't have the money. Then I would have to get persuasive, communicating the message I'd been authorized to send: your money or your life. And after a while I got used to their reactions, so now in spite of the clear peril I was in, I was not very intimidated.

But there was no sense letting him know that. "Okay," I said, cringing like I was in the habit of obeying Neanderthals.

The dog was barking again. Chad snatched a leash from a hook on the wall and stomped outside. When he'd gone I made a hard beeline for the coffeemaker on the counter, then found a clean mug and poured.

The coffee was strong, and also stone cold, which was good; I could drink it faster. Meanwhile, I rummaged the refrigerator.

Liverwurst, mayonnaise, Swiss cheese—the Cunninghams were a screwed-up family but they understood sandwich material. While I was at it I made one for Ellie, then bit into mine.

By now the three adult women in the room—Maggie, Melissa, and Dot—were all staring, thinking, I supposed, that I ought to be paralyzed with fear, not happily chowing down.

Maggie and Melissa looked thoroughly bruised and bloodied; not as badly as I'd have liked seeing, of course, but it was a start. Getting out of that burning house couldn't have been fun.

I held half the sandwich up. "Anyone want a bite?"

Nobody took me up on it. Arlene was there, too, sniffling sullenly from a chair by the back door. Abandoning the coffee, I cracked open the root beer I'd found in the fridge and slugged down gulp after gulp of the cold, sweet liquid.

Then the door to the deck thumped open and Ellie stumbled in, shoved by Chad Cunningham and followed by the Cunninghams' dog, a large, shaggy brown specimen of no particular breed. Dancing and jumping around Ellie's feet, he seemed to find all this great fun.

"I made you a sandwich," I told Ellie while a grimacing Chad seized her arm to sit her down at the kitchen table.

Ellie looked down at his hand as if meaning to bite it off, and the startled way he jerked it out of range warmed my heart.

"You girls stay here," he ordered, meaning everyone but

Maggie and Melissa. He stomped back to the door and locked it with a key, which he pocketed.

"And you two, you come with me." They followed him from the room, neither of them looking happy about it and Maggie's look frankly murderous.

"Looks like you picked up an unwanted partner," I said as she passed, and her answering glare should have incinerated me.

Yeah, right. "Arlene, you okay?" Ellie said when they'd gone.

A sniffly nod from Arlene, her face swollen with tears, answered this. Ellie was right about her, I thought; she was a child, she was ill, and she needed a hot bath, something to eat and drink, and to be put to bed with soothing music and a night-light on.

Instead I suspected that Melissa and Maggie together had made Arlene the pawn in their fatal game, with millions of dollars' worth of real estate the prize, land that wouldn't have been available to plunder if Rafferty hadn't died.

From the front room raised voices erupted, Chad's bass note rumbling with threat, Maggie's raging in reply.

Their volume encouraged me. Maybe they'd go on long enough for us to—

"Jake, c'mere." Ellie spoke quietly, beckoning me over to the door to the Cunninghams' basement, just off the kitchen. She'd opened it—Dot Cunningham still hadn't so much as looked in our direction from the kitchen table where she sat smoking cigarettes one after another—and now Ellie started downstairs.

I gestured silently at Arlene to follow, which to my surprise she got up alertly and did; she still seemed wretchedly ill. She was about halfway down and I was putting my foot on the first step when—

"Hey!" Chad Cunningham was crossing the kitchen toward me with a look of outraged surprise on that dully belligerent mug of his. He grabbed for me but I threw myself off the top step—hey, that worked pretty well last time—and he missed me by inches.

Landing at the foot of the steps on one knee wasn't so bad. Getting up, though; ye gods. But he was still right behind me.

Ahead, Ellie had opened the bulkhead door leading up and outside. I got there mere steps ahead of my pursuer, started through, and went down all at once in a bright, white explosion of pain.

Falling onto that knee hadn't been such a good move after all. Desperately I began scrabbling up six concrete steps to the outside and safety, dragging one leg.

Being the charming fellow that he was, Chad grabbed the leg and yanked on it, eliciting a scream that they probably heard on Campobello. Then with an arm around my neck he hauled me back down off those steps.

"Oh, gi-irls," he called out the open bulkhead to Arlene and Ellie. "I've got her. And I'll shoot her," he warbled sourly, "unless you both get the hell back down here right now."

He put a meaty hand in the center of my chest and pushed. Flailing, I stumbled backward and sat down, and when I looked up it was into the barrel of a gun.

Two barrels, actually. It was a shotgun; oh, of course it was. I leaned back tiredly, wondering why I'd bothered getting up this morning.

Yesterday morning, actually; through the bulkhead, the sky was paling to predawn gray. *The people at my house must be wild with worry by now*, I thought.

"Okay. Don't shoot her." It was Arlene's voice, shaky but under control. Ellie appeared and started down; when she reached the bottom step Chad grabbed her and flung her away from him.

"Now you!" he yelled to Arlene. "Get down here, you hear me? Or I'll give you a taste of the belt you'll never forget!"

Hearing all the shouting, Maggie and Melissa had ventured partway down the cellar steps to see what was going on. Slowly Arlene began descending through the bulkhead, wincing painfully and cradling one arm, her jacket wrapping the wrist.

"Honey, are you hurt?" I asked as she came toward me, but she only had eyes for Chad Cunningham and didn't answer.

He reached for her with one meaty hand and raised the other hand to strike, but before he could follow through she dropped the jacket, exposing the handgun she gripped.

"Arlene," Ellie said, but the girl didn't react. While Chad stared, still disbelieving, she pulled the trigger, and when Maggie roared fury and hurtled down the stairs at her, she pulled it again.

Through the ringing in my ears I watched Chad stagger and step back, put a hand to his temple, and bring it down bloody. But then he realized he hadn't been badly hurt and a terrible grin spread on his face.

Arlene stood frozen, the gun still in her hand, watching in horror his unsteady approach, his big, reddened hands reaching. His bloodstained fingers brushed crimson marks on her throat.

She raised the gun. I saw her finger tighten steadily on the trigger, the look on her face: *Don't make me do this.*

Then came the final gunshot.

Just one.

But one was all it took.

Thirteen

Two weeks later, winter arrived with a bang, ignoring the calendar, bringing ten inches of snow and a wind chill of two below.

"Mom!" cried my daughter-in-law, Mika, hurrying out from the kitchen as I came in stomping and shivering. She took my coat and hugged me. "Guess what?" she asked excitedly.

Her mood was contagious, and the warmth from the woodstove didn't hurt, either. Out in the kitchen, kids and dogs mobbed me, hugging and jumping up on me, and little Punky ran in from the parlor, yapping happily.

"What's going on out there?" Bella called in stern tones from the annex, but I heard the smile in the question, and right about then I could've laid down and wallowed in the safety and affection of my home and family, not to get too corny about it.

I'd just come from a juvenile hearing at the courthouse in Machias. All three shots fired in the Cunninghams' basement that night were in self-defense, the grand jury had opined, and I'm not sure what else happened but at the end of it, Arlene was free to go.

Minutes later outside the courtroom I overheard two of the attorneys talking. It seems that Steven Clute, Jr., had written a letter in support of his friend Arlene, and the judge not only read it but believed it and agreed with its sentiment: that parents (Steven's words) should help kids, but if they don't or can't then someone else should.

Ipso fatso, as Sam would've said. Heading for their car amidst a crush of newspeople, Arlene and Dot looked happy and relieved at getting the result they'd hoped for.

Or as happy as they could be under the circumstances, what with Chad being dead and all. Dot had some legal difficulties ahead of her, too, and none of them were minor.

Having met Chad, though, something told me the mother and daughter were still pretty darned happy.

"Mom!" Mika repeated, tugging at my sleeve. "Guess what? It turns out that Ephraim and Nadine are *not* going to have a little brother or sister!"

She didn't quite add a musical "tra-la" at the end. The song was in her heart, though, and in mine, too, that we weren't going to have to start putting people's beds in the basement to make room. More children were fine in theory, I supposed, but in real life we were full up.

"Excellent," I said, standing back to admire her outfit. For tonight's get-together here at home she wore slim black pants, a peony-pink leotard top, and a tie-dyed lavender T-shirt with a peace sign stenciled on the front.

With her glossy black hair pulled up in a high ponytail, she looked adorable. "Now, what's the status of the martinis?" I asked, looking around hopefully.

This evening's gathering was a martini party followed by dinner, and my dad often made early-bird specials. In fact, just then Wade came from the butler's pantry carrying one.

He offered it to me. "Hey," he said softly, his gray-blue eyes crinkling.

Our foreheads touched. "Hey," I murmured back, sipping my martini and feeling my knees weaken.

"I hear you've been having adventures."

"Yeah." But my eyes still gazed into his so it was hard to keep my mind focused. "I'll tell you all about it later," I managed, pulling away from him with an effort, and he grinned wickedly, following me.

But then Ellie came in behind us, laden with containers of German potato salad, bratwurst for the broiler, and a salad from her little greenhouse: spinach, arugula, radishes, tomatoes.

Outside, snow swirled through the street lamps' cones of yellow light. She closed the door, stomping snow off her boots, and went on into the kitchen; not long after, Dylan Hudson and Lizzie Snow arrived. By then, there was just time for another drink while the tantalizing aroma of broiling bratwursts and warm, bacon-laden German potato salad filled the air.

"I still can't believe Arlene shot Chad," Ellie said, "even though I saw it myself. She was the last person I'd have expected to be able to help."

You never know, I guess, what'll make someone say "enough." For Dot, it happened when Chad reached for Arlene's throat.

Sam looked confused; between working, worrying about Mika, and being a dad, he'd been following the high points of the drama, but not the details. "Who shot who, now?" he asked, and Ephraim looked up alertly, whereupon Mika ushered him and Nadine into the parlor, to eat in front of the TV.

"Okay, now," said Sam once they were gone, "give me the high points."

So we told him the whole thing again from the beginning, about Rafferty's party, about him getting killed, and about how first Arlene had been suspected and then Dylan was.

"I wanted to help Arlene, and Jake wanted to help me," said Ellie. "And then, kind of by accident, Jake met Maggie Davies."

Tactfully, she did not say I'd been axle-deep in driveway mud at the time.

"And Maggie Davies knew Chad Cunningham how?" Sam asked skeptically.

"They don't run in the same social circles," I agreed. "But you know those newish houses out at Goose Point?"

It was a cluster of water-view homes where the land crew, brought in from nobody knew where, cut trees in the shoreline zone against regulation and got fined for it.

But that didn't bring the trees back. "I asked at city hall," I said, "and guess who developed that land?" Maggie Davies, of course. "It's what she's done in her home state, too. Small projects, not a lot of care taken."

"But now," Lizzie Snow put in, "she'd hit the big time. If she could swing it."

She looked pale and drawn; sorting out Dot Cunningham's troubles plus dealing with the suspicious-seeming stuff we'd found under the house in Quoddy Village was taking a toll.

The broken-open crates had indeed turned out to be very interesting, especially the residue of explosives that had been found when Lizzie, working on a hunch, had one tested.

So now she had federal ATF agents in and out of her office all day long. "When Rafferty inherited Stone House, his long-estranged sister, Maggie, didn't care."

Maggie and Melissa were talking to prosecutors, each trying to make the other one look guiltier to get leniency themselves.

"Just a falling-down old pile of granite, she thought. But she'd been here before—she had roots here, after all, and even had those houses built—so she came up to take a look."

"Okay, wait a minute," said Sam, "Chad Cunningham worked with her on those first houses?"

"Right," said Lizzie, "that's how she knew him. From back then. He put in the driveways."

He chuckled. "Yeah, the ones that wash out every year."

She nodded, sighing heavily and running the crimson-tipped fingers of one hand through her black curls. Dylan put a hand on her shoulder and for once she didn't twitch it off impatiently.

"Anyway," she said, "when Maggie saw the land that went with the old heap, she knew she'd hit pay dirt. She was next in line, so if Hank could just, you know, die . . ."

Ellie spoke up. "What I still don't know is, what about the body in the shed that burned? Back at the start of all this?"

"Specifically," Wade agreed, "why'd someone shoot him and then set a fire to hide the body? Not that it would work— a fire like that wouldn't be hot enough. Still . . ."

He stopped as Mika and the two kids came back to the table, the youngsters having wolfed down their "hot dogs" with good appetites. Now Mika glanced at Dylan and Lizzie, then at me, her eyes sparkling at whatever she'd seen.

Sam's mood seemed suddenly upbeat, too, and the old folks beamed at Lizzie and Dylan's tender looks toward one another. It was all so peaceful and full of warm sentiments, in fact, that of course Dylan had to put a wrench in the monkeyworks.

"So," he turned brightly to Lizzie, "will you marry me?"

We knew what she would say: when hell freezes over. He'd pulled this stunt before. But this time she didn't say it. She looked at him instead, biting her lower lip. Then she spoke.

And what she said knocked our socks off. "Yes, Dylan. I'll say it right here in front of all these people. I'll marry you."

A tension that I'd never realized was there melted out of Dylan's face. "You . . . will?" he managed, taking her hands.

"I just said I would, didn't I? Don't go making a whole big thing out of it."

I could see it in her eyes already: *What have I done?* But she'd been shilly-shallying for over a year now, with Dylan hanging around patiently. Even I thought it was time, as Wade often said about them, to fish or cut bait.

Mika reached over and patted Lizzie comfortingly on the shoulder. "Don't worry, honey, it won't be so bad. You'll get used to it."

"Yeah," Sam agreed, and for him of course it wasn't. "Not bad at all," he said, glancing around at his friends and his family and rolling his eyes across the table at me as if wondering if he'd died and gone to heaven.

"Hey, wait a minute," said Wade, who'd had enough of the mushy stuff. "Cunningham had worked for the Davies woman before, so now just on her say-so he gets his stepdaughter involved in murder? How does that follow?"

Dylan shook his head. "It doesn't. It was sneakier than that."

My father came back from the annex where he'd set up the chairs on opposite sides of the chessboard; I'd thought that second martini that he'd served to Hudson probably had a motive.

Not that he needed a handicap; Hudson liked getting trounced, was my inescapable theory. Dylan went on:

"Once she had seen it, she drove up to Stone House to meet Melissa when Hank wasn't there. Just checking her out, you know? Just in case Hank's wife might be useful to her."

"Because Maggie already knew what she meant to do," Ellie said, and Hudson nodded. "Not the details yet, of course, but a general notion. Melissa must've seemed heaven-sent."

"Maggie says Melissa brought up how dissatisfied she was with her situation, " Dylan continued, 'that right away she was complaining about Eastport, so tiny and remote and so on—"

She was absolutely right, and we didn't care; in fact, we liked it that way. ". . . and then started talking about Rafferty," Hudson added. "Killing him was Melissa's idea, Maggie said."

He knew this because one of the state cops had told him; while in their custody he'd taken the opportunity to mend some important fences, it seemed to me.

"And then maybe Melissa caught Arlene snooping around inside the house?" Wade guessed. He ran a hand back over his graying brush-cut. "From what you've said, it sounds like she'd gotten obsessive enough."

It was out of the blue. Lizzie aimed an index finger at him. "Correct."

Big, broad-shouldered Wade didn't look like a Rhodes Scholar; she'd underestimated him at first.

But not anymore. "They saw right away how a completely unrelated person could be useful. In fact, they couldn't do it without her, or someone like her," he went on.

He said it straight to me with a smile in his eyes. *You know,* that look said, and then suddenly I realized that I did.

"A gun," I said. "They needed a gun, but not that atrocious pink pistol she had. They were afraid it could get traced to her somehow."

Most likely it couldn't. If a gun's not in the system—that is, no crime committed with it is in the records—you can't match a bullet to it. Still, when you're plotting murder you probably get paranoid about these things.

"But why not just buy one? Think about it," Wade said, so I did and came up with the women visiting a gun store, applying for permits, sitting through the waiting period, and only then getting the weapon.

Not to mention how memorable a couple of gun-buying strangers would be if anyone asked about them later. But Chad Cunningham did have guns.

"So they ask her to steal one?" I said. "Or what, they'll call the cops, say she was trespassing?"

"Not quite," Dylan joined in again. "It's worse than that,

unfortunately. Arlene's stepdad was in on the whole thing, he gave Arlene the gun. He's who drove her out to Rafferty's party."

"Oh, Lord," Bella breathed in disgust. Me too, but now I knew who'd killed the guy in the burned shed: Chad Cunningham.

I said so. "Maggie must have told Chad that the handyman saw her when she first visited. Chad took care of it."

The handyman was a loner and not from around here, so he wasn't looked for, but his body was identified through the dog tag on a chain around his neck, Lizzie had told me.

Poor guy. Dylan nodded, then said, "That's what she says happened. She also says she didn't pull the trigger on Hank. She meant to shoot him, but . . . it sounded like she felt she got cheated out of it, to tell you the truth."

Huh. An unpleasant new suspicion struck me. "Okay, so let's pretend we believe her. Then who could have . . ."

My dad's wise old eyes met mine from across the room where he was upending the martini shaker, straining the last drops. The look emanating from beneath those bushy white eyebrows dared me to say what I was suddenly, inescapably thinking:

That the time-honored two motives for murder were love and money, and in this case maybe the money-motivated folks hadn't done the dirty deed. But then . . .

"Steven Clute, Junior," I said while my dad dropped olives into the martinis. Who says they can't be an after-dinner drink, anyway?

After Dylan left his post at the front door, Steven could have slipped in, made his way upstairs, found Rafferty on the balcony with Arlene, and fired three times in quick succession.

Afterward in the confusion he'd gotten out unnoticed, likely by the back stairs, then slid on his blue-jeaned backside down the old, too-steep driveway to his bike waiting below.

I summarized all this for my dinner companions. Then:

"He had a gun of his own, knew how to shoot, and already despised Rafferty. He told us he thought Arlene was going to get hurt or in trouble mooning around after Hank the way she did."

"You think that's enough?" asked Lizzie Snow. Steven Clute hadn't even been on the cops' suspect list.

"For murder?" I replied. "Maybe not. But when Arlene told him about the plan he'd gotten involved in—because of course she did, she was a scared teenage girl, for Pete's sake—*that* was definitely enough."

"So," my dad put in; he'd sat again and was listening with his eyes closed. "Maggie Davies had a team and a plan to get rid of Hank Rafferty so she could inherit the Stone House land, then turn it into half-acre house lots and make big money on them."

"Right," said Wade, "but things went wrong."

Even he had no idea how wrong. The woman in white on the doorstep in Quoddy Village floated back to me in memory, just as it had been doing in dreams lately.

I got up and began clearing plates while Ellie pulled on an apron and turned on the hot water at the sink. Ephraim and Nadine climbed down from their chairs and ran full-speed into the parlor, hooting and hollering like the half-wild, barely housebroken little savages they were.

But not, I noticed, rampaging into the annex. I looked questioningly at Bella, but she just smiled privately as if at some funny little secret she was keeping.

"Anyway," said Lizzie, getting up. Tonight she wore a black cashmere sweater with pearls, a green-and-black plaid skirt and black tights, and high, shiny black boots; with her pale skin, black hair, and flashing dark eyes plus the bloom now coming back into her cheeks, she looked like the international-spy version of a wild Irish rose.

"I guess I might need to have a chat with Arlene's young friend Steven," she added to me.

"Yeah, I guess," I said regretfully. "I hope I'm wrong," I said, but I didn't think I was.

Sometimes nice guys really do finish last, I thought. But on the other hand, here was Dylan, now looking as if lady luck had found him, taken his face in her two hands, and kissed him on the mouth.

He put on his coat, a long black wool number that made him look fabulous, darling, plus black leather gloves and a black-and-white herringbone scarf.

"Come on, kiddo," he told Lizzie, putting his arm out. She stepped into his embrace just as if she'd been doing it all her life, while he smiled stupidly with happiness.

But before they could go, Bella piped up from the rocking chair she'd retired to, so she could watch us do dishes. "What about old Mrs. Boyd? What happened to her?"

"She's actually fine," Lizzie answered. "She did have a minor stroke, but they're bringing her home shortly," Lizzie went on, "and she's hiring some people to help her when she gets here."

Lizzie smiled wryly. Really, she was looking much better than when I'd first seen her this evening; getting engaged to be married suited her, apparently.

"She can afford it now, after all," Lizzie said.

Which was the funny part: Maggie Davies wasn't the old woman's daughter, as she'd claimed. But she was Mrs. Boyd's niece, and once Rafferty died the two women were each other's only remaining living relative.

And a clause in the original will prohibited anyone who'd ever harmed Stone House from inheriting it, so once Maggie had admitted to setting the fire that burned the place down—to distract everyone while she was busy getting the hell out of Dodge, it turned out—she was disinherited automatically and Mrs. Boyd became the will's sole beneficiary.

Just then Ellie's husband, George Valentine, came in. A short, powerfully built fellow with a ready grin and a bluff, bantyrooster way of facing the world, he greeted the assembled company cheerily, then went to the refrigerator and got himself a beer before loading a plate with leftovers.

Assembling his meal, he wore a wise, private expression that I recognized; clearly he knew something we didn't and was enjoying it very much.

"Well," he said after swallowing some of the beer and setting the bottle down firmly. "I just came from a planning board meeting. You know that stretch of land from Stone House all the way down to the water there."

Oh, did we ever, having nearly died several times in or near that very location recently.

"Looks like the state wants it for land preservation," he said, chewing. "You know, nature and all that."

It was the first I'd heard of it; Ellie, too, I saw from her face, now full of wonder.

George ate some bratwurst, followed it with potato salad and more beer. Then:

"State wants to trade it for acreage near Shackford Head," he declared.

"But Eastport doesn't own the Stone House land," Ellie objected, to which George had a ready answer.

"Back taxes, though. Nobody's been paying property tax for years. City owns it several times over, really."

"So the city can trade it," I said. "That does make sense, but I hope Mrs. Boyd isn't too upset."

George shook his head. "Somebody's already gone and talked to her, she said take it. She's talking again, recovering pretty good, but she's old, she said. All she wants is her own home, doesn't care about anything else."

"Couple of people from the nursing home went down in their ambulance to get her from the rooming house where Maggie stuck her," Lizzie said.

She shuddered communicatively, to give us an idea of what kind of place it was; the kind, I thought, that would take an old, stroke-damaged woman off your hands without asking a lot of pesky questions.

"But why didn't she call someone?" Ellie wanted to know. "Anyone in Eastport would've helped her."

George shrugged. "She's talking now, but for a while she couldn't speak or write."

Silence descended as each of us, I supposed, imagined it: silenced, trapped. But then George spoke once more.

"Who's for ice cream?" he asked, jingling his truck keys, and the next thing I knew we were piling into vehicles: Sam and his little family, Ellie and me with our husbands—Bella and my dad stayed home to enjoy some well-earned peace and quiet—and in the third car Dylan and Lizzie.

She'd stopped me on our way out. "One last thing I thought you might like to know. I had those crates tested for a few things, and two came up positive: mescaline and ayahuasca."

The names rang a bell. Back in New York, Sam got a box once from Mexico. I intercepted it, luckily, and inside found enough hallucinogens to incapacitate an army.

Suddenly I knew where the woman in white had come from: inside my head. When those crates got broken open, dust would have floated—probably throughout the house. Then we'd walked in, stirred up dust, and inhaled enough leftover eggbeater-in-your-brain chemicals to stun a horse.

And there you had it: instant phantasms. The rest of it could be explained naturally, too: the woman screaming from the window that first night was Melissa, of course, and then there was the drug residue we'd probably absorbed. Even the lights in the windows that Hudson had seen turned out to be from faulty wiring, the fire marshal had informed Lizzie soon after the investigation was finished.

"Thanks," I told her now as she got into Dylan's car. Then, not to my surprise, the newly engaged pair drove off in the opposite direction from the ice cream shop.

"Guess they weren't up for dessert," George quipped.

"I have," I answered Ellie's unspoken question, "no idea."

Why Dylan had chosen that moment to propose yet again when he'd had so many refusals, why Lizzie had said yes to an idea she'd always rejected—

Ten minutes later we were all at the ice cream parlor, and nothing about chocolate ice cream with hot fudge and maraschino cherries answered any of our questions.

But for the time being, anyway, it made their answers seem inconsequential and all that had happened seem far away. In fact, by the time we got home again and Ellie and George had departed, I'd nearly managed to forget almost getting burned up in a fire.

But not quite. Sam and Mika went right upstairs, and my dad and Bella had already retired for the night; while Wade turned on the Patriots game in the parlor I went around checking smoke alarms, carbon monoxide detectors, and the little gadget on top of the woodstove that whistles if the stovepipe gets too hot.

I locked the doors, too, but with enough dogs in the house to scare off a platoon, it was hardly necessary. Finally I went back to Wade and the TV, where a famous quarterback was passing a football and other guys were catching it.

The famous quarterback had the narrowed eyes of a carnivore searching for prey as he looked down the field. His arm cocked, and the ball sailed pointy-end-first over everyone's heads.

And then the game was over, I didn't see quite how. Wade snapped the TV off. Upstairs, faucets hammered and water swirled down drains, doors clicked shut, and a hanging stars-

and-moons mobile over the baby's crib started playing the theme from *Star Trek*.

"Everything okay?" Wade asked into the bedroom darkness when I got up there.

I dropped my clothes and crawled in beside him. "Sure. I just don't understand some things, that's all."

He wrapped his arms around me. "Like what, ghosts?"

He knew me very well. "Sort of. Because ghosts mean life after death, right? You die, but something about you still hangs around." I raised myself up on one elbow. "And that right there is the part I simply do not understand."

"Caterpillars don't get how they turn into butterflies, either, do they?" he asked. "But they still do it."

"Oh." He nodded drowsily against me.

"That," he said, his voice fading so I thought he might be talking in his sleep, speaking out of a dream, "is the point."

Beyond the naked branches outside the window, a sharp slice of moon hung halfway into the sky over Campobello. Cold, woodsmoke-scented air leaked in under the barely raised sash.

A foghorn hooted; a bell buoy clanked. I rolled over into Wade's embrace and was instantly asleep. Until:

"Jake?"

"Yes, Wade."

"Just tell me this. Do we have to put another addition on the house?"

And that, in a nutshell, was Wade. He lived with his wife, his in-laws, his wife's kid, the kid's wife, and their three kids. But he'd have built another addition onto the house if I'd asked him to.

"No, Wade." I resettled myself against him. "I have it on good authority that we are not having another grandchild anytime soon." Because of course he'd noticed Mika feeling and acting so poorly. "And Mika's fine," I added.

Gallstones, she'd told me, but they could be dealt with easily, she said; she already had the appointment.

Wade nodded slowly against the pillow. "S' good," he mumbled. "I'm glad."

"Me too," I said, but he didn't hear, already snoring. I turned my pillow over, smoothed out the blankets, and closed my eyes, sparing a silent good night for the thin crescent moon.

Glazed Chocolate Pumpkin Muffins

Ingredients

- ²/₃ cup pumpkin puree (not pumpkin pie filling)
- ²/₃ cup sugar
- 4 tablespoons canola oil
- 2 large eggs
- 1 teaspoon vanilla extract
- 1 cup flour
- 1 teaspoon pumpkin pie spice
- ¹/₂ cup cocoa powder
- 2 teaspoons baking soda
- ¹/₂ teaspoon salt
- ¹/₂ cup semisweet chocolate chips

Makes twelve muffins.

Preheat the oven to 350 degrees. Put paper muffin tin liners in a twelve-hole muffin tin or two six-hole tins.

In a large bowl mix all the dry ingredients together very thoroughly. Beat the eggs. Then in another bowl mix all the wet ingredients including the eggs together thoroughly and add the result to the dry ingredients. Stir until well blended. Then stir in the chocolate chips.

Divide the batter evenly into the muffin tins. Bake for 20–22 minutes or until a toothpick inserted into the middle of a muffin comes out clean.

For the glaze:

- 1 tablespoon unsalted butter
- 1 ounce unsweetened chocolate, broken into pieces

- ¹/₂ cup confectioners' sugar
- 1 tablespoon boiling water

Melt the chocolate and butter over low heat. Stir in the sugar. Stir in the boiling water a few drops at a time until the glaze is the thickness you want.

Drizzle the glaze in thin lines over the cooled muffins.